INSPECTOR
AN

Inspector Ghote stands alongside Hercule Poirot and Adam Dalgleish as one of the best-loved fictional detectives. But he appears to have by far the most extraordinary cases to solve—chasmed by chance, tied up in red tape and undermined by his own human and unorthodox methods of inquiry. For India is the land of the bureaucrat, as well as the snake charmer and the rope trick. Little is as it appears. So how has Ghote, over the years, still managed to track down his wrong-doers?

To celebrate twenty-five years in print, the best of Ghote's shorter adventures have been brought together for the first time. From 'The All-Bad Hat' to 'Murder Mustn't At All Advertise, Isn't It?', these stories serve as a complete biography to our Bombay detective. Through H.R.F. Keating's Introduction, we see the whys, hows and wherefores of life as an Indian policewalla. Why, for instance has the surface of Ghote's desk had to change over the years? Why has his police dwelling, once so spacious, begun to shrink? And how did Ganesh Ghote, Bombay CID, first find his way in to print?

INSPECTOR GHOTE, HIS LIFE AND CRIMES

H.R.F. Keating

ARROW BOOKS

Arrow Books Limited
20 Vauxhall Bridge Road, London SW1V 2SA

An imprint of Random Century Group

London Melbourne Sydney Auckland
Johannesburg and agencies throughout
the world

First published in Great Britain by Hutchinson 1989
Arrow edition 1990

Printed and bound in Great Britain by
Courier International Ltd, Tiptree, Essex

ISBN 0 09 971080 3

Contents

INTRODUCTION

His Life and Crimes

Inspector Ghote came to life one day in 1963. I was sitting in my study, in the red armchair by the window – I have told this story so many times that some of it must be true – reading a geography book. I had decided that my next detective novel was to take place in India, a country I had never set foot in, and I was hard at work mugging up some facts.

Up until that moment I was convinced that my reason for taking this odd and even hazardous step was a strictly commercial one. American publishers had rejected my previous four titles as being 'too British'. So how to avoid that stigma, and enter the lush transatlantic pastures? India seemed one answer, especially as I had had it in mind to write a crime story that would be somewhat of a commentary on the problem of perfectionism, and one of the few notions I had about India was that things there were apt to be rather imperfect. Good symbolic stuff.

Then, out of nowhere, into my head there came this man. Or some parts of him. A faintly worried face. Certainly, a pair of bony shoulders. A certain naïvety, which should enable him to ask the questions about the everyday life around him to which my potential readers might want answers. And he also brought with him a name: 'Inspector Ghosh'. Oh, gosh, he would keep saying, wide-eyed.

It was only when I sent the outline of my Inspector's adventure to a friend, an Englishman just back from Bombay, that I learnt that Ghosh is a Bengali name. It would be as unsuitable for a Bombay detective, at the other side of the Indian sub-continent, as Ivan Ivanovitch would be for a Parisian sleuth. He suggested the similar, but appropriate Maharashtrian name of Ghote. So, from birth we had advanced to christening or, more correctly, to the naam-karana, the name-giving ceremony.

At that point, however, I saw Ghote's life as being a short one, a single book's span. My speciality in 1963 was detective novels without a running hero, but with in each a different, more or less exotic background. There had been a coach-and-four trip, Zen (if in an English country house bleakly devoted to further education), the playing of croquet and a provincial opera venture. I saw India as just one more in that series. But the book, called of course from that running-thread of perfectionism *The Perfect Murder*, unexpectedly won the Gold Dagger award for 1964, and an Edgar Allan Poe award in America where, yes, it did get published. Ghote was granted an indefinite extension of life.

So in 1966 he underwent *Inspector Ghote's Good Crusade*, in which he investigated the murder of an American philanthropist, was harassed by a fearful squad of Bombay street urchins, was grossly deceived when he gave all he had saved for a refrigerator to the apparently poverty-stricken 'paramour' of a fisherman and learnt (alongside, I hope, the reader) that giving is not always a straightforward business. He also solved the case. This was something he was contracted with his public to do, and because of that I was beginning to realise he would have to lose a little of his naïvety. Or, rather, he would have to develop an inner toughness and shrewdness not at first apparent.

I once heard the distinguished and delightfully reticent novelist, V. S. Naipaul, pronounce – in answer to a television interviewer who had asked what was the most important quality a novelist needed – the one word 'Luck'. I think he was right. Certainly, it was my immense luck that the man who entered my head that day as I sat in my armchair proved to be a person with enough of myself in him to be able to turn this way and that, confronted by new aspects of life, and find new things in himself to match up to them.

So, in 1967 it was *Inspector Ghote Caught in Meshes*, when he looked at life as a tugging of different loyalties and became involved for the first and only time in something approaching the espionage novel. In 1968 it was *Inspector Ghote Hunts the Peacock*, where he came to London and discovered not only who had murdered a distant relation of his wife, a young woman known as 'the Peacock', but also the pluses and minuses that go with a sense of pride (Pride = peacock. Geddit?).

It was in the course of this book that I hit on a nasty little snag which I had in my innocence – or indeed sheer ignorance – created for myself. Needing a name for the wife I found that Ghote had, or had to have, while writing *The Perfect Murder*, I had chosen at random the pretty 'Protima'. Only to be told later by one of the kindly readers who send me what I call 'But' letters – *Dear Mr Keating, I much enjoyed . . . But I must point out an error . . .* – that Protima is a Bengali name. So in *Hunts the Peacock* I boldly stated that Maharashtrian Ghote had, unusually, married a Bengali.

It was twenty years later, while I was writing the script for the film of *The Perfect Murder* with the director, Zafar Hai, that I learnt there is in fact a Maharashtrian version of the name, Pratima. So in the film Ghote's wife is a Maharashtrian, as different from a Bengali as Spaniard from German, and is deliciously played as such by Ratna Pathak, the wife of Naseeruddin Shah, our star. So is the film-Ghote not the book-Ghote? Knotty philosophical point. Certainly, in Naseer Shah's performance he is very much the Ghote I had in mind. Or perhaps the Ghote I had inside, because Naseer said once that he had been given the clue to the man by looking in the eyes of his creator.

But there is a complication, or even two: a radio-Ghote and a TV-Ghote. In 1972 I was asked (I think) to write a radio play about Ghote and produced *Inspector Ghote and the All-Bad Man*, followed by *Inspector Ghote Makes A Journey* and *Inspector Ghote and the River Man*. Feeling with the latter that I could not see the situation sufficiently without being able to describe its setting as well as entering into Ghote's head, I began to write in narrative form before making it into radio dialogue. That torso tale, completed, is one of the stories here. In the second play I had Ghote coming to London a second time, as a planted stowaway among a party of illegal immigrants; and in a television play I wrote in 1983 (a semi-pilot for an abortive series), Ghote came to London yet again as a paying guest in the home of an ancient British Raj couple.

There was, too, an earlier television appearance in a version of *Hunts the Peacock* written by the Irish playwright, Hugh Leonard (who kept Ghote mercifully as he is in the book), with

3

my hero acted by Zia Moyheddin. (Incidentally, he gave Ghote a moustache, which he just has in *Inspector Ghote Goes By Train*, but which he has never had at all by the time of the following books.) Now did he, my Ghote, book-Ghote, come to London more than once? His other visits certainly do not seem to be in my mind when I embark on the business – absurdly daring if you let yourself think about it – of holding in my head that whole different world in which there is a person called Ghote who has a wife called Protima, perhaps Pratima, and a son called Ved.

Here again we are back to complications. How old is Ved? Seen first in *The Perfect Murder*, he was big enough to sleep in a bed. When filming the scene in which Protima accuses Ghote of leaving her to cope on her own with a suddenly fever-ridden Ved – as an illustration to a BBC documentary about myself and the Bombay police – he appeared to be as old as ten or eleven (the only boy we could easily get hold of). But in the film of *The Perfect Murder*, because Naseer and Ratna Shah had a charming baby about a year old, Ved slid rapidly back to early infancy. Just one in 1988, but ten in 1974?

Whereas I can keep Ghote himself more or less stationary in age (though what exactly that age is depends, I suspect, as much on who is reading about him as on who writes about him) and I can keep his Protima ever elegant, ever her same self, a small boy must grow. So as the years pass my book-Ved gets bigger, though not by quite as much as the passing years dictate. If he did, his poor father would reach the early retirement age of the Indian Police Service much too soon for me, and the ore I mine so happily would abruptly prove exhausted.

It was shortly after *Inspector Ghote Hunts the Peacock* – to abandon the chronological complications – that I happened to write a short story called 'The Justice Boy' for a contest for British writers organised by that splendid American publication, *Ellery Queen's Mystery Magazine*. Set in an English prep school, it won the second prize, running-up to that Golden Age great Christianna Brand. As a consequence Fred Dannay, the other half of the pseudonymous Ellery Queen who then edited the magazine, wrote to me asking if I had any more stories.

So, in response, Ghote was set to begin a parallel life at shorter length and the story I eventually sent was the one that opens this volume, 'The Test'. It illustrates the amount of Harry Keating that there is in Ganesh Ghote (although he had not in fact discovered his first name as early as this), because the incident in which the small Ved is overcome by horror when he thinks his father has vanished happened to me when I was much that age and my mother, not usually a practical joker, took it into her head to hide from me.

However, Ghote did not live any more of his life in short stories for a year or two after that first small, but quite characteristic, appearance. Instead there was *Inspector Ghote Plays A Joker*, in which he solved the murder of a rajah who, unlike my mother, was an inveterate practical joker. Hovering, as it were below the surface here, there were thoughts about games and games-playing in life.

Then there was *Inspector Ghote Breaks An Egg*, which took him out of Bombay to a small town in Maharashtra. This was one of the problems I faced: not to use and re-use the same setting, especially as my knowledge of never-visited Bombay was still confined to what I was able to discover about it from books, from the occasional Indian art-film featuring the city, from scraps of friends' talk, from TV glimpses and from the pages of the Sunday edition of the *Times of India*, which I had begun to take. But in any case half my research went not outward, but inward. And there I discovered for my pages things about violence, the evil of violence and the good that sometimes cannot be brought about without it.

It was not until the end of 1971 – when I was asked by a friend, Desmond Albrow, then editing the *Catholic Herald*, to write a Christmas story for him – that short-story Ghote came to life again. The story, called variously 'Inspector Ghote and the Miracle Baby' or just 'The Miracle', is the second in the pages ahead. In it I incorporated – rather impudently, since I was writing for a religious paper – a quality I had had to give to Ghote which is not particularly characteristic of Indian police officers, or of most Indians. I made him an unbeliever. Since I had arrived at that state myself, I found I could not – seeing Ghote as I do from an angel-over-the-shoulder position – enter properly into his mind if it was to be filled with simple belief. Imagine, then, my dismay when at last I got to India three years later, met Bombay CID officers and saw almost invariably under the glass tops of their desks a picture of a god. Imagine, too, my slightly lesser dismay when I realised their desks had the glass tops necessary in a stickily humid climate, as Ghote's had never had.

Short stories about Ghote were not exactly pouring from my pen, principally because there was hardly anywhere for them to be published. So he continued his life in books. In 1971 it had been *Inspector Ghote Goes By Train*, when I was able to make use of the mountain of Indian train lore I had accumulated – the extraordinary Indian railway system sets people a-writing and a-filming by the score – and send him (possibly moustached) all the way from Bombay to Calcutta and back, beset as ever with the difficulties that are a condition of his existence but triumphing finally, if not always to the complete satisfaction of his superiors.

Indeed in the next of his adventures, *Inspector Ghote Trusts the Heart*, in which he is put temporarily in charge of a child-kidnapping case – I had read a three-line story in *The Times* about the son of a rich man's chauffeur in Japan snatched in mistake for his own boy – he ends in terrible hot water for having continued to hunt for the victim unofficially, and successfully: for, in fact, trusting his heart over his head.

One other short story then followed, written originally with an airline while-away in mind, though it eventually appeared in *Ellery Queen's Mystery Magazine*: 'The Hooked Fisherman', as Fred Dannay (who never could resist altering a title) called it in place of my 'The Not So Fly Fisherman'. I had hoped that with its gentle knocking of the bucket-shops which got round the law – as it then stood – about cheap seats, BOAC would lap it up. But airlines stick together and my ingenious use of the cover of the Bombay telephone directory, a volume I had discovered in my local library, never entertained any in-flight passengers.

One more book carried Ghote onwards before I too, became a passenger to Bombay. This was *Bats Fly Up for Inspector Ghote*, a consideration of suspicion, suspiciousness and its consequences – good and bad – occasioned by dinner-party talk with a senior Pakistani Customs official in London. It begins with a wild inaccuracy. As I had already hinted at in 'The Miracle Baby', I put poor Ghote on anti-pickpocketing duty. But this, I was soon to discover, was as unlikely as detaching a Scotland Yard Murder Squad man to move on the traffic.

Then one morning, some time in 1974, I got a letter from Air India saying they had heard of this author writing about Bombay without ever having seen the sub-continent, so would I like a flight there in exchange for whatever publicity there was to be made? Immediate reaction: marvellous, now at last I can overcome the financial difficulties of staying in India for adecent period. Subsequent reaction: Oh God, but what if those real smells, those real crippled beggars, those real lepers so appal me that I can no longer write about their city? A justifiable fear. Holding imaginary worlds in your head is achancy business at best.

But I thought eventually that it would be chicken indeed to turn down such an offer. So on 12 October 1974, with eight novels, three radio plays and four short stories about Inspector Ghote behind me, I set foot for the first time on Indian soil. On landing, I had intended to say, if possible not aloud, 'One small step for Harry Keating, a giant stride for Inspector Ghote.' But instead, struck as if by an immense hot, damp wash-cloth by Bombay's post-monsoon humidity, all that emerged was amuttered 'Cripes.'

However, I spent three splendid weeks thereafter learning alot, mopping up atmosphere, filling notebook after notebook and finding there was not so much to correct in my notion of the city – only, rather, things to enhance what I had managed to put into my subconscious and thence onto the pages. Everything was more than I had believed. The colours were brighter. The clamour was louder. The rich were richer. The poor were, yes, poorer and occasionally more outwardly wretched than I had been able to conceive of. Yet I was able to accept that. My fears had proved grou dless. I credit the power of the imagination. I had seen in my mind's eye the worst, if not quite the whole, already. I suffered no crippling culture shock.

In fact, I followed up that first visit with another soon afterwards. I had had the temerity to put to BBC Television the idea of making adocumentary about this writer who had, for so long, chronicled the life of a Bombay detective without ever having seen his stamping ground, and who now at last was doing so. The BBC had taken up the idea, but tactfully left me to make my first visit unencumbered. Now, seven months later, we pretended to maks that visit again. In between and during filming, I filled yet more notebooks. And I had abonus.

As a strand in the documentary, we filmed the work of the Bombay police as it really was. So I got to see, amid much else, the office, the 'cabin' of the head of Crime Branch CID, Ghote's boss. I got to interview him, too, and Deputy Commissioner Kulkarni said, on air, 'I would like to have Ghote on my team. He has the essential quality of being able to put himself into the mind of the criminal he is seeking.' Delicious praise.

But some of Ghote's everyday circumstances did have to change as a result of what I saw. His boss's rank shot up from Deputy Superintendent to Deputy Commissioner. His desk had mysteriously become glass-topped, losing the whorled, scratched and ink-stained top it had had as at the opening of the story 'The Not So Fly Fisherman', relic of school desks where I had sat learning amongst other more forgettable things the elements of English composition.

Ghote's home, too, had to undergo a sea-change. In my earliest days with him I had read of houses in Police Quarters somewhere. But what I had failed to realise was that in incredibly crowded, sea-surrounded Bombay, where property values now compare with Manhattan, police officers, however high their rank, live in flats. So the house Ghote once occupied became for a while simply a 'home' and eventually took on bit by bit the characteristics of a flat, such as the ones in which flattered – and flattering – Crime Branch inspectors had entertained me.

So, how would all I had learnt affect what I was to write about Ghote after India? I worried. So I decided to try my unprentice hand on a short story. 'Inspector Ghote and the Noted British Author' has in it a version of a case Crime Branch was handling at the time of my visit, with the addition of a visiting author (one of the Bombay papers had described me with the delightful expression of the title) who makes more of a nuisance of himself than I hoped I had done, and is rather fatter than I hope I was.

When I had written some dozen pages of the story and Ghote was still in that cabin I now knew so well, receiving orders, I began to realise that visiting the scene of the crime has its pitfalls as well as its perks. I had put into those pages every detail of that big room, the positioning of the chairs in front of the desk (significantly different in Indian offices, but . . .), the map on the wall and what it showed, even the names of the police dogs on the duties-board. And it was then that I understood that absence from the scene can be a help to the writer; automatically cutting down the dross that obscures the picture. I had to go back and be pretty severe with the blue pencil. But in the story I was now able to show a side to Ghote, until then not in evidence, that he shares with real-life Indian police officers, the ability to obtain answers at the end of a fist. Or of an open slapping hand. It is something he and I do not have in common.

I gave the first post-India novel a background I had scented long before but had hung back from using till I had had a chance to see the real thing – Bombay's film world, the *filmi duniya* as, picking up a few words of Bombay Hindi (a fearful bastard language), I had learnt to say.

Luckily, I had had an introduction to a film distributor who in turn introduced me to one of the superstars of the Bombay studios. Thus when Inspector Ghote became infected with an echo version of the dizzying ambition that is apt to afflict quite ordinary men and women who get caught up in the swirling spiral of stardom, I had in *Filmi, Filmi, Inspector Ghote* plenty of circumstances to place him in. He goes, for instance, to a star's party – 'Come. Come, Mr Keating,' my star had said to me. 'A small party, sixty–eighty people' – and that affair is truthful to reality in every particular. On the other hand, when the star in the book is late for the auspicious ceremony that starts a film, the *mahurrat*, which must be held to the minute, it was my idea to have the clock stopped in the studio. And afterwards I think – I think – I heard this was done in reality.

Bit by bit, then, Ghote was learning about himself and about life. Or I was learning about Ghote. Sometimes a lot, sometimes just an extra detail, such as the chewy *paans* that can (filled with aphrodisiac and thus called 'bed-smashers') cost as much as a hundred rupees. They are to be found in the story I wrote for broadcasting in 1976, 'The Wicked Lady'. Originally this was to be a pilot for a series where the authors would interrupt just before the dénouement and invite listeners to guess who done it. Shamelessly, I had pinched a plot from Agatha Christie and Indianised it. The series was abandoned, so I turned the tale into a straight story. It proved to be the last about Ghote for some years, while instead I contributed tales about a charlady sleuth, Mrs Craggs, to *Ellery Queen's Mystery Magazine*.

Back in his novel life, in *Inspector Ghote Draws A Line*, the poor fellow – in the unlikely disguise of Dr Ghote, research scholar – is sent to the home of an ancient and cantankerous judge deep in the Indian countryside when the aged relic is threatened with assassination. There my alter ego came to ponder (with the reader?) at what point and how firmly you should say, 'Thus far and no further'.

Ghote also makes a fleeting appearance, the most fleeting appearance possible, in *The Murder of the Maharajah*, a book set in 1930. In its last lines the Maharajah's umbrella-toting schoolmaster expresses a hope that if he is ever to have a son to add to the tally of his numerous daughters that boy will become a police officer. It is then revealed that his name is Ghote. Safe to write this much pre-history. But later, when I came to set down incidents from my hero's childhood, I am not sure that I didn't occasionally add confusion to what is called in India his 'bio-datas'.

Two more book-length accounts add to the picture before Ghote appeared in a short story again. In *Go West, Inspector Ghote* he found himself ordered off to America, California even, and discovered that that extraordinary part of the world is a place steeped in a mysticism which strongly contrasts with materialist Bombay. He only solved the locked-room murder when he admitted to the existence of that mystical phenomenon translocation of the body (instantaneous travel, if you like, often over hundreds of miles). Atheist with all the ardour of the convert that I am, this was something that I had had to acknowledge as likely when during my first visit to India I met the representative of a pharmaceuticals firm. He had hailed me out of the darkness of the evening, recognising me from smudgy newspaper photos, and then recounted to me unabashed stories of a friend capable of summoning out of the very air money and sweets and more. Why should he have told me tarradiddles? He was a serious fellow, and not unscientific. (His job I borrowed for one of the suspects in 'The Wicked Lady'.)

In *The Sheriff of Bombay*, which appeared in 1984, Ghote encountered his most harassing experience 'till date', as we say in India. He met sex. This was something I had not been able to bring myself to put into his world before, but during my second visit to Bombay I had been asked by one of the Crime Branch inspectors if I would like to see 'the Cages', the red-light area of Bombay regularly produced as one of the city's sights, along with the Hanging Gardens (cover for a huge reservoir on top of Malabar Hill) and Elephanta Island. I had thought it my duty to succumb. The so-called cages – they are in fact no more than the barred windows behind which the girls display themselves – proved both sordid and lively, depending on the way I looked on them. So when ten years later I felt ready to use what I saw that night, *The Sheriff of Bombay* (that name I had seen on a plaque in the stern splendour of Bombay's Gothic-style Old Secretariat) taught Ghote, myself – and, I trust, my readers – that much in life can appear either black or white according to the way it is seen.

Now, for some reason or another, I entered on a whole spate of short stories about the man who over the space of some ten years had come to occupy such a deep niche in my mind. Frequently now, seeing some sight or hearing a few words that particularly caught my attention, I would ask, 'How does Ghote react to that?' and know the answer. Some such questions have already resulted in books or stories. Others lie waiting, either like the pearls maharajahs were apt to hide away too long in the dark strongrooms of their palaces only to fade into colourlessness, or else perhaps to prove ever-shining diamonds.

In answer to a request from the editor of the magazine of the Townswomen's Guilds, Ghote had an encounter with a party of ladies touring India and demonstrated that latent toughness that gives the tale its title, 'The Cruel Inspector Ghote'. I think that quality came to Ghote's surface when it lodged itself in my mind as I read a life of Rudyard Kipling, which pointed out that in *The Jungle Book* fatherly Baloo the Bear is wholesomely strict with young Mowgli. Then, in answer to a request for something filmable from a charming young woman rejoicing in the typically Indian nickname of Pooh, I wrote 'Murder Must Not At All Advertise, Isn't It?'. It was a passing tribute to my predecessor in detection, Dorothy L. Sayers, and set in the Bombay advertising world where Pooh Sayani made her living. In it, of course, was a charming creature called Tigga.

Although no film eventuated, the story, which shows a

Ghote who has now just about got the balance between softness and shrewdness right, winged its way across the Atlantic to see the light of day there, complete with the third or fourth villain I had called Budhoo. So I crossed out that name in the long list I have in the front of my alphabetical notebook of things Indian. Ghote, lucky fellow, must have learnt the infinite complexities of Indian nomenclature as he grew up. But somehow he has been slow in passing on his knowledge to me, though nowadays, with care, I think I get most names right.

At much this time, too, I transcribed one of my old radio plays into short-story form, making *The All-Bad Man* into 'The All-Bad Hat'. The story sums up, I think, where Ghote had got to by 1984. I also contrived, when the *Police Review* asked members of the Crime Writers Association for stories with a police setting, to get into words a small project I had long meditated – a story to be told purely in telephone conversations. 'Hello, Hello, Inspector Ghote' is my tribute to the magnificent imperfections of the Bombay telephone system, now considerably improved as Ghote notes in his 1988 appearance, *Dead on Time*.

In 1986 Ghote experienced existence in what, I suppose, has been his most comprehensive coming-to-life yet. In *Under A Monsoon Cloud*, I set out to consider the theme of anger, a quality which, looking back, I see was something in others which Ghote had singularly failed to come to terms with. But anger had also given him on more than one occasion an impetus helping an essentially nice man to take the sharp action which often brings about success in an ugly world.

So I recalled an episode I had been told by a former Commissioner of the Bombay Police, for whom I had felt bound to write a disclaimer as a preface to *Inspector Ghote Trusts the Heart*, which featured in a rather poor light such a Commissioner. Mr S. G. Pradhan, with immense kindness, had contacted me in Bombay and given me several hours of his time, for much of it explaining complications of Indian police life which I found dauntingly difficult to get into the pages of an onward-pressing story. One particular illustration he used certainly lodged in my mind. It concerned an officer of great promise who in a moment of rage had killed a subordinate. Now was the time to regurgitate those facts-from-life as fiction-facts in the life of Inspector Ghote.

In the story that unwound itself in my head as a consequence of a similar rash act on the part of Ghote's admired superior, 'Tiger' Kelkar, Ghote finds himself arraigned before a disciplinary tribunal. Conducting a defence of himself – as well as considering whether he ought to defend himself at all – I found he was bringing to the surface his whole attitude to life. 'What good would I be as a security officer?' he demands of his wife in the dark of the marital bedroom when the idea of resignation is in the air. 'Oh, I could do that job all right, but what satisfaction would be there?' (The phrasing comes from a notebook I have kept for twenty years, labelled and re-labelled 'A Little Book of Indian English'.) Then he flares out: 'It is not as if I have not been a good officer. Have I taken bribes? . . . Have I toadied and treated reverently superior officers? No, I have never so much as held open one car door to them. Have I had suspects beaten up even? . . . Did I buy my posting to the CID? And now am I to lose everything after I have sweated every ounce of my blood?'

It was while I was in hospital having a ruptured knee-tendon hooked back into place and dealing, a little bad-temperedly, with my editor's queries about the next Ghote novel, *The Body in the Billiard Room* (in which in the appropriately lingering Britain-of-the-1930s atmosphere of Ooty hill station Ghote finds himself harassed, as it were, by the shade of Agatha Christie and solves a murder in more or less the manner of a Great Detective), that I conceived the notion of the short story I called 'Nil By Mouth'. Those words, odd when you come to think about them, I saw day after day above the beds of patients about to go to the operating theatre, and from the fascination the phrase exercised over me grew that quite intricate little tale. It shows once more, at one and the same time, the just-tough Ghote – tough enough by now to defy at least hospital authorities – and the perhaps too-easily-moved Ghote.

Ghote's major adventures appear at about yearly intervals, giving me time between books sometimes to embark u asksd on ashort story such as 'APresent for Santa Sahib', another Christmassy tale.

A gap between books was the origin, too, of 'The Purloined Parvati and Other Artefacts', though its deeper beginning-point lay in a visit I paid to an extraordinary private museum when I was attending, as chairman of the Society of Authors, the conference of our Indian sister organisation in Jaipur. I said to myself (as the enthusiastic owner took me round, together with a solemnly appreciative lady from UNESCO), that somehow I must give the place a parallel, scarcely exaggerated existence in fiction. Some eight years later Inspector Ghote, standing outside the little Press hut I had noticed during the filming of *The Perfect Murder*, was able to set out on that brief morning's work. It enabled him to bring to the fore a capacity for critical judgement that had lain underneath the almost totally uncritical attitude he had possessed when authority figures had pronounced at the start of his career.

This capacity for objective judgement he retains, if sensibly inside his head, when in *Dead on Time* he dares to assess as mighty a figure as the Director General of Police for the State of Maharashtra. There he comes to terms, too, with his own attitude to the ever-pressing minute in time-ruled (though often time-flouting) Bombay, seeing that pressure in contrast to the almost timeless life of India's villages. And it is in one of those, I discovered as I planned the book (or Ghote brought reminiscently to mind as he lived its events, as he does again in my final little tale 'Light Coming', where he is something of an authority figure himself), that Ghote had experienced various formative happenings. His life began there. Or did it begin one day as I was sitting in that red armchair in my study?

1989

1

The Test

From the very beginning Inspector Ghote had doubts about Anil Divekar and the Test Match. Cricket and Divekar did not really mix. Divekar's sport was something quite different: he was a daylight entry ace. Excitement for him lay not in perfectly timing a stroke with the bat that would send the ball skimming along the grass to the boundary, but in the patient sizing up of a big Bombay house, the layout of its rooms, the routine of its servants, and then choosing the right moment to slip in and out carrying away the best of the portable loot.

But here Divekar was, as Ghote on a free day stood with his little son Ved outside the high walls of Brabourne Stadium, ticketless and enviously watching the crowds pouring in for the start of the day's play. He even came up to them, smiling broadly.

'Inspector, you would like seats?'

At Ghote's side, clutching his hand, little Ved's face lit up as from a sudden inward glow. And Ghote nearly accepted the offer. Ved deserved the treat. He was well-behaved and already working hard at school – and it was only a question of a pair of tickets. Some of his own colleagues would have taken them as a right.

But Ghote knew all along that he could not do it. Whatever the others did, he had always kept his integrity. No criminal could ever reproach him with past favours.

Angrily he tugged Ved off. But, marching away from the stadium, he could not help speculating as to why Divekar should have been there at all. Of course, when every two years or so a team from England or Australia or the West Indies came to Bombay, Test Match fever suddenly gripped the most unexpected people. But all the same . . .

The crowd outside the stadium had not been all college students and the excited schoolboys you might expect. Smart business executives had jostled with simple shopkeepers and grain merchants. The film stars' huge cars had nosed their way past anxious, basket-clutching housewives, their best saris already looking crumpled and dusty.

Fifty thousand people, ready to roast all day in the sun to watch a sedate game that most of them hardly understood. Waiting for someone to 'hit a sixer' so that they could launch into frenzied clapping, or for someone to drop a catch and give them a chance to indulge in some vigorous booing, or – the height of heights – for a home player to get a century and permit them to invade the pitch with garlands held high to drape their hero.

Where did they all get the entrance money, Ghote wondered. With even eighteen-rupee seats selling for a hundred, getting in was way beyond his own means. Little Ved's treat would have to be, once more, a visit to the Hanging Gardens.

But when they reached this mildly pleasurable – and free – spot, everywhere they went transistor radios were tuned teasingly to the Test Match commentary. Nothing Ghote offered his son was in the least successful.

He bought coconuts, but Ved would not even watch the squatting naralwallah dexterously chop off the tops of the dark fruit. He held out the gruesome spectacle of the vultures that hovered over the Towers of Silence where the Parsis laid out their dead, but Ved just shrugged. He purchased various bottled drinks, each more hectically coloured and more expensive than the previous one, but Ved drank them with increasing apathy.

He even attempted to enliven things by starting a game of hide-and-seek. Disastrously. After he had twice prolonged finding Ved – whose idea of hiding did not seem to stretch beyond standing sideways behind rather too narrow trees – as long as he possibly could, he decided that the game might go better if he himself were to be the one to go into hiding. So while Ved was temporarily absorbed in examining a cicada which, in a moment of aberration, had mistaken day for night and emitted its shrill squeak, he dropped to the ground behind a nicely sturdy bush and crouched there keeping a paternal eye on his small son through the leaves.

For some time Ved stayed deeply engaged with the cicada,

squatting beside it and turning it over with one delicate finger in an effort to see how such a small stick of a creature could produce that single extraordinarily loud squeak. But then he looked up, as if he were going to consult the parental oracle. For an instant he looked round merely puzzled. But then . . .

Then it was plain that the end of the world had come, the end of his small safe world. He lifted up his head and gave vent to a howl of pure, desolate anguish.

In a flash Ghote was beside him, hugging, patting, reassuring. But nothing seemed to restore that confidence there had been before. Not another offer of a cold drink. Not pointing out half a dozen 'funny men', though none of them was in fact particularly odd. Not promises of future treats, not stern injunctions to 'be a little man'. Ved's face remained tear-stained and immovable.

At last Ghote gave up in a spasm of irritation.

'If that is all you care, we will go home.'

Ved made no reply.

They set off, Ghote walking fast and getting unnecessarily hot. And still, going down Malabar Hill with its huge garden-surrounded mansions and great shady trees, there were passers-by with transistors and the unwearying commentator's voice.

'What a pity for India. A glorious captain's knock by the Rajah of Bolkpur ends in a doubtful decision by Umpire Khan.'

Ved swung round on him with an outraged glare. Whether this was because of the umpire's perfidy or because of simply not being there it was hard to tell.

And at that moment Ghote saw him. Anil Divekar. At least the figure that he half glimpsed ahead, sneaking out of a narrow gate and cradling in his arms a heavy-looking sack looked remarkably like Divekar. Ghote launched himself into the chase.

But the sound of running steps alerted the distant figure and in moments the fellow had disappeared altogether.

Ghote went quickly back to the house from whose side entrance he had seen the suspicious figure emerge. And there things began to add up. The big house had been rented temporarily to none other than the Rajah of Bolkpur himself, and a few minutes' search revealed that all the Rajah's silver trophies and personal jewellery had just been neatly spirited away.

Ghote got through to CID Headquarters on the telephone and reported. Then he and Ved endured a long wait till a squad arrived to take over. But they did get away in time to go down to the stadium again to see if Ved could catch a glimpse of the departing players.

And no sooner had they arrived at the stadium, just as the crowds were beginning to stream out, when there was Anil Divekar right in front of them. He made no attempt to run. On the contrary he came pushing his way through the throng, smiling broadly.

No doubt he thought he had fixed himself a neat alibi. But Ghote saw in an instant how he could trap Divekar if he had slipped away from the game just long enough to commit the robbery. Because it so happened that he himself knew exactly what had been occurring in the stadium at the moment the thief had slipped out of that house on Malabar Hill.

'A bad day's play, I hear,' he said to Divekar. 'What did you think about Bolkpur?'

Divekar shook his head sadly.

'A damn wrong decision, Inspectorji,' he said. 'I was sitting right behind the bat, and I could see. Damn wrong.'

He looked at them both with an expression of radiant guiltlessness. 'That was where you also would have been sitting,' he added.

You win, Ghote thought and turned grimly away. But on his way home he stopped for a moment at Headquarters to see if anything had turned up. His Deputy Superintendent was there.

'Well, Inspector, they tell me you spotted Anil Divekar leaving the house.'

'I am sorry, sir, but I do not think it was him now.'

He recounted his meeting with the man at the stadium a few minutes earlier; but the Deputy Superintendent was un-impressed.

'Nonsense, man, whatever the fellow says, this is Divekar's type of crime, one hundred per cent. You just identify him as running off from the scene and we've got him.'

For a moment Ghote was tempted. After all, Divekar was an inveterate thief: it would be justice of a sort. But then he knew that he had not really been sure who the running man had been.

'No, sir,' he said. 'I am sorry, but no.'

The Deputy Superintendent's eyes blazed, and it was only the insistent ringing of the telephone by his side that postponed his moment of wrath.

'Yes? Yes? What is it? Oh, you, Inspector. Well? What? The gardener? But . . . Oh, on him? Every missing item? Very good then, charge him at once.'

He replaced the receiver and looked at Ghote.

'Yes, Inspector,' he said blandly, 'that chap Divekar. As I was saying, he wants watching, you know. Close watching. I'll swear he is up to something. Now, he's bound to be at the Test Match tomorrow, so you had better be there too.'

'Yes, sir,' Ghote said.

A notion darted into his head.

'And, sir, for cover for the operation should I take this boy of mine also?'

'First-rate idea. Carry on, Inspector Ghote.'

1969

2

The Miracle Baby

What has Santa Claus got in store for me, Inspector Ghote said to himself, bleakly echoing the current cheerful Bombay newspaper advertisements as he waited to enter the office of Deputy Superintendent Naik that morning of December 25th.

Whatever the DSP had lined up for him, Ghote knew it was going to be nasty. Ever since he had recently declined to turn up for 'voluntary' hockey, DSP Naik had viewed him with sad-eyed disapproval. But what exact form would his displeasure take?

Almost certainly it would have something to do with the big Navy Week parade that afternoon, at the moment the chief preoccupation of most of the ever-excitable and drama-loving Bombayites. Probably he would be sent out into the crowds watching the Fire Power demonstration in the bay, ordered to come back with a beltful of pickpocketing arrests.

'Come,' the DSP's voice barked out, in response to Ghote's knock.

He went in and stood squaring his bony shoulders in front of the papers-strewn desk.

'Ah, Ghote, yes. Tulsi Pipe Road for you. Up at the north end. Going to be big trouble there. Rioting. Intercommunity outrages even.'

Ghote's heart sank even deeper than he had expected. Tulsi Pipe Road was a two-kilometres long thoroughfare that shot straight up from the Racecourse into the heart of a densely crowded mill district. There badly paid Hindus, Muslims by the thousand and Goans in hundreds all lived in prickling closeness, either in great areas of tumbledown hutments or in high tottering chawls, floor upon floor of massed humanity. Trouble between the religious communities there meant hell, no less.

'Yes, DSP?' he said, striving not to sound appalled.

'We are having a virgin birth business, Inspector.'

'Virgin birth, DSP sahib?'

'Come, man, you must have come across such cases.'

'I am sorry, DSP,' Ghote said, feeling obliged to be true to hard-won scientific principles. 'I am unable to believe in virgin birth.'

The DSP's round face suffused with instant wrath.

'I am not asking you to believe in virgin birth, man. It is not you who are to believe: it is all those Christians in the Goan community who are believing it about a baby born two days ago. It is the time of year, of course. These affairs are always coming at Christmas. I have dealt with half a dozen in my day.'

'Yes, DSP,' Ghote said, contriving to hit on the right note of awe.

'Yes. And there is only one way to deal with it: get hold of the girl and find out the name of the man. Do that pretty damn quick and the whole affair drops away to nothing, like monsoon water down a drain.'

'Yes, DSP.'

'Well, what are you waiting for, man? Jump to it.'

'Name and address of the girl in question, DSP sahib.'

The DSP's face darkened once more. He paddled furiously over the jumble of papers on his desk. And at last he found the chit he wanted.

'There you are, man. And you will find here the name of the Head Constable who first reported the matter. See him straight away. You have got a good man there, active, quick on his feet, sharp. If he could not make that girl talk, you will be having a first-class damn job, Inspector.'

Ghote located Head Constable Mudholkar one hour later at the local chowkey where he was stationed. Mudholkar at once confirmed the blossoming dislike for a sharp bully that Ghote had been harbouring ever since DSP Naik had praised the fellow. And, what was worse, the chap turned out to be very like the DSP in looks as well. He had the same round type of face, the same puffy-looking lips, even a similar soft blur of moustache. But the Head Constable's appearance was nevertheless a travesty of the DSP's. His face was, simply, slewed.

To Ghote's prejudiced eyes at the first moment of their encounter, the man's features seemed grotesquely distorted, as if in distant time some god had taken one of the Head

Constable's ancestors and wrenched his whole head sideways between two omnipotent god-hands.

But, as the fellow supplied the details of the affair, Ghote forced himself to regard him with an open mind, and he then had to admit that the facial twist which had seemed so pronounced was in fact no more than a drooping corner of the mouth and one ear being oddly longer than the other.

Ghote had to admit, too, that the chap was efficient. He had all the circumstances of the affair at his fingertips. The girl, named D'Mello – now in a hospital for her own safety – had been rigorously questioned both before and after the birth, but she had steadfastly denied that she had ever been with any man. She was indeed not the sort – the sole daughter of a Goan railway waiter on the Madras Express, a quiet girl, well brought-up though her parents were poor enough. She attended Mass regularly with her mother, and the whole family kept themselves to themselves.

'But with those Christians you can never tell,' Head Constable Mudholkar concluded.

Ghote felt inwardly inclined to agree. Fervid religion had always made him shrink inwardly, whether it was a Hindu holy man spending twenty years silent and standing upright or whether it was the Catholics, always caressing lifeless statues in their churches till glass protection had to be installed, and even then they still stroked the thick panes. Either manifestation rendered him uneasy.

That was the real reason, he now acknowledged to himself, why he did not want to go and see Miss D'Mello in the hospital, surrounded by nuns amid all the trappings of an alien religion, surrounded with all the panoply of a newly found goddess.

Yet go and see the girl he must.

But first he permitted himself to do every other thing that might possibly be necessary to the case. He visited Mrs D'Mello and, by dint of patient wheedling and a little forced toughness, confirmed from her the names of the only two men that Head Constable Mudholkar – who certainly proved to know inside out the particular chawl where the D'Mellos lived – had suggested as possible fathers. They were both young men; a Goan, Charlie Lobo, and a Sikh, Kuldip Singh.

The Lobo family lived one floor below the D'Mellos. But that one flight of dirt-spattered stairs, bringing them just that much nearer the courtyard tap which served the whole crazily leaning chawl, represented a whole layer higher in social status. And Mrs Lobo, a huge, tightly fat woman in a brightly flowered Western-style dress, had decided views about the unexpected fame that had come to the people upstairs.

'Has my Charlie been going with that girl?' she repeated after Ghote had managed to put the question, suitably wrapped up, to the boy. 'No, he has not. Charlie, tell the man you hate and despise trash like that.'

'Oh, Mum,' said Charlie, a downtrodden teenage wisp of a figure suffocating in a necktie beside his balloon-hard mother.

'Tell the man, Charlie.'

And obediently Charlie muttered something that satisfied his passion-filled parent. Ghote put a few more questions for form's sake, but he realised that only by getting hold of the boy on his own was he going to get any worthwhile answers. Yet it turned out that he did not have to employ any cunning. Charlie proved to have a strain of sharp slyness of his own, and hardly had Ghote started climbing the stairs to the floor above the D'Mellos where Kuldip Singh lived when he heard a whispered call from the shadow-filled darkness below.

'Mum's got her head over the stove,' Charlie said. 'She don't know I slipped out.'

'There is something you have to tell me?' Ghote asked, acting the indulgent uncle, turning back to the boy. 'You are in trouble. That's it, isn't it?'

'My only trouble is Mum,' the boy replied. 'Listen, mister, I had to tell you. I love Miss D'Mello. Yes, I love her. She's the most wonderful girl ever was.'

'And you want to marry her, and because you went too far before –'

'No, no, no. She's far and away too good for me, mister. I've never even said "Good Morning" to her in the two years we've lived here. But I love her, mister, and I'm not going to have Mum make me say different.'

Watching him slip cleverly through his door, Ghote made his mental notes and then continued up the stairs to tackle Kuldip Singh, his last comparatively easy task before the looming interview at the nun-ridden hospital.

Kuldip Singh, as Ghote had heard from Head Constable Mudholkar, was different from his neighbours. He lived in this teeming area from choice, not necessity. Officially a student, he spent all his time in a series of anti-social activities – protesting, writing manifestoes, drinking. He seemed an ideal candidate for the unknown and elusive father.

Ghote's suspicions were at once heightened when the young Sikh opened his door. The boy, though old enough to have a beard, lacked this symbol of his faith. Equally he had discarded the obligatory turban. But all the Sikh bounce was there, as Ghote discovered when he identified himself.

'Policewallah, is it? Then I want nothing at all to do with you. Me and the police are enemies, bhai. Natural enemies.'

'Irrespective of such considerations,' Ghote said, 'it is my duty to put to you certain questions concerning one Miss D'Mello.'

The young Sikh burst into a roar of laughter.

'The miracle girl, is it?' he said. 'Plenty of trouble for policemen there, I promise you. Top-level rioting coming from that business. The fellow who fathered that baby did us a lot of good.'

Ghote plugged away a good while longer – the hospital nuns awaited – but for all his efforts he learned no more than he had done in that first brief exchange. And in the end he still had to go and meet his doom.

Just what he had expected at the hospital he never quite formulated to himself. What he did find was certainly almost the exact opposite of his fears. A calm reigned. White-habited nuns, mostly Indian but a few Europeans, flitted silently to and fro or talked quietly to the patients whom Ghote glimpsed lying on beds in long wards. Above them swung frail but bright paper-chains in honour of the feast day. These were the only excitement.

The small separate ward in which Miss D'Mello lay all alone in a broad bed was no different. Except that the girl was isolated, she seemed to be treated in just the same way as the other new mothers in the maternity ward which Ghote had been led through on his way. In the face of such matter-of-factness, he felt hollowly cheated.

Suddenly, too, to his own utter surprise he found – looking down at the big, calm-after-storm eyes of the Goan girl – that he wanted the story she was about to tell him to be true. Part of him knew that, if it were so, or if it was widely believed to be so, appalling disorders could result from the feverish religious excitement that was bound to mount day by day. But another part of him now simply wanted a miracle to have happened.

He began, quietly and almost diffidently, to put his questions. Miss D'Mello would hardly answer at all, but such syllables as she did whisper were of blank inability to name anyone as the father of her child. After a while, with a distinct effort of will, Ghote brought himself to change his tactics. He banged out the hard line. Miss D'Mello went quietly and totally mute.

Then Ghote slipped in, with adroit suddenness, the name of Charlie Lobo. He got only a small puzzled frown.

Then, in an effort to make sure that her silence was not one of fear, he presented with equal suddenness the name of Kuldip Singh. If the care-for-nothing young Sikh had forced this timid creature, this might be the way to get an admission. But instead there came something approaching a laugh.

'That Kuldip is a funny fellow,' the girl said, with an out-of-place and unexpected offhandedness.

Ghote almost gave up. But at that moment a nun nurse appeared carrying in her arms a small, long, white-wrapped minutely crying bundle. The baby.

While she handed the hungry scrap to his mother Ghote stood and watched. Perhaps, holding the child, she would . . .

He looked down at the scene, awaiting his moment again. The girl fiercely held the tiny agitated thing to her breast and in a moment or two quiet came, the tiny hand applied to the life-giving source. How human the child looked already, Ghote thought. How much a man at two days old. The round skull almost bald, as it might become again towards the end of its span. The frown on the forehead that would last a lifetime. The tiny, perfectly formed plainly asymmetrical ears . . .

And then he knew that there had not been any miracle. It was as he had surmised, but with different circumstances. Miss D'Mello was indeed too frightened to talk. No wonder when the local bully, Head Constable Mudholkar, with his slewed head and his one ear so characteristically longer than the other, was the man who had forced himself on her, not the anti-social Kuldip Singh, not the timid worshipper Charlie Lobo.

A deep smothering of disappointment floated down on Ghote. So it had been nothing miraculous after all. Just a sad case, to be cleared up painfully. He stared down at the bed.

The tiny boy suckled energetically. And with a topsy-turvy welling up of rose-pink pleasure, Ghote saw that after all there had been a miracle. The daily, hourly, every-minute miracle of a new life, of a new flicker of hope in the tired world.

1971

3

The Not So Fly Fisherman

The telephone on Inspector Ghote's scratched and whorled little desk in his tiny office tucked into an out-of-the-way corner of Bombay CID Headquarters shrilled out alarmingly. Ghote swallowed once, squared his shoulders and picked up the receiver. Before he even had time to say his name a voice barked out at him from the earpiece. It was Deputy Superintendent Samant, sharp as a terrier dog and not to be argued with even if the truth were not on his side.

'Ghote? I will not have my officers in their seats all day. Goondaism is getting worse and worse, and you are just sitting there. What is it you are doing now? Answer, man, answer.'

'It is figures for you, DSP sahib,' Ghote replied. 'You were making most urgent request this morning. Correct figures for goondas arrested while committing violence in the second quarter of last year.'

'Figures, figures,' snapped the voice at the other end of the line. 'What good are figures only? We want action, man, action.'

'Very good, DSP sahib.'

'Ghote?'

'Yes, DSP? Here, DSP.'

'There is a man in the building, an Englishman. He has some sort of complaint to make. I have told them to send him to you. You are to deal with it. Understood?'

'Yes, DSP. And what is the nature–?'

'And, Ghote, he has demanded to see the Commissioner himself.'

The phone clicked dead with total abruptness and at the next moment, after only the most perfunctory of knocks, the office door was thrust open by an extremely scared-looking peon. Then a big-bellied Englishman strode in, his bright-banded straw hat still jammed above a florid, sweating face.

'You the Commissioner or whatever he's called?' he demanded at once in a voice so loud that it seemed to fill the little office from dusty floor to fly-haunted ceiling fan.

'No,' the Inspector said quickly. 'Unfortunately I am not the Commissioner. My name is Ghote. It is spelt G-H-O-T-E, but it is pronounced Go-tay.'

'To hell with spelling,' the Englishman battered in. 'What good did that ever do, I'd like to know? How about someone payin' some attention to me for a change? I'm the one who's been cheated out of every penny he's got.'

Ghote could hardly have been paying more attention to the cataract of sound that swirled and eddied all round the room, but he made an effort to assume an expression of even greater interest and begged his visitor to take a chair.

'If you will be so good as to supply full details,' he said, rapidly zipping open the drawer on the right-hand side of his desk where he kept his paper for note-taking.

'Right,' said the Englishman, plumping down like a sack of coal on the stout chair in front of the desk. 'Now get this. My name is Harper. Joe Harper to his friends, and they're many. And I saw this advert stuck on a wall like. Back in Batley where I come from. You'll have heard of Batley, I dare say.'

'Oh, yes. Yes, indeed,' Ghote replied with an inaccuracy all the more sweeping for the qualms he could not help feeling in employing it.

'Aye. Well, as I was sayin', I saw this advert and I gave a ring-up to the number it said. And the moment the feller told me he'd call me back I knew I was on to something. That's an old trick, you know. Ring back so as to make sure you aren't gettin' an inquiry from the police or any nasty, poke-nose lot of that sort.'

'Oh, yes, that would be most regrettable,' said Inspector Ghote.

'It would,' Joe Harper agreed with sledgehammer blitheness. 'Aye. So, as I was tellin' you, I fixed up with this feller. Golightly his name was, but he wasn't proper English. More one of your Indian half-and-halves. And what–'

'One moment, please,' Ghote interrupted, looking up from his note-taking. 'That name, Golightly. It seems to me extremely unusual. Would you be so kind as to spell it?'

'First you want to spell your name to me, and now you want

me to spell his to you. What do names matter? It's catchin' the feller I want.'

Nevertheless, in response to the Inspector's mutely poised pen the Englishman did at last oblige with the spelling of Golightly. As soon as Ghote had finished writing the name he invited Joe Harper to go on.

'Right. Then I joined this club, the Budleigh Regis Fly Fishermen's and Deep Sea Anglers' Association. And off we went. Well, when we got to Bombay we had to change planes to go to this place that begins with a K. You know, where all the filthy carvings are.'

'Khajurao?' Ghote suggested. 'That is a great tourist attraction. K-H-A-J-U-R-A-O.'

'Aye, that'd be it. Though why you want to go chanting out letters again is more than I can say.'

'I was thinking it might be of assistance,' Ghote explained. He committed this one name more to paper and looked up. 'But there is not any fishing at Khajurao,' he said.

'I'll say there isn't,' Joe Harper agreed with a heavy wink. 'Not that I'll ever see the place now, because when we got to Bombay I thought I'd drop off like and go later on my own. Joe Harper's no one's dogsbody. And then, when I went to collect my return ticket I found–'

'You had to collect your return ticket in Bombay? Surely that was most peculiar?'

'I'll say peculiar. 'Specially when it turns out there's no such address as 346 Taj Mahal Street.'

'Ah,' said Ghote, 'now I am seeing. You have become the victim of that miscreant with the unusual name.'

'Aye. Golightly. And you'd better set about gettin' hold of him, pronto.'

'Getting hold? But surely that is a question for the UK police. We will be in instant telegraphic communic—'

'UK police? Don't be daft. He's here, in ruddy Bombay. I've told you that a hundred times. He came on the flight with us. That's why I thought the whole deal was above board. Because, I tell you, I had my doubts from the first. There's no flies on Joe Harper.'

Looking across at the belly-jutting, puce-faced Englishman, Ghote could not help registering that in fact there were flies on the Budleigh Regis fly fisherman. Half a dozen had been buzzing round him ever since he had settled down, and at this moment a couple were resting on his perspiring neck.

'Mr Harper,' he said, bringing his mind back to the matter in hand, 'you are a fisherman and you—'

'Fisherman? I've never so much as hooked a tiddler in my life.'

'But the Budleigh Regis Fly Fishermen's and Deep Sea Anglers' Association?' Ghote asked, consulting his notes.

'Oh, that,' said Joe Harper.

'Yes. Well, what I was about to say was that, as a fisherman, you would understand how difficult it would be to catch one particular fish out of all the many in the sea, and that is precisely the problem you are setting us.'

'Aye, I am,' said Joe Harper uncompromisingly. 'I've given you the feller's name, I've told you he's here, and I've said he's cheated me. Now get after him. And if he's not caught in less than no time I'll be in to that Commissioner of yours wantin' to know the reason why.'

A leaden chill welled up in Ghote. He could easily conceive that someone who appeared to be as utterly self-centred as this fat, sweating and aggressive Englishman might well force his way to the Commissioner himself, with fearful repercussions for anyone who had not succeeded in keeping him out.

'Mr Harper,' he said firmly, 'if I am to find this one Anglo-Indian from among the thousands in this city, not to speak of the millions of Hindus, the hundreds of thousands of Muslims, the tens of thousands of Goans, the thousands of Parsis and the hundreds of Jews, then you must tell more than you have so far.'

'I've told you the lot,' Joe Harper replied in a fresh squall of aggressiveness.

'No,' said Ghote. 'I think not.'

'Not? What do you—'

Ghote cut into the sharply rising voice.

'For example, you did not tell that you came here on a cut-price flight,' he said.

'Cut-price—' The big Englishman suddenly sagged. 'Yes, you're right,' he said. 'How did you know?'

A hollowly anxious note had replaced the bluster.

'A great deal of information comes into Headquarters here and is duly circulated,' Ghote replied. 'For some time we have been hearing about these false clubs that are set up to tempt people to pay only about half the fare Air India or BOAC charges. When someone is putting themselves outside the law in this way there is scope for many varieties of fraud, as you have found.'

'Aye, that's true enough,' agreed Joe Harper mournfully. 'I'll have to ask the British Consul or somebody to stake me my fare home, and heaven knows where I'll find the money to pay them back. I'm right cleaned out.'

'Well, is there anything more you have to tell me now?' Ghote asked more gently. 'Let me assure you, the full truth can only be helpful to you.'

'Oh, I don't know,' the big Englishman answered. 'There's not much more I can tell you, and that's a fact. You were right about one thing, though. It wasn't fishing I came here for. It was what the advert called a glimpse of the Erotic East, that place beginning with K. Blessed if I can get my tongue round it yet. Only when we got to Bombay, I found I'd somehow lost heart.'

He looked across at Ghote, his face wrinkled like a deflating balloon with this painful effort to get to the bottom of things.

'You come to know it in the end,' he went on. 'That it won't make all that much of a difference, even if you do go off where nobody knows who you are. Well, any road, that's what I got to thinkin' when I decided to follow that Golightly out of the airport.' He brightened a little. 'But you should have seen his face,' he said, 'when he realised I was going with him. A right crosspatch. And no wonder, I suppose.'

He gave a rueful grunt of a laugh, as if he had seen his situation clearly for perhaps the first time.

'He told me he had to go and phone his old mother,' he said. 'I suppose it was just to get rid of me. What a reason.'

His eyes dropped to where the shirt stretched across his great floppy belly was patched with dark sweat.

'Do you know,' he said, 'I believed him at the time. He seemed sincere like. It made me think, what if my mother could see me now? Aye, I thought that. I did truly.'

He looked up at Ghote as if seeking, despite all odds, some sort of assurance that he had not been too foolish. But Ghote was busy with a large yellow and white volume that had on its front cover a purple advertisement for Nirodh family planning requisites.

In a moment he slammed its pages together, quickly picked up his telephone and dialled a number.

In the stuffy heat of the little office the sound of the distant ringing could be heard clearly. Joe Harper shifted his bulk on the hard chair.

'Hello? Golightly here.'

Inspector Ghote put his hand on the mouthpiece.

'It looks as if the news is good for you,' he said to the erstwhile Budleigh Regis fly fisherman. 'If there was only a single one of that unusual name in the Bombay Telephone Directory, it was certain to be your man's mother.'

He gave the Englishman an almost timid smile.

'You could be saying,' he ventured, 'that we have got your fish on the end of our line.'

1973

4

The River Man

Deputy Superintendent Samant looked at Inspector Ghote with a starkly obvious effort to keep under control the terrier sharpness of his usual manner.

'I think I have only to say to you,' he uttered, almost pushing the words back down his own throat, 'to say one name, that of Dr P. R. Kumaramangalam.'

Total blankness abruptly occupied the whole of Ghote's mind. Above him in the Deputy Superintendent's office in Bombay CID Headquarters the big ceiling fan whirred with an insistent drone that seemed to blot out every coherent thought.

At last he forced himself to reply, licking his parched lips.

'Dr P. R. Kumaramangalam, DSP sahib?'

With audible relief the DSP allowed a quick spurt of rage to escape him.

'Yes, yes, man, Dr P. R. Kumaramangalam. Are you going to tell me you have never heard of him? The newly-appointed head of the All-India College of Surgeons? Inspector, do you never read books? Do you never browse even through the pages of *Times of India Who's Who*?'

'Yes—. No, sir. Not the *Who's Who*, sir.'

With joy, DSP Samant let loose a single cutting blast of sarcasm.

'Then you can take it from me, Inspector, the day will never come when you feature in those pages. Never. Never in one hundred years.'

'No, sir.'

It was a comfort to be able to agree without reservation. Even the DSP seemed to lose some of his bottled impatience. He leant back in his heavy wooden armchair and surveyed Ghote across his desk with something like calm.

'Dr Kumaramangalam, Inspector,' he said, 'besides being

33

the head of the All-India College is also a close personal friend of the Commissioner.'

His voice rose to an incisive peak on those last two words and Ghote irradiated his face with a look of proper awe.

'Yes, sir,' he said.

'And the Commissioner, Inspector, has asked me, me personally, to undertake a certain assignment on behalf of Dr Kumaramangalam. An assignment not strictly official, Inspector, and one requiring the utmost discretion.'

The pouncing sharpness was building up again under the effort to speak of the matter with a calm equal to the discretion it required. The DSP's hands were holding hard on to the arms of his chair.

'The utmost bloody discretion, man,' he repeated.

'Yes, sir,' said Ghote.

Deep down a little flicker of delight began to play inside him. A matter requiring utmost discretion, and he had been summoned by the DSP to be told about it. No doubt to take part in whatever inquiries were necessary.

'It seems, Inspector,' the DSP said, once more making an effort to regain a fitting calm, 'that some weeks ago our friends the Customswallahs were chasing some gold smugglers in a boat up the mouth of a certain river not a hundred miles from Bombay, and in the course of the chase they came upon an aged Englishman living, all on his own and in conditions of considerable destitution, on a tiny island in the river mouth.'

'Yes, sir,' Ghote put in with caution.

'Yes, Inspector. Now, in the course of inquiries the Customswallahs heard mention in connection with this individual – generally known to the fisherfolk in the vicinity only as the River Man – of another name.'

The DSP paused.

Another name, thought Ghote. And he had already betrayed a lamentable ignorance over Dr Kumaramangalam. Please, oh please, let him get this one right.

'The name Valsingham Doctor, Inspector.'

'Valsingham Doctor. But, DSP . . . But, sir, that name is known to me. It—'

'Of course it is known to you, man. Have I not heard it from your own lips? And more than once. Much more than once. For what other reason did you think I was requiring your assistance, Inspector? Because you are renowned for your ability to handle a matter requiring discretion?'

DSP Samant laughed. Long and loudly. He enjoyed himself.

'Yes, Inspector,' he continued at last. 'You and your precious Dr James Walsingham. You and your precious eye-surgeon who cured the whole of your village, was it, when you were a boy? Your hero, Inspector. On an island, Inspector. Somewhere in a river nobody ever goes to, Inspector. The River Man, Inspector, your Dr James Walsingham.'

'Yes, sir,' Ghote said.

Could it be true? Surely Dr Walsingham, that benefactor, must be dead? Yet he had not heard that he was, and if he had been he would certainly have known. A man who had meant so much to him as a boy. Someone he had – how could he have done? – even mentioned so often to DSP Samant that he had been marked down for it? But it was certainly possible Dr Walsingham was still alive. After all, he had looked hale and hearty in newspaper pictures, with that neat beard no more than grey, some twenty years ago. So he could well be alive. A man of perhaps eighty or more. Alive and well.

Or not well . . .

'Sir, you have said destitute, sir. Is he not well, sir? Sir, a man like Dr Walsingham – oh, sir, a public benefactor, not too much to say a saint, sir – ought not to be left alone and ill.'

'Precisely, Inspector. The point, of course, that Dr Kumaramangalam made to his friend the Commissioner. And that the Commissioner made to me. Only . . .'

'Only, DSP sahib?'

'Only this man, this River Man, is he truly Dr James Walsingham, Inspector? Because he certainly appears to take pains not to own to that name, to any name. And that is creating a certain difficulty.'

'Yes, sir,' Ghote said.

Later that day Ghote, propelling forward with difficulty a commandeered fisherman's boat, little more than a hollowed-out log, felt himself becoming more and more perturbed by the problem that the identity of the River Man presented. He had seen him already, a figure that could have been no one else, prowling haggardly about the tiny island out in the wide river mouth. With DSP Samant he had watched him through binoculars for some considerable time. But the gaunt, long-bearded emaciated old man he had seen at that distance was nothing at all like the trim Dr Walsingham he had followed through the village when he had come there to carry out eye operations on the afflicted brought from miles around.

He looked mad, the old River Man. There could be no doubt about it. They had seen him through the glasses muttering to himself. While 'Valsingham Doctor' – as the non-English speakers among the poor always called him – had been far from mad. A dynamo of concentrated energy, selfless, tireless, working all the hours of light and falling asleep exhausted almost as soon as darkness had come. A powerhouse of good-doing, giving everything, asking nothing.

Except for Garibaldi biscuits.

Ghote glanced down at his feet. There on the rough-hacked bottom of their lumbering boat was a super-smart shiny packet of Garibaldi biscuits. DSP Samant had ordered him to get them – and a fearful chase he had had to find any – because he had remembered that once Ghote had mentioned the great healer's touching liking for just this sweet, currant-filled biscuit. A gift of this kind would perhaps ensure their welcome in what might be extremely difficult circumstances.

'There. Make for that tree.'

The DSP pointed. Ghote plunged his crude paddle into the swirling brown water and pushed with all his might. Their heavy craft swayed alarmingly and Ghote almost hurled the paddle at the water on the other side. The boat, which hitherto had moved no faster than a buffalo watering in some pond, suddenly surged forward and plunged suckingly on to a submerged bank of mud two full yards clear of the slimey-rooted tree.

'Idiot,' said the DSP. Ghote back-paddled desperately, sweat pouring down him. The log-like boat remained exactly where it was.

'Damn it,' the DSP shouted. 'I cannot remain here all afternoon.'

He stood up, eyed the firm platform of the tree's exposed roots and jumped.

The force of his departure did what Ghote's paddling had

been unable to do. The heavy boat slid sharply off the mud bank. Deprived at the last instant of a firm footing, the DSP landed with a splash and a long slow squelch about half-way between boat and bank.

He forced his way to dry land in terrible silence, then turned.

'Get that boat to where I ordered,' he exploded. 'Get it there. And then come to join me. And do not come barging in when I am talking. This is a matter that requires discretion. Discretion, Ghote. Discretion.'

He marched off. His trousers, till now immaculate and wonderfully smart, were up to the knees black as sin.

For ten dispiriting minutes Ghote manoeuvred his intractable craft in and out, splashing and cursing, sweating from head to foot and sometimes feeling near to tears. But at last he got it right up to the tree the DSP had indicated and tied the sopping rope at its prow to one of the roots. He got himself carefully ashore and set off cautiously across the little island towards the sole building on it, a tumbledown hut of palm leaves.

He had hardly set out, however, when he heard the DSP's voice. And as he neared the wretched hovel the words came more and more clearly to his ears.

'. . . cannot go on saying nothing, man. What is your name? Come on, you must have a name. You must. Now, answer up. Answer up.'

The voice rang all about the tiny, densely overgrown island.

Discretion, Ghote thought. Oh, DSP sahib.

But the fury apparently produced no answer. After a little, the DSP began again.

'Very well, I will go over the whole thing once more. Just once. Yes? Yes?'

Again he seemed to receive no answer. Ghote stood where he was in the shade of a stubby banana palm. Insects hummed and whined in his ears. In a moment he heard the DSP's voice once more.

'Oh, very well then. But listen to me. Acting on information received, I came to this disgraceful shack on this island in the middle of nowhere and I find one inhabitant, aged approximately eighty years, apparently of European extraction, not in a good state of health or of cleanliness, wearing a pair of old khaki shorts only, lying upon a charpoy which is in a state of disintegration. I put it to this individual "You are Dr James Walsingham?" And what does he do? He refuses to make answer.'

The DSP's voice paused . . . and then resumed on a note of rising indignation.

'I put a perfectly polite question. Are you or are you not Dr James Walsingham? It is perfectly easy to answer. Yes, I am. Or no, I am not. Whichever applies. But you refuse to answer. Why is that? What in God's name, man, can there be in such a question that you refuse altogether to make any answer whatsoever?'

Another pause. Shorter this time. Then again.

'The days of the British Raj are over. The Angrezi Sarkar is no more. I am an officer of police duly authorised to question. I am DSP Samant, Bombay CID. And you are committing an offence. Under Section 179 Indian Penal Code. So answer up. Answer up.'

The voice rang and rang, but not the faintest murmur of reply followed. Silence stretched. Ghote heard, down in the river, the heavy plop of a fish rising.

'Oh, very well then,' the DSP's voice had a note of familiar sarcasm in it now. 'Oh, very well. But I am not finished yet. I have something still that you have not at all thought about.'

And then with total abruptness the voice changed.

'Ghote. Ghote. Inspector Ghote.'

The shouts rang out.

'Yes, DSP. Coming, DSP. Here, DSP sahib.'

Ghote ran towards the sagging palm-leaf hut. He tripped over the root of a tree, staggered, righted himself and arrived, panting, at the dark entrance.

'Yes, DSP? Can I be of assistance, sir?'

It was yet darker in the hut and he could make out little beyond the DSP who was standing just inside. Only down near ground level the glint of what must be two eyes, like the glaring eyes of some animal.

'Now then, Mr River Man,' the DSP said. 'Here is something you were not expecting. Ghote, what was it at the age of six years or seven you were privileged to witness? Hm? Eh? What?'

Ghote swallowed.

'Sir,' he said. 'DSP, I take it that you are requesting me to refer to the time when our village was visited by the great Dr James Walsingham?'

'Exactly, man,' the DSP snapped. 'And at that time you saw a good deal of Dr Walsingham? Eh? Eh? You followed him round like a faithful dog only, yes?'

'Yes, sir. Yes, I did.'

'Good. Fine. Excellent. And now, tell me, who is that individual you can see lying on that charpoy there?'

Ghote took a step forward and looked down. He was quickly able to see a good deal more, the spreading tangled beard of the man he had watched through the binoculars, his bare and ribby chest, the torn khaki shorts. Soon all that remained of the face as it emerged from its frame of matted hair was fully visible.

'Sir, it is difficult,' he said.

'Nonsense, man, nonsense,' DSP Samant snapped. 'Go nearer. Take a damn good look.'

Ghote obeyed. He did not feel altogether happy to do so, but nevertheless he put his face close to that of the man on the charpoy and peered hard. Two red-rimmed eyes looked back at him, blankly and ferociously.

'Well?' barked the DSP.

'Sir . . .'

'Come, man, tell him you are well recognising him as Dr Walsingham and that this tactic of silence on his part is now altogether useless.'

'But . . . But, sir,' Ghote said.

He took a great swallow.

'Sir, I cannot say that.'

'What? What? You mean the fellow is not Dr Walsingham? You mean I have come all the way out here on a wild-goose chase? That the Commissioner . . .'

'No, sir,' Ghote said, wondering how he could produce the words. 'Sir, it is not that. It is that I cannot be sure, sir. It was a long time ago, DSP. Dr Walsingham was a neat English sahib with a trimmed, pointed beard, sir. But this – but the River Man, sir . . . Well, you have only got to look. He is dirty, sir. Filthy. You can hardly—'

But with the suddenness of a springing beast a voice came from behind him, low, growling, fury-filled.

'How dare you? Standing there. Peering at me, prying, poking. Talking about me as if I was—'

But as suddenly as he had begun to speak the old man came to an abrupt halt. It was as if something else had been forced between him and the words he had been saying like a descending steel barrier.

He gave a long shuddering sigh that seemed to have in it something of the very mark of the end of a life. And then he spoke again. But now the words were murmured, tentative, hard to catch.

'As if I was . . . As if I was what? What? What?'

DSP Samant firmly ignored the doubtful content of what the old man had said and seized on an essential.

'Ah, so you are able to talk.'

He bent over the charpoy, but the River Man ignored him.

'As if I was what?' he murmured again.

'Now look here,' the DSP said, keeping himself somewhat in check. 'If you please, are you or are you not one Dr James Walsingham?'

'Dr James Walsingham?' the aged, lined, cracked and matted-bearded figure answered, his voice wavering at first but gathering strength and purpose. 'No, I am not Dr James Walsingham. Who is Dr James Walsingham? I know nothing of any Dr Walsingham.'

The DSP was shocked.

'But – but – but, look here—'

Daringly Ghote forestalled the coming lava flow.

'Sir. Sir, no. Sir, he has denied. I think, DSP sahib, with respect, all we can do now is to go.'

In the darkness a sharp gleam seemed to come into the River Man's eyes.

'Yes,' he said, more briskly than anything yet. 'Yes, go. Leave me in peace.'

DSP Samant looked at him in bafflement.

'But then how was it . . .' he began. 'Oh, damn and blast. The Commissioner would have . . . Well, look here, in any case, what is your name, then?'

'Yes, go, peace,' the River Man answered.

'Sir,' Ghote ventured again, 'I think since he has asked . . .'

'Peace,' the River Man muttered, seemingly far away now. 'Peace. Ponder. Think it out.'

'Yes, but all the same,' the DSP persisted, answering Ghote. 'Why did the fellow not give a straight answer in the first place?'

He swung round to the River Man again.

'Look, you, are you not after all truly Dr Walsingham?'

'Go, go,' he answered. 'What do you want here? How could I be the great Dr Walsingham? Look at these hands of mine. They shake, they tremble. Are these Dr James Walsingham's hands?'

In the sun-shaded gloom Ghote could see the River Man was holding out both hands. The nails were long and curling, split here and there and grimed with earth. And certainly they shook.

But DSP Samant pounced.

'Hands,' he repeated, with rising delight. 'Hands that shake. Never heard of Dr James Walsingham? Those were your words. Then how was it that you knew it mattered whether his hands would shake? A surgeon's hands, an eye-surgeon's hands? Eh? Eh?'

He glared down at the thin-armed old man on the bed. It was some time before the aged, tired voice could get out more than a few broken words. But at last more came.

'No, no. I did not say that. A mistake. All a mistake. I take it back.'

'What is said is said,' returned the DSP. 'There can be no taking back of the truth, Dr Walsingham.'

Ghote bobbed in.

'But, please, Dr Walsingham,' he said, 'please do not think we are meaning you any harm whatsoever. That is far from the case.'

'Yes, yes,' the DSP added, coming back to the realities of the situation. 'We are here to help only. To act with the utmost discretion.'

'No.'

'No?' the DSP asked. 'What no is this?'

The old man raised himself a little and looked at them with a new steadiness.

'No,' he said, 'you think you've got me trapped, don't you? Think you've got a poor old man trapped?'

'It is not at all a question of trap,' the DSP replied.

'But you haven't,' the old man went on. 'You have not. That's a trap I can walk right out of.'

'I repeat,' said the DSP with a touch of returning asperity. 'There is no question of trap, Dr Walsingham.'

Down on the charpoy what could only be an expression of animal cunning came over the dirty aged features.

'No,' the old man said. 'Not Dr Walsingham. Not at all. Listen to me. I deny that I am Dr James Walsingham. I tell you that I am not. I walk out of it.'

'But, look here—' the DSP began.

'No. If I say that I am not that man, what can you do about it? Ha? Who should know better than I who I am? And I say that I am not Dr James Walsingham. There.'

The River Man's pleasure was malign.

'But . . . but, Mr River Man,' Ghote said, 'we are not at all meaning to accuse.'

'No,' he almost snarled back. 'No, I shall hear not a word more. I am not Dr James Walsingham, and there you will have to leave it. You must.'

'But then, Mr River Man, who are you?' Ghote asked simply.

For a palpable moment the River Man did not reply. Then he spoke, and his voice once again had taken on a plaintive note.

'Who am I? Young man, you ask more than you know. There you are – what are you? A police inspector? There you are, going about your business of arresting people, detecting crimes, whatever it is, and never for one moment do you stop to think. Do you?'

Ghote saw that the ancient, staring eyes were demanding an answer.

'Well, excuse me,' he said, 'but often I am attempting to consider my whole position in this world. But on the other hand there are a great many duties I have to undertake. Statistics to compile, reports—'

'Routines,' snarled the River Man. 'I was caught in them myself – once.'

'But, no,' Ghote protested. 'Saving the sight of so many people, that was not at all routine.'

At once the cunning look came back into the old, old face.

'Hah, you think you can catch me that way? Saving sight? That was Dr Walsingham. That wasn't me; I am not Dr Walsingham.'

'Dr Walsingham,' Ghote said, 'please. Please, DSP Samant has already proved. But, Doctor, why is it that you do not wish to admit to being what you were? Sir, if ever I have hoped to do good to my fellow men, sir, it was from you that hope came.'

But the River Man only glared back at him malevolently.

'Look, please, Dr Walsingham,' Ghote went on. 'Here is proof of how much you were meaning to one small boy. All these years he has remembered this.'

And he abruptly thrust forward the glinting, shiny-packed Garibaldi biscuits.

'Sir, you liked,' he said.

'What? What?' the River Man blurted out, reduced suddenly to an old, confused creature.

'They are Garibaldi biscuits,' Ghote explained.

'Garibaldi biscuits.'

There was – plain to hear – a note of wonder in the River Man's voice. A chord struck and faintly reverberated.

'To us boys you were calling them always squashed flies,' Ghote said. 'It was joke.'

'Yes,' murmured the River Man. 'Yes, seeing them there, holding them now, the taste buds tingle. And so long ago that I . . . So is it the same thing in me that quickens to these absurd, flat, currant-filled sweet things? In me? Is it?'

DSP Samant stood above him and rocked gently back once on his heels.

'Good,' he said. 'Excellent. And now, Dr Walsingham, now that we have finally dealt with the matter of identity, perhaps I could ask a number of questions? Now, have you been in residence on this island since the date of your retirement, I understand in 1945?'

The River Man looked up at him from his clutching at the shiny packet with the bright picture of its contents.

'I retire in 1945?' he returned. 'And who are you to say that that was me?'

The DSP sighed.

'I much regret, Dr Walsingham,' he said. 'But the matter of identity has now been thoroughly established. All that I am asking is have you been resident here since 1945?'

'No,' said the River Man, 'I cannot answer. It is too hard.'

'Too hard? What non—'

The DSP remembered where he was. He began again.

'Dr Walsingham, I think there must be a misunderstanding.

43

All I have asked is how long you have been in residence here. There can be nothing difficult to that.'

'Nothing difficult? You pup.'

The River Man spat back the words.

For one long instant Ghote watched the DSP's face, saw the blood come up into it, the cheeks puff hard, the eyes widen.

'DSP sahib,' he said hastily. 'I am sure that Dr Walsingham did not mean . . .'

The DSP rounded on him.

'Mean? Mean?' he barked. 'He said it, man. He said it. He said that that simple question was too hard to answer. Pah!'

He wheeled back to the River Man.

'That is nonsense, Dr Walsingham,' he declared. 'Altogether nonsense.'

The River Man rose, still holding the shiny packet, till the top half of his rib-revealing body was almost upright. He gave the DSP a look of sweeping contempt.

'Oh, you poor certainty-monger,' he said. 'What do you know? I am Dr Walsingham, am I? The great, benevolent eye-surgeon, the friend of the poor? Is that it? Is it? Is it?'

In face of these demands the DSP straightened his back.

'If you are stating, then yes,' he said.

'And what if I say no?' the River Man roared back, his voice high and cracking. 'What if I say, no, I am as different from that man as cheese is from chalk? What if I say I am a killer? A mass-murderer? The foulest of killers? Eh?'

'Dr Walsingham,' the DSP said, 'that is thoroughly ridiculous.'

'Ridiculous? You pig-headed jackass. I tell you that I am. I am one Jack Curtin. Jack Curtin. Never heard the name? No? Then perhaps you've heard of my title? The title they gave me? The Beast of the Beaches.'

And the instant the words were uttered Ghote, at least, knew that he had heard of Jack Curtin.

'DSP,' he said, feeling himself floating in an unknown sea, 'DSP, that is a well-known case of past times. But I was reading of it only recently. In the *Illustrated Weekly of India*, DSP sahib. It was a case that occurred in Bombay itself some sixty years ago.'

'Yes, that's so, read it myself,' the DSP said slowly. 'A celebrated case.'

Ghote looked at the scrawny figure on the dilapidated charpoy.

'Dr Wals— Mr River Man,' he said, 'are you telling that somehow you were the perpetrator in that affair?'

The River Man looked at them both with blazing scorn.

'Well, what do you feel now, you cock-sparrows?' he asked.

'Sir,' Ghote said doubtfully, turning to the DSP, 'I suppose it is possible. He is looking as if he is in excess of eighty years of age, and the killer was a youth of twenty only. And that man was never apprehended. That is the point. He was never apprehended.'

The DSP pulled his face into a semblance of stern inflexibility.

'Am I to understand,' he asked the matted-bearded old man, 'that you are confessing to be the killer of six Anglo-Indian girls on the beaches in or near Bombay during a period of some four months in or about the year 1910?'

'Sir, no,' Ghote burst in. 'I see what he is doing now. He is attempting only, for reasons of his own, to persuade us to leave. He is attempting to create a state of confusion.'

'You fool,' snarled the River Man. 'I am making it clear. At last I am telling you everything. And you will hear.'

His lean body was taut now with the passion of what he was saying. The eyes under the tangled eyebrows were wide and fierce.

'DSP sir,' Ghote said softly and quickly, 'I think that we ought to leave without delay. If this River Man is truly Dr Walsingham, sir, he is telling something he ought not.'

The DSP made an apparent effort to put the affair on a level of normality, shrugging his shoulders loosely and assuming a man-of-the-world expression.

'Now, look here, Dr Walsingham,' he said, 'I do not know what all this is about, but let me assure you it is altogether unnecessary. Inspector Ghote and I are here simply to help. Here are you, living in appalling conditions, and your friends in Bombay are anxious about you. All we need is a few particulars.'

'Anxious about the Beast of the Beaches?' the River Man answered with a cutting edge to his voice. 'Anxious about the man who within one month took six lives for his pleasure?'

'I do not know anything about all that,' the DSP persisted.

'You have shown me to my own satisfaction that you are Dr Walsingham, and that is all there is to be said. This other business is sheer tommy-rot.'

'You need convincing still, do you? It was here, you know. Here, to this island, that I came, came when they were hunting me.'

'Doctor, Mr River Man,' Ghote said urgently. 'Do not utter one more single word.'

But the old man appeared not even to have heard him.

'The last one of them, the seventh one, screamed,' he went on in a voice that was low but terribly clear. 'Screamed and screamed. People were coming down to the beach. I had to leave her and run. To run through the heat of the night. And then I saw the boat, and got out to sea in it. But they brought up a steam launch. If it hadn't been for the mist they would have caught me like a wriggling fish. But in the mist I left that boat and swam for it, and when the sun came through I was here in the river mouth. And on this island I found shelter.'

'Sir,' Ghote asked the DSP in a whisper, 'do you think this fellow has been here for sixty years, that he is someone else?'

'No, no, man, nonsense. I have proved he is Dr Walsingham.'

The River Man had caught the words; he glared at the DSP.

'You block of wood,' he said. 'You still do not understand, do you? What do you think I did here? What do you think Jack Curtin – the lad who had been a butcher's apprentice in England before he took that job as a liner steward – what do you think he did?'

The wild eyes were glaring at Ghote now. Ghote swallowed.

'Please,' he said, 'I do not know.'

'No, you lily-livered creature,' the River Man spat at him. 'No, you wouldn't know, wouldn't have the guts even to guess. Why, I carved at myself, man, carved at myself.'

'Carved?' Ghote asked.

'Carved my face, you loon. I still had my butcher's knife, my killing knife, and I carved the flesh of my own face, looking down into the water of the river there, carved it and let the cuts heal, and carved again. I made myself a new face.'

'DSP,' Ghote whispered. 'It is possible. Inside that beard Dr Walsingham's face was somewhat lumpy.'

'Yes,' said the River Man, dropping a little from his rigid

pose. 'Yes, I tricked them. I went back to Bombay and I walked the streets, safe as safe. I got myself work, made money, enrolled at Grant College. I studied.'

The voice abruptly took on a new note. The tinge of almost childish pride dropped away, to be replaced by a wondering.

'Yes,' he said, 'I became a different man.'

Again he paused. Neither Ghote nor the DSP made the least sound.

'Yes, tricked them,' the River Man said. 'Became a new man. But who else did I trick? Did I trick myself as well? What did I do to myself?'

And there was now, plainly, an appalledness in the old, old voice. If the DSP and Ghote had been silent before, they were now doubly held so. Only able to stand and to try to grasp just what they had heard.

So that two women's voices, talking loudly, were already within twenty yards of the shack before either Ghote or the DSP was aware that they were no longer the only visitors on the island.

The DSP wheeled round on Ghote.

'What do you mean by it, Inspector?' he let rip. 'Allowing persons to land here? Did I not specifically say this was a matter requiring the greatest discretion?'

'But, sir, how could I prevent?'

The DSP was saved from explaining how easily Ghote could have been at one and the same time down by the shore and in the old man's shack by one of the two women outside saying loudly, 'It is here,' and the opening to the hut being at the next moment blocked by the figure of a woman aged about thirty-five, dressed in a sari at once expensive and functionally neat, wearing a pair of heavy spectacles on her smooth-skinned face.

She stood for a moment blinking at the shadowed gloom inside. Then she turned and addressed her companion.

'Intruders, Dr Abrahams,' she said. 'It seems we have intruders.'

'Well,' came a thick voice from outside, speaking English with a strong Germanic accent, 'well, it would seem so, my dear.'

A moment later she came into the hut, a tough-looking old lady of perhaps seventy-five, dressed in old-fashioned white clothes, a blouse and thickly pleated skirt, and a sun helmet.

47

'Ah,' she said, as soon as she had got accustomed to the gloom, 'but one of these intruders is known to me. Deputy Superintendent Samant, is it not?'

The DSP stiffened.

'Dr Frieda Abrahams,' he replied. 'And what are you doing here?'

'I imagine,' Dr Abrahams replied, with a certain heaviness, 'that I am on the same business as you yourself.'

'But—' the DSP stammered. 'But how was it that you knew there was any question of . . . of Dr Walsingham being here?'

Dr Abrahams gave him a smile that was at once pitying and comforting.

'It was you who came to me with a lot of questions about a colleague I thought was dead. An old woman who has seen something of the world can draw conclusions, you know.'

Appalled and ashamed at hearing this revelation of how indiscreet the DSP had been in a matter so heavily labelled 'Be discreet', Ghote hardly listened as the formidable German lady went on to explain that, with the aid of a few inquiries at CID Headquarters, she had been easily able to find out where the DSP had said he was going, and that she had followed post-haste with the young woman who had first entered the hut, Dr Sooni Doctor, a specialist in the care of the aged, just back from Britain and America with a string of impressive qualifications. He was only fully aware of what was going on when Dr Abrahams turned to the darkest corner of the hut where the River Man now lay flat on the old charpoy, only a pair of red-rimmed, wide-open eyes betraying that he was at all aware of the invasion of his lonely home.

'Well,' she said, 'all this talk, all these introductions, and I have not yet greeted my old friend.'

She moved across to the charpoy and looked down at the silent, bearded, hostile-looking form of the River Man.

'James,' she said. 'My old friend. It is Frieda Abrahams after these many years.'

The River Man said nothing.

'James?'

'Dr Abrahams,' the DSP said, quietly and quickly, 'you are in no doubt that this is Dr Walsingham?'

Dr Abrahams turned to him.

'It is many years. He is much changed. Indeed, I do not

think he is in a very good state at all. So, well, really, if it was a court of law I could not swear. But, before this, why is he staying so silent?'

She looked at the DSP with sharp shrewdness and concern plainly stamped on her square battered face. Then Dr Sooni Doctor, who had stepped briskly forward and given the River Man a quick professional scrutiny, turned round.

'There will doubtless be a good deal of loss of hearing,' she suggested.

'If it was that only,' said the DSP.

'That only?' Dr Abrahams queried. 'There is something wrong here, I think. When I first came in I sensed something. An old woman develops a certain feeling for tensions, for trouble.'

She turned authoritatively back to the River Man and picked up one emaciated hand.

'James,' she said. 'My old friend, what is it?'

But the River Man still obstinately remained silent.

Ghote took it on himself to explain.

'Madam, DSP Samant and myself came here at the request of Dr P. R. Kumaramangalam, as perhaps he has told you. When we arrived Dr Wals— this person, who in the neighbourhood they are calling the River Man, at first refused to speak at all. Then, when the DSP most ingeniously proved, truly and beyond doubt, out of this man's own mouth, that he must be Dr Walsingham, suddenly he told us that . . . Madam, he told us that he was the Beast of the Beaches.'

'The Beast of the Beaches,' Dr Abrahams said, 'but didn't I read . . .'

'In *Illustrated Weekly of India*, madam.'

'Really, Inspector,' Dr Doctor put in, 'do you think Dr Abrahams would waste her time on publications of that sort?'

'But nevertheless an old retired lady has time to waste,' Dr Abrahams answered. 'Or rather she had time to waste till now. Now she sees a very nasty situation.'

'Dr Abrahams,' the DSP said thoughtfully, 'does it then seem possible to you that he could indeed be both? Both Dr Walsingham and the Beast of the Beaches?'

'Possible?' the old German lady answered slowly. 'As a matter of pure chronology it could be so, if I remember the article correctly. And then . . . There always used to be something mysterious about James Walsingham's origins. I remember he would never state a date and place of birth. We used to make jokes about it.'

She sounded extraordinarily sad.

'But, madam,' Ghote broke in, swept by feelings of unfathomable dismay, 'madam, is it possible as more than a matter of dates only? Madam, could two such people, two such totally different people, truly be one?'

Dr Abrahams shook her head in bewilderment.

'I am an old woman, Inspector,' she answered at last. 'And perhaps I no longer know what to believe. Dr Doctor here has more experience in such matters. What do you say, Doctor?'

The young England-returned doctor looked as gloomy.

'In Europe,' she said, 'I read many accounts of such people as the guards at Nazi concentration camps who later appeared to be model citizens, kindly even. Then there is the famous American murderer Leopold, of the Leopold and Loeb kidnapping and murder case, who became a medical missionary when he had served his prison term. You cannot ignore such examples.'

Ghote sadly looked at the ground. Even the DSP seemed a little pensive. But, surprisingly, Dr Abrahams looked up with sudden decisiveness.

'Well, well,' she said, 'all that is a matter requiring much thought. In the meantime there are things to be done. Plainly James . . . plainly the River Man, as you call him, is not at all well. He needs hospital care. Hospital care at once. Is that not so, Doctor?'

'Why, yes,' Dr Doctor answered, after a moment's hesitation 'Yes. Yes, his condition is decidedly morbid. Immediate hospitalisation is indicated.'

'No.'

It was DSP Samant. The forceful syllable rang through the hut.

'What do you mean, no?' Dr Abrahams asked.

'If,' the DSP explained with stiff formality, 'it is possible that this man, as you have just said, is both Dr Walsingham and Jack Curtin, the Beast of the Beaches, then the whole matter becomes a police affair. Offences in contravention of Indian Penal Code Section 302.'

'Murder,' Ghote bleakly explained.

For a moment no one spoke. Then Ghote turned earnestly to the DSP.

'Sir,' he said. 'Sir, if he – the River Man is Dr Walsingham, if he is that great benefactor, well then, sir, he has asked us to leave him in peace. And . . . and, sir, I am thinking we ought to do same.'

'Nonsense, Inspector. A serious allegation has been made. A confession, even. It must be investigated. And, back in Bombay, there would be plenty of corroborative evidence once I am starting to look.'

It was, however, Inspector Ghote who in fact did the looking for corroborative evidence. In the ancient, crumbling, ant-mined reports of the Beast of the Beaches murders, written out long before by hand by babus who had learnt regularity of script but had evidently no conception of the need to be readable.

'. . . sent to the Chemical Examiner,' he pieced out, and realised with a faint shock that what had been sent to that dignitary of years gone by, for what reason it was impossible to conceive, was an entire rowing boat, the one that had been found drifting after the escaping Beast had made off in it.

He raised his head and wondered aloud.

'So after all was that fellow drowned, and was Dr James . . . Was the River Man . . .?'

He plunged back to his task. The DSP had said that, although they had put a guard on the river bank opposite the little island, he wanted to get out there again as soon as some corroborative material had been found.

But, at last, there were only the newspapers of the time to be gone through. He had nearly finished his search of their columns, forcing himself to be totally thorough however repetitive they were, when the door of his cabin burst open and DSP Samant was there.

'Well, man?'

'Sir, there is nothing.'

'Nothing? Nothing? Well, that's excellent. There is nothing that contradicts the confession we were both hearing.'

'Yes, sir,' Ghote sadly agreed. 'Nothing in the case papers is contradicting that.'

'Very well. So you've finished, eh? I will order transport to be here in five minutes.'

'Sir, almost. Just one or two more newspapers to check.'

'What can newspapers only have to tell? Pack up, Ghote.'

'Yes, sir. But I will just only . . .'

Once more Ghote plunged into the tall yellowed pages.

He had believed the DSP had been away less than five minutes when his door was flung open once more.

'Damn it, Inspector. I have been waiting out in the compound for one half-hour. One half-hour. What the devil have you been doing?'

'Sir, I was reading only.'

'Reading? Reading? I'll give you reading, Inspector. Wasting my time in this fashion, I'll—'

'No, sir, no.'

Ghote was unable to stop himself cutting the DSP short.

He saw the fierce eyes beginning to blaze with redoubled fire.

'Sir,' he jabbered hastily. 'Sir, I have proof. Proof. I have just only realised it, sir. Sir, in each and every one of the newspaper accounts there was not one mention of one thing.'

'What the hell are you talking about, man? Come along, we'll never get to that island at this rate.'

'No, sir. Sir, it is this. There is no mention in any paper whatsoever of the Beast having been a butcher in his early days. But, sir, he – the River Man, sir. He was saying *Do you think Jack Curtin, the lad who had been a butcher's apprentice* . . . Sir, I heard. You also heard. Sir, it is proof. Proof, I am altogether afraid.'

Back out on the island once more there had been no sign of the River Man prowling his little kingdom as there had been when they had first watched him through binoculars. And, when their boat had touched the shore – Ghote managed it more adroitly this time – there was still no sign. It was only when they had reached the hut and peered inside that they saw why. The old man was lying on his charpoy, feebly coughing from time to time and looking yet worse in health than when they had left him the day before, after the DSP had persuaded the two doctors that their ruse to take him to some private hospital had failed.

Ghote ducked his head, entered the hut and went across to the sick man.

'Dr Walsingham,' he said, deciding in an instant that this was the only form of address he wanted to use. 'Dr Walsingham, you are not well? Can I get you tea?'

He checked himself.

'Well, there does not seem to be any fire for making such. But can I fetch you some water? Or . . . Or perhaps one Garibaldi biscuit? May I open this packet?'

He pointed down at his still unopened shiny purchase.

'Quiet, man,' the DSP said, coming to his side and looking at the emaciated figure on the bed.

He cleared his throat loudly.

'Now,' he said, 'I have one or two questions to put. You were informing us yesterday that the Beast of the Beaches had been in youth a butcher, yes?'

The old man on the charpoy was silent.

'Well,' the DSP said eventually, 'you can take it from me that you were making such a statement. Inspector Ghote here witnessed the same. Now, tell me. How do you account for your knowledge of that when none of the published records describe the Beast as other than a ship's steward?'

There was another silence.

But at last the old man broke it himself.

'Perhaps,' he suggested feebly, 'it was somewhere in the papers at the time?'

'Ghote here conducted a cent per cent thorough search.'

'You're hard. A hard man.'

'Perhaps,' the DSP answered. 'But it was you yourself who started this. Did you expect a police officer to take no notice of such a confession?'

'Yes,' the River Man answered, coughing dryly and hard. 'Yes, I suppose I did.'

'Please, Dr Walsingham,' Ghote put in. 'Please, is there not an explanation of how you knew the Beast was a butcher also?'

'Before I came here, to this island, the second time,' the River Man responded with a new meanderingness. 'Before. I never had time to think.'

'Come,' the DSP barked. 'This is not a matter requiring thought. You told us the Beast had been a butcher. The records confirm the killings were expertly done. But there was nothing of that in the newspapers. Unless you are the Beast itself, how do you account for that?'

'I was busy,' the River Man went on, apparently not having heard. 'I was always working. Working.'

He looked up abruptly at Ghote.

'You,' he said. 'You as a boy saw that.'

'Yes, I was seeing. From dawn to dusk you worked. But – but, please, tell us one way you could have known the Beast was this butcher's apprentice.'

'Then my hands went,' the old man continued wanderingly. 'The processes of age. And what use was there for an eye-surgeon with shaking hands? So I left. I came here again. To think. At last. To think. And when you start to think the world begins to look very different.'

'Are you about to say the world looks like a place where the Beast of the Beaches did not exist?' the DSP cut in.

'Yes,' the old man said, seizing on the words. 'Yes, yes. Where that young man does not exist.'

'Now, look,' the DSP said, his famous terrier anger evidently rising once more. 'I am asking one simple question, and I require an answer. How did you know the Beast of the Beaches was a trained butcher?'

'I have given you your answer. People who once existed cease to exist.'

'Pah.'

'Look at me. Old. An old man on an old and rotten charpoy. Can you see it, this thing, me, pulling down ripe young girls in the darkness of the night?'

'It is not a question of what I am able to imagine. It is a question of what you were or were not doing.'

'But, sir,' Ghote felt obliged to offer. 'Sir, is there not something in what he is saying? Can you charge such an old man with a young man's crimes?'

'I can, Inspector. And I will, unless he can explain how he knows what no one but the murderer should know.'

But the River Man was paying no heed.

'Time to think,' he muttered. 'Out here. What we are. That's the centre of it. What can we say for certain that we are? We change. At every instant. I am changing now. I feel it. A cold slow heaviness creeping on.'

Ghote leant forward.

'Dr Walsingham,' he said. 'There is no need for any more. He is understanding what you are meaning now.'

He was hardly sure that the DSP was beginning to have any doubts. But at least he was now silent. However, the River Man ignored everything.

'Change. Everything changing. The river. The old conundrum. The water flows. Is it the same stream that it was a moment ago? Am I the same man?'

'Dr Walsingham, do not tire yourself. Lie back. Take rest. Look, DSP sahib is convinced.'

'An old man is not a young man. *Is* not. Once, long ago, somewhere, there was a young man tormented by desire, who came in the end to be called the Beast of the Beaches. The Beast.'

'The Beast, yes,' the DSP broke in. 'That is what we have to cling to. That man committed six murders. Offences under Section 302. The law does not have these doubts.'

He thrust his face down at the River Man's.

'Now,' he jabbed out, 'are you or are you not the Beast of the Beaches? Yes or no?'

'Sir, he has said it is no.'

'Let the chap speak for himself, Inspector. He has been attempting to spread confusion, and it is plain he has succeeded. But some of us can see through such fancy work.'

'Wait,' the River Man replied, looking up at his interrogator. 'Just you wait thirty or forty years, and then you won't talk about fancy work. Then you will know.'

'But now I am only knowing what I know. That it is my duty as a police officer to charge a murderer.'

'Oh, you poor fellow,' the River Man answered with more fire. 'Things are not so simple. No, they are not.'

'Yes,' the DSP shot back. 'Yes, they are simple. There is a logic to things. It is only when you start playing with logic that you come unstuck. Like when you forgot no one could know you were a butcher by training.'

'That,' said the River Man, with a stirring of his matted beard that might have been a smile. 'That. Now that is something simple.'

'Simple enough to catch you out.'

'No,' Ghote broke in again. 'Dr Walsingham, you were

saying there is a fault in our claim, that it does not show you must be the Beast?'

'You forgot one thing.'

'Impossible,' the DSP snorted.

'No, no. You see, if you were in Bombay at the time and followed the newspaper reports—'

'No,' Ghote said. 'I must state clearly. There was not one single mention of butcher.'

'No, I dare say there was not. But there would be one man who could have deduced from all those accounts that the Beast was in fact a butcher.'

'Nonsense, nonsense.'

'Dr Walsingham, who?'

'Why, another trained butcher, you ninny. Another man who knew the ways a knife could be used.'

'But you . . .' Ghote said. 'But is it that you are saying Dr James Walsingham was once also a butcher's apprentice?'

'There. There, Mr Deputy Superintendent of Police. There's a hole in that logic of yours.'

'And, Doctor,' Ghote hastily added, 'was it because you had once been a simple butcher that you were concealing your origins, as Dr Abrahams was stating was the case? I can see it would not have done for a surgeon to be known as a butcher only.'

'I knew a case like this was altogether too much of good luck,' the DSP muttered, seeing all his happy suppositions apparently deflated. 'Come along, Inspector. Come along, for God's sake.'

They were on the point of beginning the awkward business of getting into the boat when they heard the noise coming from the hut. A monstrous bout of coughing.

'Sir,' Ghote said, one leg in the boat, one in the mud. 'Do you think he is all right?'

'Yes, yes, man. Why not? He's been out here for years, why should he be any worse now?'

'Yes, DSP sahib. Yes. But – but it is altogether most quiet there now.'

'Yes.'

Ghote heaved his leg from the mud.

'You think we really should go now, sir?'

'Yes. Yes, I suppose so, Inspector.'

Then in the still air there came the sound of a distinct groan.

'What was that? Did you hear, Ghote?'

'From the shack, sir?'

'Quiet, man.'

They listened.

And it was quite plain that from the shack the River Man was calling to them.

'Come on, man,' the DSP snapped. 'Can't you hear? The fellow needs help. He's ill.'

The River Man plainly saw that they had come back into the hut. But he seemed to speak as much to himself as to any listener.

'When I go back I can see it all as if it was yesterday. The first. She was stupid, a stupid girl. Able to think of nothing but her stomach. I got her down to the beach with a promise of Turkish Delight. A box of Turkish Delight. The fool.'

'What is it you are saying?' Ghote heard himself whisper.

'After her, after the timid boy had killed, I thought I would never be able to stop. And each one made it worse. But then . . . Then when I came to this island, rowing in that boat, swimming in the end, then, then I found I could stop. I was someone different. Afterwards, back in Bombay, I used to think about those girls sometimes. But not often. I was too busy. You. You remembered how hard I worked.'

'Yes, I remembered.'

'So there was little time to think. Till my hands went. And since then, out here, I have had something else to think about. The change. The two selves I had been.'

'So you were truly both?' Ghote asked, though he knew he had no need to.

'Oh, yes, I was both. But was each of them the other? And which was I really? They were very different, you know. The Beast, poor little Jack Curtin, was a sorry sort of chap. Good for nothing but his trade, cutting up meat. And timid. Now a surgeon cannot be timid. And James Walsingham was not. He was a driving man. A force. Was that not so, Inspector? You saw him.'

'Yes, it was so.'

'Then did he blot out the other? Tell me. Tell me the truth.

Isn't that timid, dark-minded butcher boy who took his prey on the warm foreign beaches in the soft dark, isn't he gone? Blotted out? Vanished?'

'Yes,' Ghote said. 'I believe he has vanished for ever.'

The DSP was adamant still. 'He has not.'

'Yes, you are right,' the River Man answered him. 'I remember it, remember it all, just as it was. So he must be here still, inside me. The Beast. In here.'

Ghote turned to the DSP.

'Are . . . are we going to take him away now?'

'Dr Walsingham,' the DSP said, his voice less harsh. 'You understand we must ask you to accompany us to Bombay?'

'Yes. I understand.'

'We had better secure some help,' the DSP said. 'Dr Walsing— the River Man had better be carried to the boat.'

'Yes, sir, I will go at once, sir.'

'No. In his condition . . . No, Inspector, you had better stay here. I will go.'

When the DSP had left, almost at a trot, Ghote turned to the old man on the charpoy again.

'You are not well, Dr Walsingham,' he said. 'We would see that it is to a hospital you are taken. I – I am sure . . .'

'Yes. Not well. Tired. Sleep a little.'

But the old man had hardly closed his eyes when he gave a startled cry.

'Dr Walsingham, what . . . DSP sahib! Sir! Come back. Sir, he is most serious. Dr Walsingham, lie back. Lie down. What is it? You have something more you are wanting to say?'

'Tell you.'

'Yes, yes. I am listening. Take your time. I am here.'

'Help.'

'Yes, yes. You are needing help. It is coming. Soon. Most soon.'

'Not that.'

'Not?'

'Listen.'

'Yes, I am listening.'

'Did – I – tell – you?'

'That you were the Beast? About the girl and the Turkish Delight? Yes, you have told all.'

'Yes. Thought – I – had.'

'Dr Walsingham, was it not true after all?'

'Fell asleep. Couldn't remember if said.'

'Yes, yes. You have told us. Do not worry any more.'

'So it wasn't dream?'

'No.'

'But what if . . .'

Behind him Ghote was aware that the DSP had returned.

'Sir,' he said, 'he is going fast.'

'But what if – imagined?' the man on the bed said with a sudden access of vigour. 'What if I imagined it all? 'Magination run riot. Believe it was all 'magination. Self- . . . Self-delusion.'

He gave a sort of laugh, appalling to hear.

'Had even convinced myself,' he said, quite clearly. 'Even convinced myself I was the—'

Then a tremendous cough broke out of him.

And ceased.

'What are you saying, man?' the DSP banged out. 'Are you telling us now that you invented the fact that you were the Beast of the Beaches? Are you? Are you?'

'Sir,' Ghote said. 'It is of no use to ask.'

'But he cannot go back on it now. He must give us the truth. He must.'

'Sir, death has taken place. We will never find out anything more now.'

But that was not to be the case. It was after a clergyman had intoned the words of burial at the funeral of the man Ghote had been reduced to thinking of only as the River Man that, standing talking to Dr Abrahams and Dr Doctor among the mournful, leaning tombs and rank undergrowth of Bombay's European Cemetery, the DSP produced his bombshell.

'Madam,' Ghote had said to Dr Abrahams, 'are you knowing what were his last words only?'

'You were there, Inspector?'

'Yes, yes. And DSP sahib also. And we are able to tell you that Dr Walsingham died stating that he had invented the fact that he was the Beast of the Beaches. One hundred per cent invention.'

'Then, after all—'

'No, madam,' the DSP had interrupted then. 'No, it is not a

question of after all. I can prove now just who he was.'

'But, sir—'

'No, Inspector.'

He turned to Dr Abrahams.

'Do you understand fingerprints, Doctor?'

'Of course, of course. That they are unique to each individual.'

'But there cannot be any prints for the Beast,' Ghote broke in. 'When it was all so long ago.'

'That is where you are wrong, Inspector. You forget that the system was first used in India. And it so happens that the Beast's prints were taken from the soft tar of the rowing boat he made his escape in and were transferred to plaster casts. They are in our museum. I looked at them this morning.'

'But – But – Dr Walsingham's prints? You cannot have taken them from his corpse.'

'No need, Inspector. There was a very fine set on a certain packet of Garibaldi biscuits you yourself were thrusting into the man's hands.'

Ghote gave a great sigh.

'So, sir, you have proved your case after all. Fingerprints cannot be lying. Dr Walsingham and Jack Curtin were one and the same individual.'

'I think so. I think so. No hard feelings, eh? I shall give you some credit when I publish my account in *Asian Crime Digest*. And I will see that you get a copy, Doctor.'

'Thank you,' Dr Abrahams said solemnly. 'But I prefer not.'

And then it was that it came to Ghote.

'Madam, no,' he burst out. 'No, kindly do not sound so down in the dumps. Listen, please. A thought has come to me, and it is this. If Dr Walsingham, if the River Man was dying believing that he had invented that whole part of his life, why then at the moment of his death he himself was not the Beast of the Beaches and never had been such. And that is what can never be taken away from him, not now or ever. When he died he was Dr James Walsingham and no one else whatsoever. No one else whatsoever.'

1974

5

Inspector Ghote and the Noted British Author

Perched up on a creaking wobbly chair in the office of the Deputy Commissioner (Crime), the peon put one broken-nailed finger against Inspector Ghote's name on the painted board behind the DCC's desk. He swayed topplingly to one side, scraped hold of the fat white pin which indicated 'Bandobast Duties', brought it back across in one swooping rush and pressed it firmly into place.

Watching him, Ghote gave an inward sigh. Bandobast duties. Someone, of course, had to deal with the thousand and one matters necessary for the smooth running of Crime Branch, but nevertheless bandobast duty was not tracking down breakers of the law and it did seem to fall to him more often than to other officers. Yet, after all, it would be absurd to waste a man of the calibre of, say, Inspector Dandekar on mere administration.

'Yes? Dandekar, yes?'

The DCC had been interrupted by his internal telephone and there on the other end, as if conjured up by merely having been thought of, was Dandekar himself.

'Yes, yes, of course,' the DCC said in answer to the forcefully plaintive sound that had been just audible from the other end. 'Certainly you must. I'll see what I can do, ek dum.'

He replaced the receiver and turned back to Ghote, the eyes in his sharply commanding face still considering whatever it was that he had promised Dandekar.

And then, as if a god-given solution to his problem had appeared in front of him, his expression changed in an instant to happy alertness. He swung round to the peon, who was carefully carrying away his aged chair.

'No,' he said. 'Put the bandobast pin against – er – Inspector Sawant. I have a task I need Inspector Ghote for.'

The peon wearily turned back with his chair to the big painted hierarchy of crime-fighters ranging from the Deputy Commissioner himself down to the branch's three dogs Akbar, Moti and Caesar. Ghote, in front of the DCC's wide baize-covered desk, glowed now with pure joy.

'It's this Shivaji Park case,' the DCC said.

'Oh yes, DCC. Multiple-stabbing double murder, isn't it? Discovered this morning by that fellow who was in the papers when he came to Bombay, that noted British author.'

Ghote, hoping his grasp both of departmental problems and of the flux of current affairs would earn him some hint of appreciation was surprised instead to receive a look of almost suspicious surmise. But he got no time to wonder why.

'Yes, quite right,' the DCC said briskly. 'Dandekar is handling the case, of course. With an influential fellow like this Englishman involved we must have a really quick result. But there is something he needs help with. Get down to his cabin straight away, will you?'

'Yes, sir. Yes, DCC.'

Clicking his heels together by way of salute, Ghote hurried out.

What would Dandekar have asked for assistance over? There would be a good many different lines to pursue in an affair of this sort. The murdered couple, an ice-cream manufacturer and his wife, had been, so office gup went, attacked in the middle of the night. The assailants had tied up their teenage son and only when he had at last roused the nearest neighbour, this visiting British author – of crime books, the paper had said, well-known crime books – had it been discovered that the two older people had been hacked to death. Goondas of that sort did not, of course, choose just any location. They sniffed around first. And left a trail. Which meant dozens of inquiries in the neighbourhood, usually by sub-inspectors from the local station. But with this influential fellow involved . . .

Emerging into the sunlight, Ghote made his way along to Dandekar's office which gave directly on the tree-shaded compound. He pushed open one half of its bat-wing doors. And there, looking just like his photograph, large as life or even larger, was the Noted British Author. He was crouching on a small chair in front of Dandekar's green leather-covered desk, covering it much like a big fluffed-up hen on one small precious egg. His hips, clad in trousers already the worse for the dust and stains of Bombay life, drooped on either side while a considerable belly projected equally far forward. Above was a beard, big and sprawling as the body beneath, and above the beard was hair, plentiful and inclined to shoot in all directions. Somewhere between beard and hair a pale British face wore a look of acute curiosity.

'Ah, Ghote, thank God,' Dandekar, stocky, muscular, hook-nosed, greeted him immediately in sharp, T-spitting Marathi. 'Listen, take this curd-face out of my sight. Fast.'

Ghote felt a terrible abrupt inward sinking. So this was how he was to assist Dandekar, by keeping from under his feet a no doubt notable British nuisance. Even bandobast duties would be better.

But Dandekar could hardly produce that expected rapid result with such a burden.

Ghote squared his bony shoulders.

Dandekar had jumped up.

'Mr Peduncle,' he said, in English now, 'I would like you to—'

'It's not Peduncle actually,' the Noted Author broke in. 'Important to get the little details right, you know. That's what the old shell collector in my books – he's Mr Peduncle – is always telling his friend, Inspector Sugden. No, my name's Reymond, Henry Reymond, author of the Peduncle books.'

The multitudinous beard split with a wide, clamorously ingratiating grin.

'Yes, yes,' said Dandekar briskly. 'But this is Inspector Ghote. He will be assisting me. Ghote, the domestic servant of the place has disappeared, a Goan known as John Louzado. They had no address at his native-place, but we might get it from a former employer. Will you see to that? And Mr Ped— Mr Reymond, who is expressing most keen interest in our methods, can attach himself to you while I talk with the young man who was tied up, the son, or rather adopted son. I think somehow he could tell a good deal more.'

Ghote put out his hand for Mr Reymond to shake. He did not look forward to dealing with the numerous questions likely to arise from that keen interest in Bombay CID methods.

As Ghote drove the Noted British Author in one of the branch's big battered cars down Dr D. N. Road towards Colaba, the area where the fleeing servant's former employee lived, he found his worst forebodings justified. His companion wanted to know everything: what was that building, what this, was that man happy lying on the pavement, where else could he go?

Jockeying for place in the traffic, swerving for cyclists, nipping past great lumbering red articulated buses, Ghote did his best to provide pleasing answers. But the fellow was never content. Nothing seemed to delight him more than hitting on some small discrepancy and relentlessly pursuing it, comparing himself all the while to his Mr Peduncle and his motto 'The significant variation: in that lies all secrets'. If Ghote heard the phrase once in the course of their twenty-minute drive, he seemed to hear it a dozen times.

At last when they were waiting at the lights to get into Colaba Causeway, he was reduced to putting a question of his own. How did it come about, he interrupted, that Mr Reymond was living in a flat up at Shivaji Park? Would not the Taj Hotel just down there be more suitable for a distinguished visitor?

'Ah yes, I know what you mean,' the author answered with an enthusiasm that gave Ghote considerable inward pleasure. 'But, you see, I am here by courtesy of Air India, on their new Swap-a-Country Plan. They match various people with their Indian equivalents and exchange homes. Most far-sighted. So I am at Shivaji Park and the writer who lives there – well, he has written some short stories, though I gather he's actually a Deputy Inspector of Smoke Nuisances and a relation of your State Minister for Police Affairs and the Arts, as it happens – well, he at the present moment is installed in my cottage in Wiltshire and no doubt getting as much out of going down to the pub as I get from being in a flat here lucky enough to have a telephone. People are always popping in to use it and while they're looking up a number in the little book, they talk away like one o'clock.'

The Noted British Author's eyes shone.

'Yes,' Ghote said.

Certain queries had occurred to him. Could there, for instance, be an exchange between a police inspector in Bombay and one in, say New York? But somehow he could not see himself getting several months Casual Leave, and he doubted whether many other similar law-enforcing Bombayites would find it easy.

But he felt that to voice such doubts aloud would be impolite. And his hesitation was fatal.

'Tell me,' Mr Reymond said, 'that sign saying "De Luxe Ding Dong Nylon Suiting". . .' And, in a moment, they had struck full on another 'significant variation'.

Desperately Ghote pulled one more question out of the small stock he had put together.

'Please, what is your opinion of the books of Mr Erle Stanley Gardner? To me Perry Mason is seeming an extremely clever individual altogether.'

'Yes,' said the Noted British Author, and he was silent right until they reached their destination in Second Pasta Lane.

Mrs Patel, wife of a civil servant and former employer of John Louzado, was a lady of forty or so dressed in a cotton sari of a reddish pattern, at once assertive and entirely without grace.

'You are lucky to find me, Inspector,' she said when Ghote had explained their business. 'At the Family Planning office where I undertake voluntary work, Clinic begins at ten sharp.'

Ghote could not stop himself glancing at his watch though he well knew it was at least half-past ten already.

'Well, well,' Mrs Patel said sharply, seeing him. 'Already I am behind schedule. But there is so much to be done. So much to be done.'

She darted across the sitting-room, a place almost as littered with piles of paper as any office at Crime Branch, and plumped up a cushion.

'Just if you have the address of John's native-place,' Ghote said.

'Of course, of course. I am bound to have it. I always inquire most particularly after a servant's personal affairs. You are getting an altogether better loyalty factor then. Don't you find that, Mr— I am afraid I am not hearing your name?'

She had turned her by no means negligible gaze full on the Noted British Author. Ghote, who had hoped not to explain his companion, introduced him with a brief 'Mr Reymond, from UK.'

'Yes,' said Mrs Patel. 'Well, don't you find . . . ah, but you are *the* Mr Reymond, the noted British author, isn't it? Most pleased to meet you, my dear sir. Most pleased. What I always find with criminological works is the basic fact emerging, common to many sociological studies, a pattern of fundamental human carelessness, isn't it? You see—'

But river-spate rapid though she was, she had met her match.

'One moment – I am sorry to interrupt – but there is a slight discrepancy here. You see, there are two different sorts of crime books involved. You are talking about sociological works, but what I write are more crime novels. Indeed, it's just the sort of mistake my detective, Mr Peduncle the old collector of sea-shells, is always pointing out. "The significant variation: in that lies all secrets."'

'Ah, most interesting,' Mrs Patel came back, recovering fast. 'Of course I have read a good deal of Erle Stanley Gardner and so forth, and I must say . . .'

She gave them her views at such length that Ghote at last, politeness or not, felt forced to break in.

'Madam, madam. If you will excuse. There is the matter of John's native-place address.'

'Yes, yes. I am getting it.'

Mrs Patel plunged towards a bureau and opened its flap-down front. A considerable confusion of documents was revealed, together with what looked like the wrappings for a present bought but never handed to its intended recipient.

Prolonged searching located first an unhelpful address-book, then 'a list of things like this which I jot down' and finally a notebook devoted to household hints clipped from magazines. But no address.

'Madam,' Ghote ventured at last, 'is it possible you did not in fact take it down?'

'Well, well, one cannot make a note of everything. That is one of my principles: keep the paperwork down to a minimum.'

She gave the British author some examples of Indian bureaucracy. Once or twice Ghote tried to edge him away, but even a tug at the distinguished shirtsleeve was unsuccessful. Only when in return he himself began explaining how British bureaucracy was a crutch that fatally hampered people like Inspector Sugden in his own books did Ghote act.

'Madam, I regret. Mr Reymond, sir. We are conducting investigation. It is a matter of urgency.'

And with that he did get the author out on to the landing outside. But as Mrs Patel was beginning to close the door with many a 'Goodbye, then' and 'So interesting, and I must try to find one of your books', Mr Reymond broke in in his turn.

'Inspector, there is a small hiatus.'

Ghote stared.

'Please, what is hiatus?'

'Something missing, a gap in the logic. You haven't asked this lady where Louzado worked before he came here. Mr Peduncle would have a word to say to you. If there's one thing he always seizes on it is the small hiatus.'

The bursting-out beard parted to reveal a roguish smile.

'Yes,' said Ghote. 'You are perfectly correct. Madam, do you have the address of John's former employer?'

'Why, yes, of course,' Mrs Patel replied, with a note of sharpness. 'I can tell you that out of my head. John was recommended to me by my friends, the Dutt-Dastars.'

And, mercifully, she came straight out with the address – it was somewhat south of the Racecourse – and Ghote was even able to prevent her giving them a detailed account of the posh-sounding Dutt-Dastars.

Since their route took them back past Crime Branch HQ, Ghote decided to risk the Noted British Author re-attaching himself to Inspector Dandekar and to report progress. Besides, if he could install Mr Reymond in his own office for ten minutes only, it would give him a marvellous respite from relentlessly pursued questions.

So, a peon summoned and Coca-Cola thrust on the distinguished visitor, Ghote went down to Dandekar.

'Well, Inspector,' he asked, 'did the son have more to tell?'

'More to tell he has,' Dandekar answered, sipping tea and dabbing his face with a towel. 'But speak he will not.'

'He is not one hundred per cent above board then?'

'He is not. I was up there at Shivaji Park within half an hour of the time he freed himself from those ropes, and I could see at a glance the marks were not right at all.'

'Too high up the wrists, was it?'

'Exactly, Inspector. That young man tied himself up. And that must mean he was in collusion with the fellows who killed the old couple. How else did they get in, if he did not open to them? No, three of them were in it together and the Goan and a notorious bad hat from the vicinity called Budhoo have gone off with the jewellery. You can bet your boots on that.'

'But the young man will not talk?' Ghote asked.

'He will not talk. College-educated, you know, and thinks he has all the answers.'

Ghote nodded agreement. It was a common type and the bane of a police officer's life. His determination to push forward the case by getting hold of John Louzado's address redoubled.

'Well,' he said, 'I must be getting back to Mr Reymond, or he will come looking for us.'

In answer Dandekar grinned at him like an exulting film villain.

But, back in his office, Ghote found the Noted British Author doing something more ominous than looking for Dandekar. He was furiously making notes on a little pad.

'Ah,' he said the moment Ghote came in, 'just one or two points that occurred to me in connection with the case.'

Ghote felt this last straw thump down.

'Oh yes,' he answered, waggishly as he could. 'We would be very delighted to have the assistance of the great Mr Peduncle and his magical shell collection.'

'No, no,' the noted author said quickly. 'Mr Peduncle's shells are by no means magical. There's a slight discrepancy there. You see, Mr Peduncle examines shells to detect their little variations and equally he examines the facts of the case and hits on significant variations there.'

'The significant variation in which are lying all secrets,' Ghote quoted.

Mr Reymond laughed with great heartiness. But in the car, heading north up Sir J. J. Road, he nevertheless explained in detail every single discrepancy he had noted in his little pad.

It seemed that, in the comparatively short time between the apparently distraught son coming to say he had been set upon and Inspector Dandekar bringing him to Crime Branch HQ, he had accumulated a great many facts and bits of hearsay. All of them must have been boiling away in his fertile mind. Now to spume out.

Most were trivialities arising from the domestic routine of the dead couple, or of his own flat or the flats nearby. To them Ghote succeeded in finding answers. But what he could not always sort out were the queries these answers produced. 'Significant variations' seemed to spring up like buzzing whining insects in the first flush of the monsoon.

Only one point, to Ghote's mind, could be said to have any real connection with the killing, and that was so slight in any other circumstances he would have thrust it off.

But it was a fact, apparently, that Mr Reymond's servant, an old Muslim called Fariqua – or more precisely the servant of the absent Indian author of some short stories – had been discovered on the morning of the murder asleep inside the flat when he ought to have been in the distant suburb of Andheri where since the British author's arrival he had been boarded out – 'Well, I mean, the chap actually seemed to sleep on the couch in the sitting-room, and I thought that was a bit much really' – and had provided no explanation.

'Now,' Mr Reymond said, turning in his seat and wagging his finger very close to Ghote's face, 'he must have hidden himself away in the kitchen till I'd gone to bed. And isn't that just exactly the sort of variation from the normal which my Mr Peduncle would seize upon, and which my Inspector Sugden would try to shrug off? Eh, Inspector?'

Ghote felt the honour of the Bombay force at stake.

'Certainly I do not shrug off this at all, Mr Reymond,' he said. 'After we have seen the Dutt-Dastars I will have a word with Fariqua. But then, since you would be at home, perhaps you would care to rest yourself for the afternoon. I know this humid weather makes visitors most extremely fatigued.'

He held his breath in anxiety. To his delight Mr Reymond, after consideration, acquiesced.

And if at the Dutt-Dastars' he got Louzado's address . . .

The Dutt-Dastars, it appeared, were a couple entirely devoted to art. Their house was crammed with Mrs Dutt-Dastar's oil-paintings, sprawling shapes in bus-red and sky-blue, and Mr Dutt-Dastar's metal sculptures, jagged iron masses inclined to rust and a considerable menace, Ghote found, to trouser bottom and shirtsleeve. And in the Bengali way their devotion was expressed as much in words as in acts.

Mr Reymond they seized on as a fellow artist, blithely ignoring any occasion when he tried to point out a discrepancy, hiatus or 'significant variation'. And equally ignored, time and again, were Ghote's attempts to get an answer to the one question he still saw, despite the somewhat odd behaviour of Mr Reymond's Fariqua, as the plain and simple way to break the case. 'Do you have the address in Goa of your former servant John Louzado?'

At last, when he had established to his complete satisfaction that a couple as utterly vague could not possibly have recorded, much less retained, a servant's address, he planted himself abruptly full in front of Mrs Dutt-Dastar just as she was explaining the full similarity between her painting 'Eagle Figure with Two Blue Shapes' and Mr Reymond's book *Mr Peduncle Caught in Meshes*, which she had yet actually to read.

'Madam, kindly to tell, who was the previous employer of John Louzado?'

'John Louzado?' Mrs Dutt-Dastar asked, seemingly totally mystified.

'The servant you recommended to Mrs Patel, of Second Pasta Lane.'

'Ah, John. Yes, what to do about John? He did not suit, not at all – it was sheer madness to have taken him on from someone like Shirin Kothawala, a dear person but with no understanding of the artist, but I could not sack the fellow just like that. And then I remembered that funny Mrs Patel. Well, she would never notice what a servant was like, would she?'

'Madam, if you do not have John's address, are you having at least the address of Mrs Shirin Kothawala?'

'Well, but of course. In one of those divine but madly expensive flats in Nepean Sea Road. A block called Gulmarg. Anybody will tell you.'

'Mr Reymond, I am departing to proceed with inquiries.'

'Oh, yes, my dear fellow. Coming, coming.'

On the way back, thanks to Ghote's unequivocal assurance that he would immediately interrogate Fariqua, for all that he privately knew nothing would come of it, the author's questions were at least confined to the sociological. But before they arrived Ghote decided to issue a warning.

'Mr Reymond, in India – I do not know how it is in UK – servants often have matters they are wishing to conceal from their masters, like for instance the true cost of vegetables in the bazaar. So, you see, it would perhaps be better if you yourself were not present when I question Fariqua.'

He regarded the author with apprehension. But it seemed he need not have worried.

'Excellent idea, Inspector,' Mr Reymond surprisingly replied. But then he as if in explanation added: 'We don't have servants in England now, so I find it difficult to know how to behave with them.'

So Ghote had the pleasure of tackling the Muslim unimpeded by any bulky British shadow. It was a good thing too, because Fariqua proved every bit as evasive as he had told Mr Reymond servants could be. He needed, when it came down to it, to use a little tough treatment. And he had a notion that cuffs and threatened kicks would not be the way Mr Peduncle conducted an interrogation.

But, after ten minutes in which Fariqua noisily maintained he had not been in the author's flat at all the previous night, he caved in quite satisfactorily and produced a story that might well be true. He had been playing cards with 'some friends' and it had got too late to catch a train to Andheri. So he had bided his time, sneaked back into the author's flat before the door was locked and had hidden down between the stove and the wall till he had been able to take what, he implied, was his rightful place on the sitting-room couch.

Ghote gave him another couple of slaps for impudence.

'Now, what are the names of your card-playing friends?'

'Inspector, I do not know.'

But this time Ghote had hardly so much as to growl to get a better answer.

'Oh, Inspector, Inspector. One only I am knowing. It is Jagdev Singh, sir, the driver of Rajinder Sahib at Flat No. 6, Building No. 2.'

'Achchha.'

Ghote let him go. He ought to walk round to Building No. 2 of the flats and check with the Punjabi gentleman's driver, but that must wait. The Noted British Author might change his mind and want to come with him. And he would get that address, the simple key to having a solid case against the three of them, much more quickly unencumbered.

It turned out, however, that the Parsi lady's 'divine but madly expensive' flat was not, as Mrs Dutt-Dastar had said, in a block called Gulmarg in Nepean Sea Road but in a block of that name in Warden Road on the twin-prominence of Cumballa Hill. But at least Mrs Kothawala, sixty, exquisitely dressed, precise as a crane-bird, was helpful. She knew to a week just how long she had employed Louzado. She knew to an anna just how much he had cheated her by. She remembered having warned Mrs Dutt-Dastar about him, and that Mrs Dutt-Dastar had clearly forgotten before the telephone conversation was half-way through. And she knew for a fact that she had never had John's address in Goa. But, of course, she was able to tell Ghote where he had worked before he had come to her . . .

Sorting out Mrs Dutt-Dastar's error had taken some hours, so Ghote found that having dutifully telephoned Inspector Dandekar and made sure there was no sign of the Noted British Author – their suspect was still unshaken too, he heard – he had time that evening to make only this one inquiry. And that proved as exasperating as the others – worse even since instead of getting at least the name of Louzado's next earlier employer he had to be content with the name only of a lady who would be 'sure to remember'.

Before trying her next morning he gritted his teeth and put in a call to Mr Reymond who, of course, was only too keen to come with him – 'I had been thinking of looking in on Inspector Dandekar actually' – and only by wantonly altering the geography of Bombay did he persuade him it would be more economical for him to stay at Shivaji Park until after he had made this one inquiry, which he promised would be rapid. But in fact the task proved immensely troublesome since the possibly helpful lady had moved house and no one nearby seemed to know where to. Application to the postalwallahs met with a certain amount of bureaucratic delay and it was not until the very end of the morning that he had an address to go to. So he telephoned Mr Reymond once more and dolefully arranged to collect him after lunch.

'No sleep for me this afternoon, Inspector,' the cheerful voice had assured him. 'I've a lot I want to ask you.'

'Yes,' said Ghote.

The first thing the Noted British Author wanted to know was why Fariqua had not been arrested. Ghote produced the fellow's explanation for the 'significant variation' in his behaviour.

'Ah, so that accounts for it,' Mr Reymond said, for once apparently happy. 'I'm glad to hear it. I wouldn't like to think I was getting my breakfast scrambled eggs from the hands of a murderer.'

Ghote gave a jolly laugh. It came to him all the more easily because he had felt sure there would be some hiatus or discrepancy to pursue. But the journey passed with no more than questions about the peculiarities of passers-by – until they were almost at their destination, a flat just inland from Back Bay in Marine Lines.

Then the author, after a long silence that had prolonged itself wonderfully, suddenly spoke.

'Inspector Ghote, I can no longer conceal it from myself. There is a small hiatus.'

'Yes?' Ghote asked, misery swiftly descending.

'Inspector, you did not, did you, check Fariqua's alibi with Mr Rajinder's chauffeur? And I think – I am almost sure – Mr Rajinder is the man who left on holiday by car three days ago.'

'Then I will have to make further inquiries,' Ghote said glumly.

But he forced himself to be a little more optimistic.

'In any case,' he said, 'perhaps we shall learn here just where John Louzado is to be found in Goa and then, who knows, a single telephone call to the police there and they would have the fellow behind bars and we will have evidence in plenty, even some of the stolen jewellery, if we are lucky.'

'Yes,' Mr Reymond said, 'but Fariqua's invented story still leaves a loose end.'

Yet the interview at the Marine Lines flat looked from the start as if it was going to be all that Ghote and Inspector Dandekar had been counting on.

'Oh, John, yes,' said the deliciously beautiful occupier, Mrs Akhtar Hazari. 'Yes, we should have an address for Goa. Not for John himself but for a priest – John was a Christian – who

73

was to provide a reference. In fact, it was when we heard that John had a criminal record that we decided he must go. My husband imports watches and we often have valuable stock in the flat.'

Ghote was possessed of a sudden feeling that everything in the world was simple. Confidence bubbled in his veins. It would not be as direct a way of wrapping up the case as he had spoken of to Mr Reymond, but the whole business might still be dealt with inside a few days.

'Of course it was two or three years ago now,' Mrs Hazari said. 'But I always seem to keep letters. I will look. Will you take tea?'

So they sat in her big cool sitting-room, Ghote on a fat pile of cushions, the Noted British Author swinging rather apprehensively in a basket chair suspended by a chain from the ceiling.

Time passed.

The servant came back and inquired whether they would like more tea. Mr Reymond hurriedly refused for both of them. Ghote would in fact have liked more tea, but even better he would have liked to see that letter. He asked Mr Reymond – who seemed to feel it necessary to speak in swift hushed tones – a few questions about his books. But the answers were not very satisfactory.

And then at last Mrs Hazari returned.

'Inspector,' she said, 'I must tell you that after all I have not got that letter. I had thought it was in an almirah where I put old papers like that. I even knew exactly the box it should be in. But my memory played me false. I threw out a lot of junk about a year ago, and it must have been in that.'

Ghote felt like a child robbed of a sweetmeat. And now, he realised with gritty dismay, he would solemnly have to pursue Mr Reymond's theory about Fariqua.

'And John came straight to you from Goa?' he asked Mrs Hazari desolately.

'No,' she said. 'He did have one short job first. He went to a family where at once the wife died and the man no longer needed so many servants. That was why we took him without a reference. It was a business aquaintance of my husband, I think. And unfortunately he's in Delhi. But if you would give me a ring tonight, I could perhaps tell you then.'

With that Ghote had to be content. That, and the dubious gain to be had from dealing with Fariqua's final lie.

Happily by the time they got back to Shivaji Park Fariqua had left for Andheri, earlier than he should have done but not so much so that there was any reason to suppose he had run off like John Louzado. To placate Mr Reymond, Ghote sadly confirmed that the Jagdev Singh with whom Fariqua had claimed to be playing cards on the night of the murders had indeed already left Bombay by then.

Perhaps, Ghote thought as he turned from saying a last goodnight, down at HQ the boy would have broken his obstinate silence and admitted the truth and then there would be no need to pursue next morning this surely – surely? – unsatisfactory discrepancy. Or was it a hiatus?

But Inspector Dandekar had no good news. Indeed he seemed considerably worried.

'I had the damned boy in the interrogation room today for eight solid hours,' he said. 'I have kept him standing up. I have been drinking tea and smoking cigarettes in front of him. I have had a trestle set up and Head Constable Kadam standing there swinging a lathi. But nothing has moved him one inch.'

'Inspector,' Ghote said with some hesitation, 'is it possible that those ropes on his wrists had been altogether badly tied by the real miscreants and not faked only?'

Dandekar sat in silence glaring down hook-nosed at his desk.

'Well, anything is possible,' he said at last. 'But, damn it, I cannot believe it, I just cannot believe it.'

So Ghote was up at Shivaji Park before eight next morning, waiting for the tricky Fariqua and telling himself that there was no reason why the fellow would not come to work as usual.

But the surge of relief he felt when the Muslim did appear made him realise how he was now expecting everything about the affair to go wrong. He pounced like a kite dropping down on a tree-rat.

It did not take long to reduce the fellow to a state of abject fear. And then he talked.

'Aiee, Inspector. No. No, Inspector sahib. I swear to God I had nothing to do with it. Inspector, I just got to know those fellows. We used to sit and talk when I was sleeping here.

Inspector, I did not know they were badmash fellows. Inspector, I am swearing to you. And then that night, that one Budhoo – Inspector, he is a really bad one that one, a devil, Inspector – Inspector, he said more than he was meaning. He said something was going to happen that night. We were in the kitchen of their flat, Inspector. All of them were out, Sahib, Memsahib and the boy. I did not know it was going to be murder, Inspector. I thought they had a plan only to take the jewellery, Inspector. They were saying she had jewellery worth one lakh, Inspector. They would hide under a bed. But no more were they telling me. And then they threatened that I should stay with them. But after they said I could go, Inspector. Then it was too late to go to Andheri. But Reymond Sahib had his door open still and I was able to creep in. I swear to you, honest to God, Inspector, I am never knowing anything about killing. But they said also that they would kill me if I spoke. Inspector, will you be saving me, is it? Is it, Inspector? Is it?'

Ghote stood looking down at the shrunken cringing figure. Was he letting the fellow trick him again? It did not really seem likely. What he had said this time had been more than simply logical, like the story of card-playing with the Punjabi's driver. This account of inconclusive talk with two of the murderers in the kitchen of the dead couple's flat had rung true through and through. No wonder the fellow had tried to set up an alibi if that had happened.

Of course, there had been no mention of any involvement by the son. But then the other two would have kept quiet about that. Yes, what he had learnt would scarcely help Dandekar.

'You will be safe enough from your friends,' he growled at Fariqua. 'In the lock-up.'

Without the rest of them there would not be a case worth bringing as an accessory before the fact. But no harm to have the fellow to hand.

He marched him off.

He gave the Noted British Author the news by telephone. A witness who had heard and not properly heard the criminals' plans, hardly the sort of thing for the pages of *Mr Peduncle Plays a Joker*. A man induced by threats to join a robbery and then let go before it had begun: not exactly the sort of event for *Mr Peduncle Hunts the Peacock*.

And indeed questions and doubts poured out so fast that he was reduced at last to pointing out sharply that Mr Reymond was now without a servant. At that the Noted British Author betrayed signs of disquiet. So Ghote explained he could get a replacement by talking to his neighbours and was rewarded by the author quite hastily ringing off.

Encouraged by this, he hurriedly set out for the address he had got from Mrs Hazari late the night before. It was, her husband had said, a Mr Dass whose wife, now dead, had first briefly employed John when he had come to Bombay. He lived in a block of flats in B Road behind Churchgate.

Climbing up the tiled stairway of the building, Ghote found he was retaining – despite the rather shabby air of the place – all his optimism. Louzado's trail had been long, but now it must be near its end. This was, after all, where the fellow had had his first Bombay job. They could go no further back. But it was equally the most likely place for an employer to have noted that Goa address.

On the door of the flat a small tree-slice name-board had painted on it in much-faded script 'Mr and Mrs Gopal Dass'. It must, Ghote reflected, have been a long while since there had been a Mrs Dass if it was her demise that had brought Louzado's first Bombay job to its abrupt end. And certainly the little irregularly-shaped board had a strong look of dusty neglect.

He rang the door bell.

There was such a long silence that he almost became convinced he was to experience yet another defeat. He was even turning towards the next-door flat to make inquiries when the door opened by just a crack.

He swung round.

'It is Mr Gopal Dass?'

The door opened a little more. Ghote saw in the bright light from the room beyond a man who had once been fat.

Afterwards he was able to account in detail for the instantly stamped impression. It had come in part from the old European-style suit, its jacket drooping from the shoulders in deep encrusted folds, the trousers hanging in baggy rucks from the hips. But even the face had shown the same signs: flesh seemed to sag from it.

'What is it you are wanting?'

The voice, too, appeared to be coming from someone no longer there, hollow and without force.

Rapidly Ghote introduced himself and stated his problem. He felt that the slightest chance might cause the tall empty man to close the door so barely opened.

Mr Dass heard him out however. Then he sighed, driftingly like a puff of night breeze with hardly the strength to ruffle lonely waters.

'Oh, no, no,' he said. 'No addresses. Everything like that went when my wife left me for another life. Everything.'

He turned slowly and looked into the room behind him. Ghote saw over his shoulder that it was almost completely bare. No curtains, no carpet, no pictures of the gods. Just a small table with a brass bowl, a brass tumbler and a packet of Mohun's cornflakes on it, and in a corner a bed-roll.

'Yes,' Mr Dass said. 'I got rid of everything. My life is at an end, you know. At an end.'

Very slowly, and without any sense of discourtesy, he turned and closed the door.

And I too, Ghote thought in the thick sadness he felt billowing from the shut door with its once gay tree-slice name-board, I too have reached an end. The end of my hunt for John Louzado.

But one part of the affair certainly was not over. The Noted British Author would undoubtedly be out pursuing his hiatuses before much longer. He might be doing so already. One conversation with a neighbour could well have found him a new servant.

He ran clatteringly down the empty echoing stairway, drove full-out back to HQ, glancing wildly at Dandekar's office as he came to a gravel-squirting halt, and ran for his telephone to stop the Noted British Author descending on HQ alone.

'Ah, Inspector Ghote.'

The British author's enveloping smile seemed to come all the way down the line. 'Ah, good. I was just setting out to see you. You're speaking from your office?'

'Yes,' Ghote answered. 'That is – no. That is . . .'

'There seems to be a bit of a discrepancy,' the plummy voice said.

'Not at all,' Ghote answered with sharpness. 'I am at office and I shall be here all morning.'

But when the Noted British Author arrived he was magnificently insulated from him. Within two minutes of his call Inspector Dandekar had asked him to take over his interrogation. It had been something of an admission of defeat for Dandekar. He had told Ghote he felt he dared no longer leave unexplored the possible trails in the Bombay underworld. If the boy was innocent despite everything, then inquiries through the usual network of touts and informers must be pursued now with extra vigour.

'Mind you,' he had concluded, 'I still swear young Raju is guilty as hell. I hope you can break him.'

So, with Dandekar gossiping to thief acquaintances in such places as the stolen goods mart of the Chor Bazaar and thus safe from any British botheration, Ghote felt perfectly justified in leaving the author to cool his heels.

And in the meanwhile he faced young Raju, cocksure graduate of Bombay University, adopted son of the murdered ice-cream manufacturer and, as Dandekar had discovered at Shivaji Park, openly mutinous at having been assigned the fairly humble job in his new father's firm of going round to shops and restaurants instead of having a fat sum given him to start up on his own.

It was with this point that Ghote began.

'Sit down, sit down,' he said. 'I have been going over your answers to Inspector Dandekar, and there is one small thing I cannot understand. You wanted a sum to start up a business. But it is not at all clear what is the business.'

The boy sat down on the hard chair in front of Ghote's table and with deliberate casualness put one leg over the other.

'You are not catching me that way, bhai,' he said. 'All along I am denying and denying I asked for money.'

Ghote sighed.

'But we have a statement from a neighbour to whom you yourself complained,' he said. 'Two others also heard loud quarrelling.'

'Lies,' Raju answered contemptuously.

Ghote did not let himself be discomposed. But for all the calmness with which he went back to the point and for all the reasonableness of every other question he asked in the next two hours, he got, it seemed nowhere. Some of the hard and shiny contempt left the boy's voice, and the two of them eventually might have been friendly acquaintances, but the answers, though different in tone, were never one whit helpful.

So when a constable came in with a chit saying Inspector Dandekar had returned Ghote felt decidedly relieved. He had not really hoped for success where Dandekar had failed, but a small gleam in him had licked at the possibility. And now he knew it would not be.

Dandekar he found equally gloomy.

'Nothing,' he said in answer to a query about his luck with the informers. 'Not a whisper. Of course there may be something still, you know. When the newspapers get on to a case people hold out. But I did not get one word.'

And if you did not, Ghote thought, no one else could.

'The boy is also the same as ever,' he said, 'I talked and cajoled and urged but he did not give one thing, except to stop back-answering.'

'That little rat. I am going to have him, Ghote. I am going to get him talking if it is the last thing I do. I am going now.'

And, all solidly compact determination, he marched out.

Ghote sat where he was on the small chair beside Dandekar's desk. He felt he could not face the waiting British author; he had used every atom of his patience with young Raju. He leant forward, banged the brass bell on the desk and when the peon came ordered tea.

He took his time sipping at the hot milky liquid and had not quite finished when suddenly the bat-wing doors clapped back with a noise like a pair of quick following pistol shots and Dandekar came striding in again.

But now his face was alight with a dark joy.

'Got him,' he said. 'Got him. I knew I would, and by God I did.'

Ghote's first feeling – he tried to overcome it – was chagrin. He had had Raju all morning and had ended up where he began; Dandekar had had him for scarcely twenty minutes and had broken him. But never mind who had done it, the boy had talked.

'He confessed everything?' he asked Dandekar. 'Faking the ropes, planning it all with Louzado and that Budhoo?'

'Everything. Thanks to you, Ghote.'

'To me?'

'Oh yes. When I heard you had taken that soft line I thought that perhaps how one good hard push would do it. And it did. They did not set out to murder, of course. But when that Budhoo found not one lakh of jewellery but four or five rings only, he went mad. That accounts for all those wounds.'

'Shabash, Inspector, shabash,' Ghote said, a rush of warmth swirling through him.

But Dandekar, slumping down into his chair, opening a drawer and pulling out a towel to dab his sweaty face, had begun to look less triumphant.

'It is all right, Ghote,' he said. 'But you know as well as I do that when it comes to court, as likely as not young Raju will shamelessly deny every word.'

'Yes,' Ghote said. 'We need Budhoo, though we would be lucky ever to find that one. Or we need John Louzado.'

He began recounting how that trail had ended. But in a minute a look of wide-eyed staring came on Dandekar's hook-nosed face. Slowly Ghote turned, though he knew almost for a certainty what he would see.

And there it was, looming over the top of the doors like a bristling hairy moon, the face of the Noted British Author.

Resignedly Ghote pushed himself to his feet.

'Mr Reymond,' he said, his voice ringing with brightness. 'I was just coming to tell you. We have broken the case.'

But congratulations did not come as freely as he felt they should. Indeed, as out in the sunshine his story progressed, the bushy beard gaped wide more than once with hardly restrained interjections.

Discrepancies, Ghote thought. Hiatuses. 'Significant variations.' Surely there could not be more.

And at last he ran out of words and had to face the author's objections.

'Inspector, I feel bound to point out a few things. You and Inspector Dandekar have been most kind to me. I can see that as soon as I get home I shall write a story called *Mr Peduncle and the Indian Inspector*. And it would be nothing short of a betrayal if I kept silent.'

'Most kind. But I assure—'

'No, Inspector, it is the least I can do. First then, let me say that I know young Raju well. He and I often had long, long talks when he came to phone friends in Delhi and other places. And I promise you, Inspector, he is not the chap to set

81

criminals on to rob his own benefactors. There's a simple discrepancy between what the boy is and what you say he did. But that's not all.'

'No?' Ghote said.

'No. You see, there's one piece of the puzzle which still doesn't fit. And time and again my Mr Peduncle has said to Inspector Sugden, "You've got to fit in every bit, my dear fellow, every bit of the puzzle."'

'But—'

'No, Inspector, hear me out. I know this can't be easy to take, but you can't get away from pure logic. What you heard from Fariqua this morning simply didn't add up. You've only to think about it. And if he's lying there can be only one reason. Young Raju wasn't the third man – Fariqua was.'

Ghote stood there fuming. Who was this detective-story writer to come telling them what was and was not so? Him and his logic and his hiatuses.

But, even as he encouraged the rage to squirt and bubble inside him, he also felt a streak of cold doubt.

Logic. Well, logic was logic. And suspects – even college-eduated – had been known to confess under pressure to crimes they have not committed, right up to murder. And Dandekar, first-class though he was, certainly could put pressure on.

Was it possible that, despite what seemed plain facts, that story of Fariqua's – seemingly unlikely but perfectly in accord with the way things happened – was just a story?

One thing was certain. The shame, the ridiculousness, of having an author of detective books get to the right answer first must not make them ignore that answer. If only they were not relying wholly on that confession but had Louzado or Budhoo in a cell too. If only the trail of addresses had not . . .

And then, like a last monsoon storm coming winding rapidly in across the sea long after the monsoon ought to have ended, bringing a last welcome sudden coolness, an idea came winding and leaping into his mind.

'Sir, sir,' he said. 'Come with me straight away, sir, if you please.'

And without giving the author a chance to reply he bundled him into the car and set off into the darting traffic.

They made it to the Shivaji Park flat in record time. There, still begging for patience, Ghote took one fast look round the sitting-room – couches spread with cotton counterpanes, bookshelves, two tables and, yes, the telephone.

And next to it 'the little book' in which, so the Noted British Author had told him soon after they met, people from nearby looked things up. His mention just now of Raju telephoning distant friends had at last brought it to the front of his mind. He flicked at the indexed pages with sweat-slippery fingers. L for Louzado. And yes. Yes, yes, yes. There it was. The address.

He seized the phone, dialled furiously, shouted instructions for a Lightning Call and miraculously was speaking to the Goa police in Panjim in minutes. And got splendid cooperation. They knew the place, they would find the man, no doubt they would find his share of the missing rings. The fellow would be behind bars in half an hour.

It was almost as if he was putting a hand on his shoulder himself.

He turned from the telephone and looked the bursting-bearded British author full in the face.

'Let me tell one thing, sir,' he said, savouring the irony to the last drop. 'Let me tell one thing: never to neglect a hiatus.'

1975

6

The Wicked Lady

Inspector Ghote sat on the terrace of the tourist hotel looking down on the loveliest beach in all the beauty-crammed little State of Goa, and did his best to look like someone on holiday. On the white sand of the beach some fifty yards away there sprawled Dattu Phadkar, the young man the newspapers never ceased to call 'The Crown Prince of Smugglers'. But he did not, Ghote reflected for perhaps the twentieth time, look at all like a big-time operator in the middle of setting up a big-time deal. Yet none of his own senior officers back in Bombay had believed that such a fellow as Phadkar would go all two hundred miles to out-of-season Goa except for the purpose of conducting some huge deal. And so under the pretence of being a holidaying civil servant, he in his turn had been sent on the same journey to keep an eye on the young smuggler whom, luckily, he had never happened to encounter in the course of their parallel but opposed careers.

Did they know, back in Bombay, that Dattu Phadkar was accompanied by Mrs Phadkar, Ghote wondered. Would that have altered their view? Because, if the young smuggler looked like an ordinary holiday maker, Mrs Phadkar looked a dozen times more like an ordinary middle-class lady. Indeed she seemed the very pattern of the obedient Hindu wife, timid, hardly speaking, never out of a sari, its end usually modestly over her head, eyes only for her husband.

Well, if back at Headquarters they wanted him to stay down here and laze by the sea, to eat huge meals and to drink a little of the local liquor, strong-tasting feni, then he would do his duty and keep a discreet watch from a distance on the young smuggler. It was really very pleasant.

Except for Miss Bhatt. Miss Bhatt, one of the few other guests here this early, taking a well-earned rest after her widower father's death had ended years of devotion, was the fly in the ointment, decidedly. Because if her weary limbs were resting now, her tongue certainly was not. And, as he was on duty watching the young smuggler's every move, he could not escape that clacking whenever she chose to descend on him.

Thank goodness she had not come out yet.

'Mr Ghote, how very very pleasant. May I join you? Ah, I see Mr Kolwar down there on the beach already, and that nice little Mrs Kolwar.'

'Excuse me,' Ghote interrupted, though he knew that to do so would only redouble the spate of chatter that awaited him. 'Excuse me, but that is Mr and Mrs Phadkar down there. Mr and Mrs— Mr Kolwar and his lady are the other guests here.'

'Oh, of course, of course,' Miss Bhatt answered. 'But I always get things muddled. My poor father, it was a wonder only that I was not poisoning him with all the different medicines that he had to have.'

She sat back with pride.

'But look,' she said an instant later, 'there go the Kolwars now. Or are we not to say "Mrs Kolwar"? Ah, what a naughty world it is.'

Only Miss Bhatt, Ghote thought – muddle-headed, talkative, rushing-in Miss Bhatt – could have believed that Lalitha the film star, elegant, sophisticated, bikini-wearing, was the legal wife of Mr Kolwar, that excessively rich manufacturer of ice-cream. No, Lalitha – though she had had long-lasting and well-publicised relationships with two male stars, one maharajah and a famous sitar-player – was not the marrying kind. Indeed, she really owed her screen success – if all that he had heard was true – to having cultivated for years the image of the Wicked Lady.

'But,' Miss Bhatt resumed, leaning closer towards him but still speaking in a voice which, he was only too well aware, could easily carry down to the beach below, 'but there can be no doubt she is a most beautiful woman. They say she is a star, you know.'

'Yes,' said Ghote. 'I know.'

'And Mr Kolwar is so rich. Did you hear him last night ordering one of those paans that cost a hundred rupees? And did you hear him chewing it?'

Miss Bhatt laughed.

'Not very educated,' she said. 'But powerful, you can tell.

Not a person ever to let go when he has something in his grasp. Ah, they have joined the Phadkars now. They seem already to know each other well.'

'No doubt they were acquainted in Bombay before they came here at all,' Ghote consoled her.

'Ah, yes, the wealthy circles. Of course, I could never . . . But, tell me, Mr Ghote, do you think that down here we might venture to join them?'

'No,' said Ghote.

Nevertheless before that day was done he found himself being forcefully introduced by Miss Bhatt to the little group. 'Mr Ghote is a civil servant, you know, most senior.'

And he was at the same time introduced to a new guest, already swept up under Miss Bhatt's vigorous wing. He was a hearty Sikh, clutching a shiny leather sample case. 'Mr Singh Anand is a pharmaceuticals representative for a very well-known German firm. Many, many of his products I have had to give to my poor father.'

Within a few minutes of their meeting Ghote found himself being nudged by the pharmaceuticals traveller and a thick voice whispered in his ear, 'Damn fine woman, Lalitha, haan?' And before he had managed to excuse himself from the group on the grounds of having to make a telephone call the Sikh had nudged him again and had whispered, even more loudly, 'Pretty little thing, Mrs Phadkar. Too bad.'

The reason for this last comment was only too clear: young Dattu Phadkar, Crown Prince of Smugglers, was paying heavy attentions to the glamorous Lalitha. Indeed, not long after-wards Ghote was an unwilling witness to little Mrs Phadkar's further discomfiture. Having ascertained from the hotel manager that Mr Singh Anand was indeed a pharmaceuticals representative who regularly stayed here on his round, he was dutifully keeping up his watch on the young smuggler from a hard bench in a corner of the lobby. And from there he saw Mrs Phadkar come out of the bar and, apparently not noticing him, turn and signal to her husband that he should come with her upstairs. But there was no response from the bar, except perhaps for an even louder shout of laughter. Ghote watched Mrs Phadkar trail sadly and alone up the stairs, and it was not until much later that he was able to end his vigil when Lalitha and her admirers at length went up in their turn. Then at last he got painfully, bones aching, to his feet.

But he had forgotten swooping Miss Bhatt.

'Mr Ghote, what a pity you had to leave us. You missed some most interesting conversation.'

She leant towards him.

'Though, if you are asking me, poor little Mrs Phadkar left because she was not understanding. We were talking in English. Naturally. And she must learn also not to demand from her husband. That is always a very great mistake in married life.'

'Yes,' said Ghote. 'And good night, *Miss* Bhatt.'

Three evenings later the murder took place. Miss Bhatt had, as was now her custom, assembled them all for drinks before dinner. All except Lalitha, still upstairs with her maid – another part of the holiday routine that had become customary. But the party was not a happy one. Only Mr Singh Anand seemed really content, having secured for himself a chair next to the one awaiting the glamorous if ageing film star. The place on the other side was hotly disputed between young Dattu Phadkar and the rich ice-cream manufacturer, each glaring at the other and constantly calling for fresh drinks. Miss Bhatt soon began to look greatly distressed by this bull-like rivalry. And serve her right, Ghote thought.

But at last Lalitha came sweeping in.

'Somebody get me a feni, please, please, please,' she called. 'I am half dead already with that stupid girl.'

Both the rivals leapt to their feet. But Lalitha's powerful protector was the more cunning.

'Sit, sit,' he said. 'Take my drink. I have not touched.'

Lalitha flung herself down, took the feni from Mr Kolwar's hand and downed it in one. 'Life saver,' she declared. Only to choke, to clutch at her stomach and to be laying dead on the floor within two minutes.

The Inspector of the Goa Police, who arrived with commendable promptitude, very quickly learnt all about the situation between Lalitha, her protector and the young Dattu Phadkar. Miss Bhatt's unstoppable tongue saw to that. And when, turning to question the young smuggler more clearly, he spotted a small bottle in the pocket of his bush-shirt and on inquiring was met with a loud denial that he knew anything about it, he arrested Phadkar there and then, grabbing the little bottle as he did so. It proved to have contained a heart remedy with – clearly written on its label – a warning against exceeding the stated dose. There were only a few drops left.

Miss Bhatt, as soon as the young man had been hustled out to the manager's office and Lalitha's beautiful body had been removed, favoured Ghote with her views.

'What a ghastly moment for him. To have decided to get rid of his rival and then to have to watch while the deadly glass was handed to the woman he loved. Should he speak and incriminate himself? Should he try somehow to prevent her sipping the fatal brew? And then, before he could utter a word, gone. Swallowed in one. No wonder that he forgot to get rid of the little bottle. Ghastly.'

'Yes, ghastly,' Ghote agreed. 'But it was not exactly like that, you know.'

And, with that, he left her.

'Stop, Mr Ghote, stop.'

Inspector Ghote, coming into the lobby an hour or so later fresh from a quiet word with his Goa Police counterpart, froze to a halt. It was Miss Bhatt. He might have known he could hardly have left for Bombay, his cover now unavoidably blown, without encountering her once more.

He turned to her with resignation.

'Yes, Miss Bhatt?'

'Mr Ghote, you cannot go out of the hotel without telling why you think this terrible business was not exactly as I have said. It is altogether plain to me that it was Mr Dattu Phadkar who was responsible. Who else could it have been? Why, we all saw them finding that deadly bottle in his pocket.'

'It was put there,' Ghote said.

'But . . . but it was quite clear also that Mr Phadkar was terribly terribly in love with Lalitha, and Mr Kolwar is not at all the sort of person to let go.'

'True, Mr Kolwar would not let go of anything he was wanting.'

'Well then,' Miss Bhatt began in knock-down triumph.

But at that moment out of the manager's office came young Dattu Phadkar with the manager himself beside him, scuttling along and assuring the Crown Prince of Smugglers that, if he felt he must leave, his luggage would be fetched at once and a taxi for the airport found immediately.

Miss Bhatt was silenced. But not for long.

The moment the young smuggler had stepped outside she swung round to Ghote.

'But–' she said. 'But he should be under arrest. What is happening? I do not at all understand.'

Ghote sighed.

'Well, you see,' he said, 'the truth is that Mr Kolwar did not any longer want Lalitha. She is no more young, you know. So now it was her who was wanting to keep him. That was why each and every evening she was taking so deplorably long to make herself look beautiful. But there is one person here who is young, and pretty also, as even Mr Singh Anand agreed, although like everybody else he felt that he had to a little bit flirt with a famous star. And that pretty young person is, of course, Mrs Phadkar. I am afraid that, for all her appearance only of being the good little Hindu wife, it was she who was in truth the wicked lady here.'

Miss Bhatt blinked in total astonishment.

'Little Mrs Phadkar attracted to Mr Kolwar?' she said.

'Yes, that was the situation. She was undoubtedly the one who obtained that medicine from Mr Singh Anand. But, of course, it was Mr Kolwar who, when we all looked at Lalitha as she came in, slipped the stuff into his own drink. Then he could easily hand to the lady who was not going to let him go what you were calling – isn't it – the fatal brew.'

'Yes,' said Miss Bhatt, 'the fatal brew.'

Ghote took a little pity on her then.

'But you were perfectly right about one thing,' he said. 'Mr Kolwar was not at all educated. He did not know fingerprints, and when we took his to compare with those on that little bottle he altogether broke down.'

'We took?' Miss Bhatt asked in new bewilderment.

'Well, yes, we took,' Ghote said. 'Appearances are sometimes deceptive, you know. I am actually from Bombay CID.'

'Oh,' said Miss Bhatt. 'Oh dear, oh dear.'

And after that she chattered no more.

1976

7

The Cruel Inspector Ghote

Inspector Ghote stood deep in thought. He was in a dilemma. It was the matter of the Hashambhai son, young Musa. Undoubtedly the young fellow was the one responsible for the theft of rupees one lakh from his own parents. But no doubt either about two other things. The first was that those hundred thousand rupees were almost certainly 'black money', the hidden-away unbankable accumulation of cash payments not entered in the books of Mr Hashambhai's watch-making business, one of the most prosperous in all Bombay. The second was that Mr Hashambhai was a person of 'influence'. He had friends in high places. Doing anything that displeased Mr Hashambhai, like getting the Hashambhai name in the papers, would bring trouble. A word in the Commissioner's ear. Something like that only.

But nonetheless, young Musa Hashambhai had stolen that money. He himself had all the evidence necessary. He ought to arrest the boy, no matter how indulgent about the whole matter his father might be. Even, he owed it to the boy himself. One big shock now, when he was seventeen-eighteen years of age, and he might behave himself well for the rest of his life.

On the other hand, Mr Hashambhai did have that influence and might well use it. Nor did he perhaps deserve to get back that tainted money.

Suddenly Ghote realised something. While he had been standing stock-still in thought here on the pavement beside Churchgate Station he had been witnessing a crime, witnessing it without taking it in at all.

Never mind that it was not the most serious crime in the Indian Penal Code. It was a crime. Never mind that the perpetrator was no more than a child, a chubby little boy of eight or so with an air of bouncy joyfulness about him, what he was doing there on the opposite pavement at this very moment was a crime.

Only, as the little devil was on the pavement opposite and half the roadway betweeen them was blocked by one of Bombay's most curious sights, there was nothing that he himself could do to stop that crime taking place. But he could probably prevent the criminal getting away.

What the boy was doing was slitting with a razor blade stuck into an old cork the underneath of a big blue leather handbag on the arm of a rather plump European lady in a boldly flower-patterned dress, who stood peering into the view-finder of her camera recording Bombay's curiosity, the *dabbawallas*.

The *dabbawallas*, who were occupying the roadway and blocking him off from his quarry, were very much worth photographing for a foreign tourist, Ghote thought. Each morning of Bombay's working week they collected up from homes in the suburbs home-cooked tiffin for husbands working in offices in the heart of the city. Each lunch was placed in four round cans fitting neatly one on top of the other into their carrier marked in red paint with its code numbers. The *dabbawallas* took them to the nearest suburban rail station and went with them to the Churchgate terminus. There, in the roadway outside, the tiffin-carriers were rapidly sorted according to destination and placed in long wooden racks which other *dabbawallas* would carry on their heads at a fast trot to offices all over Bombay's commercial and administrative heart. It was a sight to see – and to record on film. Only, unfortunately, while you were concentrating on doing that you were at risk of having your pocket picked. Or handbag slit open.

Ghote stepped through the criss-cross jumble of wooden racks. He waited impatiently while half a dozen trucks clattered by on the clear side of the road. At last he darted over, keeping his eye all the while on his chubby little target. Then, as the boy made off with suspicious nonchalance in the direction of the pavement-dwellers' huts standing in tumble-down confusion some quarter of a mile distant, he launched himself forward at a run. In less than a minute he had the little thief firmly by the ear, digging a finger sharply in, a trick he had long ago learnt to make sure no slippery captive got away.

Even as he made his catch he was aware that the little thief's crime had been discovered. From behind his back, some fifteen or twenty yards away there rose a wail of purest English anguish.

'My bag. It's empty. My purse. It's gone. My passport.'

Keeping the urchin firmly held in his special grip, Ghote wheeled him round and marched him back towards the outraged lady in the flowery summer dress, her indignant voice joined now by other shrill comments. 'It's too bad, too bad.' 'I just hope they catch him, whoever it is.' 'Yes, and put him where he belongs – for as long as they can.' 'If they want tourists they should make sure they protect them.'

'Madam,' he said to the outraged victim, 'kindly be no longer worrying. I am a police inspector, Inspector Ghote by name, and I have had the jolly good luck to catch the thief of your possessions.'

He reached down with his free hand, grasped the little criminal's ragged khaki shorts by their top and gave a good tug. Passport and purse, cunningly tucked away, fell to the ground. The boy opened his mouth in a big round 'O' and let out a howl of dismay.

The circle of British ladies – they all looked much alike to Ghote, large, pink-faced, heads tight with curls golden or greying, all flowery-frocked – peered down at the small figure.

'Oh,' said a voice from among them. 'The poor mite.'

A chorus broke out at once. 'Yes, the poor little thing.' 'Oh, he can't be more than six or seven.' 'Was it him really?'

The lady with the razor-ripped blue bag was as transformed as any of her companions.

'Inspector,' she said, bending forward and addressing Ghote confidentially, 'Inspector, don't you think – he's only a bit of a thing, isn't he? – don't you think you could let him go? I've got my purse back. I don't mind.'

Ghote, finger crooked hard in the boy's ear, looked at her stone-faced.

'Madam,' he replied, 'I have caught the little riff-raff red-handed only.'

'Yes, I know Inspector. But all the same . . . I'm sure he'll never be so naughty again. He's got such a sweet little face.'

And it was true that the boy, who probably hardly understood a word of English but who knew a tone of voice when he heard one, had stopped howling and was looking up at the ring of large pink faces with the hint of an endearing smile trembling on his chubby features.

'Madam,' Ghote said once more, 'I am suspecting that you are wanting this little anti-social to go free because you are thinking what a very, very great nuisance it would be for you to give evidence tomorrow morning at Esplanade Police Court.'

'Inspector. What a suggestion.'

And the lady was supported by a new chorus asserting her public-spiritedness on numerous occasions, and explaining that they were a group on a tour of India specially designed for ladies with 'inquiring minds' and that they were not due to leave for Agra and the Taj Mahal for another three days.

But Inspector Ghote's countenance remained unmoved.

'No, no,' he said. 'It is no good your hearts becoming pools of tears. I must hand the culprit to some passing constable to be kept in custody until his appearance before the Magistrate. Yes, definitely.'

And indeed, as if by magic, at that moment a constable hove into sight, not at all Bobby-like in his floppy blue uniform and little boat-shaped blue and yellow cap, but a formidably tough-looking figure for all that.

Ghote led his captive away. By the ear.

But, somewhat to the surprise of the British ladies, after speaking to the constable for a minute or so he returned still gripping the little chubby bag-slitter.

'That fellow was not at all suitable,' he said, jerking his chin in the direction of the departing policeman.

And then, apparently thinking it was not quite the proper thing to imply to these foreign visitors that any of the Bombay police force was not ready for whatever task they were called on to perform, he added hastily, 'He had many, many other important duties at this time only.'

So they waited, a fairly silent little crowd, while the *dabbawallas* in the roadway completed their sorting-out, swept up their long wooden racks on to their heads and departed briskly for where lunchers waited at their desks. Once or twice one or two of the group tried suggesting again that the little thief, now looking doubly appealing, should be let off after all. But one glance at Ghote's stern face shrivelled their pleas half spoken.

'What is your good name, please?' he inquired firmly of the theft's victim.

'And at which hotel are you staying?'

Name and address were supplied, and once more silence fell. But before long another constable came into view, a stout old veteran by the look of him. Ghote called out sharply and the man broke into a slow, dignified trot, only to arrive puffing and panting.

The little thief was handed into his custody. He grasped him by the arm and set off at a ponderous pace. Ghote took a rapid farewell of the assembled British ladies and departed, rather hurriedly, in the direction of the distant tumble of pavement-dwellers' huts.

The visitors stood where they were, watching the sad little thief being led off and clucking in helpless dismay at his fate. But he was hardly fifty yards distant when, with a swift wriggle and a sharp jerk, he slipped from the grip of the puffing old veteran constable, whirled round and headed away in the direction he had first made off in, weaving through the crowds on the pavement and in the roadway like a tiny tadpole slipping between slow-moving carp.

'Well, I never,' exclaimed the lady with the ruined blue handbag.

But time was getting on. There were other items on the group's morning itinerary, more for 'inquiring minds' to see and assimilate. The hire cars that had brought them to Churchgate Station were waiting with the guide that the tour operator had supplied.

'We are now going to Victoria Gardens Zoo,' he announced. 'It is very, very interesting.'

Some of the ladies appeared to doubt this. They looked as if they felt Bombay ought to provide something meatier for their inquiring minds than a mere zoo.

But they were destined to see a sight that would provide them with plenty of mental fodder, and plenty to talk about, well before they reached Victoria Gardens.

In fact, they had gone less than a quarter of a mile on their northwards journey before, with their cars stuck in a minor jam, they had the unexpected sight of Inspector Ghote once more.

He was loping along on the far side of the road, looking

somehow simultaneously intent and uninterested, but moving all the time with tremendous purposefulness. And then – there, only some ten yards ahead of him – the keener-sighted of the touring ladies spotted the little chubby escapee pickpocket.

They had better luck than that even. Before the bullock pulling a little kerosene-tank cart that had been holding them up had been persuaded to move on, the craning ladies actually saw the boy dive into one of the pavement shacks, a desperately slanting affair of sagging bamboo poles, pieces of rusted corrugated iron, stretched gunny sacks and odd lengths of soiled plastic. A moment later Ghote plunged in after him to emerge grasping this time, not the chubby eight-year-old but a tall, hangdog individual in a greasy European-style suit.

Then, surprise on surprise, who should come running up from behind but the very constable Ghote had not handed the little thief over to, the tough-looking one who had had 'many, many other important duties'. And in a trice a pair of handcuffs was round the wrists of the man in the greasy suit and the constable was marching him off, a grin of triumph on his face.

'How very strange,' one of the ladies in the first car said.

'It certainly is,' another echoed.

'I wonder what's happened,' said a third.

The next day, after a letter had been delivered to the hotel summoning the victim of the bag-slitting to the Esplanade Police Court, the ladies of the tour, accompanying her en masse, had their inquiring minds happily satisfied.

First, the summoned witness had had to give her evidence. Then Inspector Ghote had recounted how he had followed the absconding thief and had tracked him down to a pavement hut in Maharishi Karve Road where he had found the accused in possession of numerous articles stolen on such-and-such dates. And finally the man in the greasy suit, which was looking even greasier for a night in the lock-up, had been sentenced to six months Rigorous Imprisonment.

As soon as the ladies had their chance, they surrounded Inspector Ghote on the courthouse steps, demanding the full story in their pink-faced clucking voices. And Ghote, with a deprecating wag of his head, eventually obliged.

'You see, ladies,' he said, 'it was like this. I was not wishing for that boy to be too much punished. He was after all seven or eight years of age only. But I was thinking that it would be a very, very good thing if we could put behind the bars the blacksheep who was making him commit those acts of thieving. As you know the golden opportunity never knocks twice. So I was wanting the boy to escape, hoping he would go straight back to the boss of his gang.'

'And that was why you handed him over to that fat old constable and not to the other?' said the lady with the most inquiring mind of them all.

'Oh, yes, madam, you are seeing that straight away. It is most sagacious of you. Very, very sagacious indeed.'

'So, when you had that little talk with the first one, you were telling him to back you up when you started to follow the boy?' asked another of the ladies, not to be outdone in the sagacious line.

'Very, very correct, madam.'

'And the boy?' asked a third lady, not perhaps as sagacious but very tender-hearted.

'Well, madam, I am thinking that finding himself caught in the act would scare him to the bones, especially when he found in the end he had not escaped so jolly easily. So I am letting him go with one cuff on the head only.'

'Oh, the poor mite,' exclaimed the tender-hearted lady.

But she was alone in her tenderness. 'No more than he deserved.' 'He'll have learnt his lesson.' 'A bit of cuff does 'em no harm.' That was the chorus.

'Well, Inspector,' said the lady who had stood in the witness-box and delivered her testimony with assurance, 'it's not far off lunch-time, and I think all of us would be delighted if you would join us at our hotel.'

But Inspector Ghote shook his head.

'Very regret, madam and ladies,' he said, 'I am still having to give evidence in a case here. You see, yesterday after we had met I was arresting the son of a certain very, very wealthy watch-maker. The boy had stolen a large sum from the house of his parents itself and, whatever they are feeling and whatever they are saying to anybody influential, it is right only that the young fellow should receive some kind of shock treatment. So good day to you, ladies. Good day, please.'

1984

8

Murder Must Not At All Advertise, Isn't It?

The Cabin Killer Strikes Again. Inspector Ghote, getting out of the police car and looking up at the sky-zooming building in Bombay's tower-jostling, rich-to-bursting Nariman Point area, found the phrase, in just those English words, pulsating in his mind.

The Cabin Killer. It was what the more sensational papers had taken to calling the fellow whose modus operandi appeared to be entering well-equipped offices, making away with the prize pickings from the boss's own cabin, and if disturbed not hesitating to attack. And just because the Press had seized on this particular criminal among all Bombays hundreds, orders had come down to the CID from the Minister for Home himself to make the case their Number One priority.

So when a jabbering voice on the telephone had reported that 'the Cabin Killer has struck again', yet one more officer had been taken off all other duties. Himself. And since Crime Branch's top investigator, the renowned Assistant Commissioner 'Dasher' Dabholkar, in charge of the inquiry, was already out in the field elsewhere, he had been sent to the offices of Shalimar Associates, the big advertising firm, whose boss – so the report had said – was the Killer's latest victim.

The Cabin Killer Strikes Again. Ghote tried to shake the headline words, soon no doubt to be seen once more, out of his mind. They were nonsense only, he told himself. The man was hardly a killer. He was a common thief only, if one with something of a new angle. No one else, so far as the clacking mechanical files in Records could turn up, had hit on the trick of making for the top man's room itself when slipping into a set of offices, at a time few people were about, intent on quick robbery. It was usually simply an unguarded typewriter that was taken, or any other obviously sellable object.

But this fellow had certainly gone one better. Somewhere he must have come to learn that in the boss's cabin of most of the posh firms in areas like Nariman Point there would be a bottle or two of the best. Generally Chivas Regal whisky. Generally in the bottom right-hand drawer of the big glossy desk.

And twice, just twice, in a career of crime that Dasher Dabholkar had had traced back over nearly three years, the fellow had been caught red-handed. And once, once only, when he had snatched up a heavy object and lashed out, his victim had died from injuries received. The second attack victim, in fact, had suffered no more than a cracked jawbone and a nasty bruise. But for some reason the papers had decided to blow up the perpetrator as 'The Cabin Killer'.

Who now had 'struck again'? Or perhaps not. You never could tell with excited witnesses phoning in. Someone had said something about a sword, too. That the Cabin Killer had used 'Shivaji's sword'.

Well, that was nonsense too. The sword reputed to have been wielded in times long ago by the hero of all Marathi-speaking Bombay, Shivaji the Great, was – it was well-known – in British hands. In some museum or other in London. And all attempts to get it restored to India had so far failed. So how could the Cabin Killer have used Shivaji's sword?

Ghote heaved a sigh.

Ah, well, better get up there and sort it all out.

At the penthouse offices of Shalimar Associates, whisked smoothly upwards in a steel-walled lift, he began to have doubts about how easy that sorting-out would be. The place was Western, very, very Western. Even the reception area was covered in one vast layer of carpet, a dark brown unblemished surface that seemed to proclaim 'No chappals here. Shoes only.' Above, from a huge expanse of ceiling broken into different panelled areas all in immaculate white, there hung curious futuristic lights, each lit even though outside the sun was beating down in its usual bleaching blaze. The closed slatted blinds in dark brown plastic were, however, taking care of the sun.

And, as if all this was not daunting enough, there were the people. There seemed to be dozens of them, almost all dressed in smart Western clothes, girls in hugging jeans and most of the men too. And all of them chattering in English, jabbering, gesticulating, and paying no attention at all to himself, a lone figure, ahead of the fingerprint and photography team, dressed – he became acutely conscious of the fact – in simple shirt and pants, a good deal the worse for a long morning in dirty, sweat-springing Bombay.

But this would not do. There had been a murder here. Or so they said. And he had come to investigate.

He marched forward over the smooth brown lake of carpet and up to the nearest person to him, a young woman – seemingly even more animated than anyone else – wearing a deep red thin silk Lucknow kurta above the obligatory jeans.

'Madam,' he said. 'Excuse me. It is CID. Inspector Ghote. A murder has been reported, isn't it?'

The girl turned.

'Well,' she said, 'it's the fuzz. At last.'

Yet, unwilling as he was to accept this form of address, Ghote could not help responding to the cheerful smile that went with it.

'Who is it, please, I am speaking with?' he asked, less reprovingly than he had intended.

'The name's Tigga,' the girl answered. 'I'm a copywriter here.'

'Very well, Miss Tigga. Now, where is the deceased?'

'Yes, the deceased. I'll take you to his cabin. He's . . . He was—' Unexpectedly the girl choked back a sudden lump in the throat. 'He was our Creative Director. Managing Director, too. The boss, in fact. Mr Patel. Known everywhere as Billy Patel. He was . . . Inspector, he was always so alive. Such a go-getter.'

'Yes, yes. I understand. But, Miss Tigga, we must please proceed to the cabin in question.'

'Yes. Yes, of course. This way.'

She began to lead him through the still jabbering throng of people, all young, all still highly excited.

After a moment she turned back to him.

'By the way, just to get it straight,' she said. 'It's not Miss Tigga, actually. It's Miss Kelkar. Neeta Kelkar. But I'm always known as Tigga. I was called it after Tigger in the Winnie the Pooh books, you know.'

'Yes,' said Ghote, who did not know.

'I ought to have one of those name badges we always seem to

get given at conferences and seminars and things,' she went on breezily. 'Then no one would have to ask, and no more long complicated explanations.'

'No,' said Ghote.

They had passed through the glossy reception counter, adorned with a huge vase of white flowers, a white telephone and nothing else, and were heading for one of the wide corridors behind it. But abruptly the ebullient Tigga halted again.

'Roger, Roger,' she called out.

A young man with a trim beard, wearing the inevitable close-fitting jeans and a crisp shirt that put Ghote's sweat-saddened one to shame, came up beside them.

He gave Tigga a wary glance.

'Friends?' he said.

'Friends,' she answered decisively.

She turned back to Ghote.

'This is Roger Rajinder, youngest account executive at Shalimar Associates,' she announced. 'Oh, wow, another name complication. Naresh Rajinder, I should have said. But known to all as Roger, on account of a tremendous resemblance to a certain British film star. Roger, this is the CID Inspector.'

Roger Rajinder gave her a mock glare of rage before turning to Ghote.

'Don't mind this dreadful girl, Inspector,' he said. 'What can I do for you? You're on your way to poor Billy's cabin?'

'Yes, yes. But, tell me please, what is this about a sword? Was the killing committed with a sword only?'

'Shivaji's sword, Inspector, no less,' Roger answered. 'Or, in point of fact, a mock-up of Shivaji's sword we had made for our new Cocopuff biscuits campaign. It was on Billy's desk, and it seems when he came back for something or other during the lunch break he disturbed this fellow who must have picked up the sword and stabbed him. It's a terrible thing.'

He glanced at Tigga as he said these last suddenly saddened words and received from her an answering look. Ghote felt a dart of warmth. These two young people were in love. He knew it as surely as if it had been written on a matching pair of the name badges Tigga had talked about. They were in love – despite that query about being friends – and out of nowhere death had entered their lives. Violent death.

100

But he was a police officer, sent to investigate an offence under Indian Penal Code Section 302.

'Take me to Mr Patel's cabin please,' he said.

They found two other people in Billy Patel's cabin, standing over the body from which, sure enough, a wide-bladed curving sword protruded. Roger Rajinder introduced them, with unexpected formality.

'Inspector, this is Mr Shantaram Das, our senior account executive – and, I suppose, now in charge of things – and this is Mr Tarlok Singh, our accountant.'

Shantaram Das was immediately pleasing to Ghote. To begin with, he was not a young man. Not young and, Ghote added to himself, irresponsible. Instead he was a dignified figure of perhaps fifty, weightily plump. And then he was not dressed in jeans. Indeed, he was almost at the opposite extreme, in flowing white kurta and calf-clasping white churidar, the very picture of tradition. The Sikh accountant, on the other hand, was as glossy as everyone else Ghote had seen, down to his wide maroon necktie exactly matching his neat maroon turban.

Ghote decided to ignore him and address himself exclusively to the dignified Mr Das.

'Tell me, please,' he said, 'the exact circumstances of the matter.'

'Certainly, Inspector. It was, in point of fact, Mr Singh here and myself who found poor Billy. We came into the cabin here to tell him about some clients we had been lunching, and there he was as you see him now. Dead. Dead on the floor and with Shivaji's sword buried deep in his back. Of course we knew at once who had done it. The Cabin Killer. We sensed that, didn't we, Tarlok, even before we saw that Billy's new desk-computer was missing?'

'Well, yes,' the Sikh agreed. 'Only, if you remember, Shantaramji, I was not actually sensing.'

'Yes, yes,' Shantaram Das concurred. 'I am the one who senses in this office and you Tarlok, have the head for detail. All those figures at your fingertips.'

He turned to Ghote with a smile of great sweetness, tinged a little with sadness.

'Inspector,' he said, 'you see in me a poet. I am, I admit, on occasion a little carried away. I exaggerate. Isn't that so, Tarlok, Roger, Tigga? I exaggerate, don't I, Tigga, my dear?'

'Yes, Shantaramji, you exaggerate,' Tigga confirmed with a heavy mock sigh.

'But, Inspector,' the self-confessed poet went on, 'Inspector, believe me, you can trust me to tell you every detail exactly of what happened to poor Billy. That vile criminal must be caught and, if there is anything I can do to help, that I will do. Even to sacrificing the element of poetic enhancement.'

'Very good, Mr Das,' Ghote replied. 'So, kindly tell me about the – what was it you called it? – the desk-computer.'

'Ah, yes. Yes. A clue for you, Inspector. A good, solid unpoetic clue. You see, poor Billy had on trial on his desk this week the very newest mini-computer. Smuggled, of course. He saw a great future for it at Shalimar Associates. Instant assessments. Files at his fingertips. All our accounts revolutionised. A very valuable piece of apparatus, Inspector. Just the thing the Cabin Killer would like. And it's gone. Gone. You couldn't have better proof than that, could you?'

'A very valuable machine?' Ghote asked. 'A very, very advanced one?'

'Exactly, Inspector. You have seized on – what shall I say – the nub. The nub of this business. I can see that you are no poet, my dear fellow, and a very good thing that is too. It is down-to-earth qualities we are wanting to get this appalling killer. Yes, down-to-earth qualities.'

'Down to earth,' Ghote said slowly, echoing the words. 'Yes, Mr Das, just a little I am wondering . . .'

Nudging the back of his mind there was a feeling that something about this particular room was different.

He turned from Billy Patel's huge glass-topped desk, where the missing computer was represented by a square cleared space, and, carefully circumnavigating the body on the floor with the false Shivaji's sword protruding from it, he went over to the room's expanse of slat-covered windows, through which the noises of bustling Bombay, furious (and illegal) horn blasts, the roar of heavy construction trucks round the ever upwards-leaping new buildings, shrill hawkers' cries, could be heard more distinctly than in the air-conditioned other parts of Shalimar Associates' offices.

'Yes,' he said suddenly, 'I thought that must be so.'

He reached out and lifted back one of the smart dark brown slatted blinds. The window behind it was wide open. It was through here that the street noises were penetrating this above-it-all eminence.

'Yes, I thought there would be a window open,' he muttered. 'A little strange, isn't it?'

He put his head through the large square opening and craned out.

'A garden far below,' he called back into the room. 'And, yes, right in the middle of a clump of what is looking like bakain bushes there is a square grey object.'

He pulled himself back in and turned to look at the four members of Shalimar Associates staff.

'Now, what would you be thinking such an object must be?' he asked.

There was a silence, broken at last by Tigga.

'The desk-computer?' she asked. 'Is that what you are saying, Inspector? That the Cabin Killer threw the desk-computer out of the window? But why should he do that?'

'Yes,' Ghote answered. 'That is excellent question altogether, Miss Tigga. Why would a fellow like this so-called Cabin Killer, a fellow who is liking to take bottles of first-class imported whisky from the desks of office bosses and then give a clean slip to all, why should he pilfer a very, very advanced computer, and then throw it through an open window only?'

'Because . . .' Tigga answered slowly. 'Because – are you saying this, Inspector? – Billy was not murdered by the Cabin Killer at all?'

'I am much inclined to be thinking that, certainly,' Ghote said.

'And if that is so,' Tigga went on, her eyes intent in quick thought. 'If that is so, is this what you call an inside job, Inspector?'

'I think it very well may be,' Ghote answered. 'An inside job, yes. Mr Patel murdered by someone in these offices.'

He would have dearly liked to have seen the reactions to his announcement. A glance of suspicion from one of the people in the cabin to another, a look of fear perhaps, or even the murmured name of some person not in the room: any fragment of a hint would have helped at that moment. But instead everyone's attention had been caught by a loud commotion outside the door, and a moment later this was thrust open by Sergeant Sawant, the fingerprint wallah, together with one of the police photographers and a pair of constables with a stretcher ready to take the body for medical examination.

While Sawant was at work, puffing and dusting, and the photographer – with a great deal of unnecessary crouching and leaping – was taking his pictures, Ghote did his best to learn something more from the poetic Mr Das, who had begun in an unpoetic way to be more concerned with re-establishing office routine. Both Roger Rajinder and the dapper Tarlok Singh had been sent to 'put an end damn quick to all that hulla-gulla outside' and only Tigga remained. It was from her that he was able to discover a little more about the dead man. He had, it seemed, been a go-getter indeed, a great figure in the Bombay advertising world, renowned for a lifestyle almost as flamboyant as a film star's.

'Inspector,' Tigga concluded, 'Billy had created more first-class ads per rupee of billing than anyone else in the industry.'

Ghote almost asked, 'What industry?' so surprised was he to learn that the concoction of advertisements and advertising films was dignified with such a description. But he was beginning, in spite of Tigga's Western ways, to like her very much, so he forbore.

At last Sergeant Sawant had covered almost every surface in the cabin with his powders dark and light, and the photographer had clicked and flashed away from every conceivable angle. 'Okay to take away body, Inspector sahib?' the senior constable asked.

Ghote waved assent, battered and inwardly furious at the way his investigation had got lost amid all the play-acting.

The constables laid their stretcher beside Billy Patel's heavy corpse and with an 'ek, do, teen' lifted it up and over.

And the moment they had done so a small object just underneath the recumbent form caught Ghote's eye.

He crouched quickly and picked it up by its edges. It was a metal lapel badge, shocking-pink in colour, with one word clearly painted on it in fancy black letters: 'Roger'.

Slowly Ghote got to his feet with the little disc cupped in his hand. He was aware that both Tigga and Shantaram Das had seen just what he had picked up. Tigga was holding herself unnaturally still, as if the blood in her veins had all in an instant turned to a steely-strong skeleton. The poetical Mr Das's eyes were flicking to and fro like a fugitive looking every which way for escape from an utterly fearful situation.

Ghote elected to address him.

'Mr Das, tell me please, this is a badge such as is worn by staff members of Shalimar Associates?'

The massively large white-clad account executive did not answer for some moments. Then he heaved a deep sigh.

'Inspector, it is.'

'And who else besides Mr Roger Rajinder is known in the firm by this British name?'

'No one, Inspector.'

'Then I must at once see Mr Rajinder,' Ghote said, turning to the door.

But he was not to get through it. Like a leaping ball of fire, red kurta-clad Tigga leapt to it before him. She stood guarding it like a panther, all claws to defend her cubs.

'Now, Miss Tigga, please,' Ghote said. 'You know that I must talk with Mr Roger Rajinder.'

'Fuzz. Bloody fuzz.' Tigga spat the words out as fiercely as that mother panther spitting defiance. 'That's all the idea you CID wallahs have of solving crimes, grab the first person your fancy takes and beat a confession out of him.'

'Miss Tigga, I am not at all beating.'

'Oh no, not yet. But wait until you get him in one of your cells. I know what sort of things go on there. Torture, torture, torture till your victim doesn't know who or what he is.'

'Miss Tigga, I am wanting to question only. Even you must see there is *prima facie* case against Rajinder sahib.'

'Faked evidence. Another rotten fuzz trick.'

'Miss Tigga, that badge was underneath the body. You must have been seeing that clearly, as was Mr Das here also. It is possible, I am willing to admit, that the badge was lying there on the floor long before Mr Billy Patel was killed. But it is not at all likely, isn't it? In such a smart cabin as this, with the clean, clean carpet and not a speck of untidiness anywhere. You must see that.'

'All right, all right,' Tigga shot back, not moving an inch from the doorway. 'The badge was there. I know that. But you are going to build up a whole case on just one thing. That, plus beating and torture.'

Ghote sighed.

'Miss Tigga, I am guaranteeing absolutely that nothing of torture will be used.'

He said the words with all the firmness he could muster, but he knew in his heart that they were not strictly true. Very well, the Bombay CID did not use the crude methods reported from distant parts of India. But there was such a thing as dangling a cigarette in front of a deprived smoker – and a hundred and one other tricks and strategies.

Still Tigga did not move. Instead she began calling out.

'Roger. Roger. Get out quick. This damn plainclothes wallah wants to get you. Roger.'

The door of Billy Patel's cabin was thick, but Ghote wondered whether on the far side someone might hear and warn Roger Rajinder. Who might then take to his heels.

'Miss Tigga, stand away from that door,' he said.

'Never.'

He did not wait for any further defiance. Two hands shooting forward to grasp the girl by her elbows, a quick flex of the knees, a lift, a swing round and she was dumped safely out of his way.

In fact he found Roger Rajinder still at his desk, and took him back at once to CID Headquarters for questioning. He had no alternative.

It was not, however, in a scream-proof cell that he questioned the young man but in his own office, its bat-wing doors open to the day – even if a wiry constable was standing outside. But it came as no surprise when Roger implacably denied that he had gone back to the offices during the time they were almost deserted at the lunch hour, even though he admitted that he did not have an alibi for the whole of that period.

No, the boy said, he could not account for his badge being under Billy Patel's body. He had worn it two days previously at a conference to present the firm's new Cocopuffs campaign. He must have taken it off afterwards, but he could not remember doing so or seeing it at any time since then. He had never wished Billy Patel any harm. He had received an increment only one month earlier from him and it had been every bit as much as he had hoped to get.

All that was worrying. The young man really did not seem to have even the shadow of a motive for killing Billy Patel. Yet there under the body there had been that badge, and there was no reason why it should have been on the floor unless in the course of the murder it had fallen there.

At last Ghote told the boy simply that he would be kept in custody overnight.

A locked door during the long hours of darkness was often enough, with a person used to a comfortable middle-class life, to reduce the proudly defiant to the readily cooperative.

And an hour or two of extra suspense when daylight came again was, too, a useful topper-up for any self-induced fears. So Ghote went first next morning not to Headquarters but back to the tower-top offices of Shalimar Associates. He asked to see Mr Das – now, he gathered, in charge following Billy Patel's demise.

He found him, indeed, in the late Billy's cabin, its wide desk already covered in papers. And with him he found Tigga. Not in the most favourable circumstances.

With the object of preventing Das donning his poetic mantle before answering some simple questions about the routines and politics of Shalimar Associates, Ghote had stopped anyone announcing him and had entered the cabin without even knocking.

He found Tigga standing closely beside the bulky seated form of Shantaram Das, with his arm round her waist.

It might have been there as the protective act of a mere uncle figure, he told himself later. Certainly, after an instant's flinching the plump poet had left the arm where it was for a few seconds and then had said, all kindness and consideration, 'Well now, you run along, Tigga, my dear, and don't worry your head. Perhaps Inspectorji had already come to tell me that young Roger would be released right away.'

'No, sir and madam,' Ghote said, 'I regret my inquiries are not yet complete.'

Shantaram Das chuckled comfortably.

'But I am sure that they will be in a few hours only,' he said, 'and then we would have young Roger in his seat again.'

Tigga made no answer before she left the room. Unless to glare long and hard at Ghote was an answer.

'Yes, yes,' Shantaram Das said as the door closed. 'The poor girl is in a hell of a state. I feel it my duty as head now of the firm to offer what comfort I can.'

Ghote did not pursue the subject. He decided that Das's attitude to Miss Tigga was something that must wait for examination when he had leisure. For one thing, it had seemed to him that the girl had not been at all averse to that friendly encircling arm. But, if this was so, it spoilt the picture he had built up for himself of young love looking all the world in the face, a picture he had by no means managed to rid himself of even when he had been questioning Roger Rajinder the night before. For all that he told himself again and again that such a notion was no more than *filmi* nonsense.

So it was in no very cordial mood that he questioned Das about the people of Shalimar Associates. Whenever the literary fellow showed signs of building up one of his towering, improbable fantasies he ruthlessly brought him down to earth. But, long though the session was, he found at its end that he had not learnt anything revealingly new. Roger Rajinder was the bright hope of the firm and had had a recent large increment. Tarlok Singh was a wizard with figures and had 'a head for detail that is positively amazing'. One or two minor employees might have small grudges about this or that, a bright idea rejected, a hoped-for increment not arriving as soon as expected. But that seemed to be all, if what Shantaram Das had told him was the truth. No one, not even Roger Rajinder, had any real motive for killing Billy Patel.

And, bar those beginnings of poetic flights, he had been exemplary in producing long-forgotten half grudges and half injustices for Ghote's consideration, even down to a peon he remembered as having been sacked some three years earlier: 'A one-eyed fellow, Inspector, a man whom I never did trust, with a distinct air of malevolence.'

'Please,' Ghote had asked sharply, 'what is malevolence?'

'Ah. Well, shall we say "ill-will"?'

'Ill-will towards which persons?'

'Oh, I do not think towards anyone in particular. A general ill-will, or as we may say malevolence. Difficult to pin down, you know. The fellow's name was Budhoo, as I recall. You would be able to locate him easily enough. I think he still uses the garden wall outside here to sleep under. I have seen him there when I have been working late. Find him, Inspector. He is a very very likely suspect for you. Very very likely altogether.'

'I do not think that will be necessary,' Ghote said.

And on that quelling note he had left. To go back to Headquarters and see what a long night's reflection and an awkward couple of hours afterwards had done for Roger Rajinder.

They seemed to have done nothing. No, the boy said again, he had no reason, conceivably, for wanting to kill Billy Patel. He had admired him. He was a man who had come up from nothing and had ended with a fine flat in the prestigious Pali Hill area. He had an imported car. He was a big success. No one had known more about creating a need and then backing it to the hilt with advertising films in every one of India's many cinemas, with newspaper and magazine ads of startling originality, with hoardings that had made all Bombay laugh.

Roger hoped he would do half as well himself and be able to marry some day and find a flat and have a family.

Ghote thought of Tigga and Shantaram Das's uncle-encircling arm. Or not so uncle-like?

He took his questioning back to the matter of the badge under the body. But Roger still had no idea, he said, how it had got from his pocket – where he supposed he must have put it two days earlier – to the floor of Billy Patel's cabin.

Ghote, increasingly exasperated, began to wonder about a bit of 'torture'. Hitherto he had let young Roger smoke as much as he wanted. Yet if he deprived him now of cigarettes . . . But the thought of Tigga's jibes made him determined to break down his suspect without the least suspicion of illicit pressure. Indeed, he went even further in the direction of scrupulous behaviour. Conscious that in all probability he was being a sentimental fool, he even allowed Tigga to come and see Roger in an interview room, unsupervised.

In the meanwhile he occupied himself in going through the list of Shalimar Associates employees, in the faint hope of finding something pointing to another possible murderer.

Then late at night, when he hoped that Roger Rajinder would be relaxing sure that his interrogation was over for the day, he had him brought to his office once again. And, bracing himself, he determined to make use of a thoroughly unfair trick.

'Well, Mr Roger,' he said, without any other preliminary, 'what do you think of your girl friend now? You know she is allowing Mr Shantaram Das all sorts and kinds of liberties, isn't it? She has deserted you altogether, I am thinking. Yes, altogether deserted.'

But Roger Rajinder simply smiled in answer.

'What for are you smiling only?' Ghote burst out. 'I am telling you that Miss Tigga is making up to Mr Shantaram Das. She has given you the push altogether. She is sure you are the guilty party. Damn sure.'

Roger Rajinder smiled again.

'In that case, Inspector,' he said, 'why do you think she is in Shalimar Associates offices at this very moment trying to find evidence that will get me off the hook? Oh, yes, I know about Shantaram. He's a thoroughly naughty old man, and yes, Tigga did this morning allow him some liberties. She was upset. But when you let her come to see me she told me each and every thing that had happened between them.'

Ghote thrust aside the fury he felt with himself for having so unwittingly strengthened Roger's resistance. Something more urgent claimed attention.

'Evidence?' he snapped. 'What sort of evidence is this that Miss Tigga is trying to find? Why did she not inform me of any evidence there is to be found?'

Roger shrugged.

'I think she doesn't like you very much, Inspector,' he said. 'Nothing personal, just a general distrust of CID wallahs. So she means to get hold of her evidence first and tell you afterwards.'

Ghote felt a sudden inward lurch of despondency.

'What sort of evidence is this? I demand to know.'

'Oh, I am not going to hold out on you, Inspector. I've learnt too much respect for you in the last twenty-four hours to want to do that, whatever Tigga feels. It's just this: she has got it into her head that Billy may have been killed by a spy.'

'A spy? A spy? What utter damn nonsense is this? Is Shalimar Associates a Secure Defence Area? What is it you are saying?'

'Well, no, not exactly a spy of that sort,' Roger answered. 'But what you might call an industrial spy, Inspector. The advertising *duniya* is riddled with spies of that sort, you know. Chaps out to pinch good ideas and use them in their own firms' campaigns. It's a serious problem.'

110

Ghote thought for an instant.

'And what you and Miss Tigga are saying is that in the Shalimar Associates offices there is someone who is such a spy, and that Mr Billy Patel perhaps found him in the act and was killed?'

'That's what Tigga thinks certainly. And I can't see any other motive for Billy's murder. Can you, Inspector?'

'Never mind what motive I am seeing or not seeing. You say Miss Tigga is searching the offices for evidence just now?'

'She is, Inspector.'

'Then I am going there myself, *ek dum*.'

At the late hour of the evening it did not take Ghote long to get from the Crawford Market CID Headquarters to the almost deserted business area of Nariman Point, its tall unlit tower buildings huge and ghostlike in the darkness. But at the top of the tower that housed Shalimar Associates a light was glinting out.

Possessed by a sudden inexplicable need to hurry, Ghote routed out the building's chowkidar.

'No lift working, Inspector sahib,' the half-asleep sulky old Pathan guard said. 'Stairs only. Many, many.'

Ghote shook him off and set out at a rapid trot up the concrete steps winding behind the gleaming lift shafts of the tall building.

Up and up he ran. But before long, his rapid trot was reduced to a steady plod. And before much longer that plod became yet slower. Sweat rich on his face and clammy round his body, he forced his weary legs on. With each step his sense of urgency had grown.

Tigga Kelkar was alone in the Shalimar Associates offices. What was she finding there? What evidence could there be that there was a spy from some other concern on the staff? And that this person, whoever they were, had murdered Billy Patel? Yet unlikely though he thought the notion to be – a spy? To discover the secret of a new advertisement? What rot – somehow he felt that all might be not well, that all was not well up in the penthouse offices above.

Mouth wide open, gasping for air, he pushed his lead-heavy legs into moving faster. And at last he was at the top of the building. The outer door of Shalimar Associates was standing wide open and, although the futuristic lights of the reception area were not on, a dim glow from somewhere further inside the offices did make it possible to see vaguely the whole of the wide brown-carpeted space.

Then as he stood, head bent, deeply breathing, attempting to decide what to do first, there came a sudden thundering sound from somewhere on the far side of the broad reception counter, its huge vase of white flowers palely visible in the gloom.

It was the sound of running feet, of feet running hard as they could along one of the wide corridors off which the various cabins lay.

But was it the sound of just one pair of running feet? It was difficult to make out, but he thought it was not. Surely a second set of steps had been thundering after the first?

He took a rapid, fiercely penetrating look all round. And, yes. Yes, there were the light switches. He darted across and with a single sweep of his hand caused them all to blaze out.

The overpowering white glare of illumination sent search-light beams down each of the wide corridors, and at the very end of the one nearest to him Ghote just detected a door swinging to and fro as if someone had held it for a moment while they ran round it and into a room beyond.

He set off at a fast run again, energy from somewhere overcoming all his fatigue.

There was silence ahead. Fleetingly he wondered whether someone, some enemy – or perhaps after all the spy, the killer spy – was waiting in the dark of one of the cabins listening, waiting. Listening and ready to attack.

But he did not let himself hesitate. Tigga Kelkar was in the offices somewhere; that he knew. And there was someone else in here too. Someone hostile. That he knew too almost as certainly.

Then, as he neared the end of the corridor where the light from the reception area hardly penetrated, he heard above the sound of his own thumping steps another noise. It was something like a squawk. A stifled scream. A sound of pain and desperation.

He thought it had come from the last cabin on the right, the very one whose door he had detected swinging. He raced up to it. He flung himself in at the open doorway.

The room in front of him was pitch dark. But by the faintest of lights coming from behind him he thought he could see something in a far corner. Figures. Two figures locked fast in struggle.

'Stop,' he called out, loudly as he could. 'Stop. Police.'

In the far corner the tense swaying movement of the struggle abruptly stilled. One figure separated from the other. It was, so far as he could see, that of a man. A tall, broadly powerful man.

Then suddenly, with the force of a cannonball shot from a gun, the figure launched itself forward. Ghote crouched, nerving himself to receive the assault, determined to bear its brunt, to reach out, grab and hold on.

But he had underestimated the strength and weight of his opponent. The man's rush, for all his readiness to take it, simply bowled him right over. On his back in the doorway, he shot out a hand and grabbed at the fellow's ankle. His frantic clutch did at least check the attacker, but in an instant his other foot came swinging hard back. A bare heel, hard as a hammer, caught Ghote fair and square on the nose.

Pain dazed and dazzled him. He felt the ankle he had grabbed wrenched from his grasp. Struggling to roll over, get to his knees and heave himself up, he heard steps running furiously away along the corridor.

Once up, he set out in pursuit. But his head was dizzy from the blow to his nose and he found himself swaying and stumbling hopelessly. He came to a halt, leaning up against the wall, almost sobbing from pain, exhaustion and anger.

A voice came from behind him in the gloom.

'Is it you, Inspector Ghote? You, you saved my life.'

He turned, reluctantly opening his eyes wide.

It was Tigga. In the half-light he could see that her kurta was ripped down half its length.

'Miss Tigga,' he said, his voice curious and croaky. 'Miss Tigga, are you all right?'

'Yes. Yes, I think I am. But he was strangling me, Inspector. If you hadn't come at just that moment I would have passed out. I couldn't struggle any more.'

Ghote took a few deep breaths. His swimming head began to clear.

'It was not your spy, was it?' he asked.

Tigga gave a short, ironic laugh.

'No,' she said. 'No, it was some barefoot fellow who must

have seen me coming in and followed me. I – I don't know who it could have been, but . . . But he had only one eye, Inspector. I saw his face close to mine. It was horrible. Horrible. That one eye, glaring at me.'

Ghote heard her crying in the half-darkness. He put a hand on her shoulder and patted it, comfortingly as he could.

'Not to worry, not to worry any more,' he said. 'The fellow has gone now. And I think I know who it would be also. Was there a peon here once by the name of Budhoo, who had one eye only?'

'No,' the girl answered, catching back her sobs. 'I don't know— Wait, yes. Yes, there was. I joined here after he had been dismissed but I remember people talking about him. A horrible man, they said.'

'Yes,' said Ghote, 'a horrible man, and I am somewhat thinking the Cabin Killer also.'

'The Cabin Killer, but . . .'

'Yes, that is what I am thinking. You see, a peon in offices like this would get a very, very good idea where a Chivas Regal whisky was to be found, and as far as we have been able to make out the pilfering activities of his particular sort began about three years ago, which is just the time this Budhoo was retrenched from here. Mr Das was telling me also that the fellow is always sleeping beside that little garden in the front of the building, so I think he would not be too difficult to find and put behind the bars.'

'Inspector, Inspector, that's marvellous. That's wonderful. Hey, I'll never make rude remarks about the fuzz – the police – again.'

With the resilience of youth Tigga was throwing off the terror of her recent experience like a puppy shaking off water drops after a run into the sea. Ghote heard her with pleasure.

For a moment.

Then a thought slid chilly into his mind.

'Well, Miss Tigga,' he said, unable to keep out of his voice the sudden sinking he had felt, 'that may or may not be good. It is depending on whether Assistant Commissioner Dabholkar and his team can find this fellow, and whether he does turn out to be the man we were looking for when we have got him. But that is not at all the end of the matter, you know.'

'Oh, a trial and all that,' Tigga answered. 'But no doubt you will get a confession, even if you have to beat it out of the brute.'

Ghote ignored this turn-about in attitude. He had something much more unpleasant to say.

'No, Miss Tigga, it is not about the Cabin Killer that I am thinking.'

'Then what—'

She came to an abrupt halt and fell silent.

'Yes, it is the killer of Mr Billy Patel who still has to be found, isn't it?' Ghote said eventually. 'Finding Budhoo here is not at all proving he was killing Billy Patel yesterday. I am supposing he was all along knowing how to get in here, and, when he was hearing about the murder, he was taking it into his head that now at night only was the time to come. It was one piece of bad luck for you, Miss Tigga, that you were deciding to look for some evidences of a spy at the same time.'

'Yes. Yes, I see all that now.'

But Ghote had not finished.

'And you were not finding those evidences, isn't it?' he went on. 'You could not have done, when you are really thinking of it. No advertisement is so important that a person is going to kill for same, is it?'

For a little Tigga made no answer, and when she did it was in a markedly subdued way.

'Yes, you're right of course, Inspector. Advertising isn't that important. It's never exactly a matter of life and death, even though here we sometimes act as if it was. But you're right. It was never a spy who killed poor Billy.'

'No,' Ghote said, sighing heavily. 'No. It was no spy. And so we are back to where we were at the beginning, holding your most good friend, Mr Roger Rajinder.'

He had half-expected another blistering attack at this, even sharp nails reaching for his face. But Tigga accepted what he had said in silence. And it was in silence that he escorted her down to his waiting car and drove her to her home.

'You are all right now?' he asked as he left her at the door of the flat.

'Yes. Yes, thank you, Inspector. I'm all right. Or, well, I will be after I've slept all night and a bit more.'

'Yes. I will take a statement from you tomorrow.'

He had not been able to think of anything more to say. 'Good luck' would have meant 'I hope your Roger is not guilty' and, though he did hope so, he knew that to voice even a hint of that would be to give the girl hope with little prospect of justification.

Next morning – and, yes, there was one headline *The Cabin Killer Strikes Again* – summoning Roger Rajinder for yet another interview, Ghote felt exactly as he had done the night before. The girl Tigga was delightful, full of life, full of confidence, pretty as could be, and somehow deserving of happiness. Of happiness in love, in the full *filmi* way even. And Roger seemed in every way right to provide that happiness – except that he was, on such evidence as there was, a murderer. However little he looked or behaved like one.

'Inspector,' he burst out now, the moment he marched in. 'Did you find Tigga at the office last night? Did she actually get hold of anything to show that a spy killed poor Billy?'

'No. No spy,' Ghote said.

'Oh well, thinking things over in the night I realised that was pretty unlikely in fact.'

'However,' Ghote said, 'thanks to that enterprising young lady we did somewhat advance matters.'

He told Roger just what had happened at Shalimar Associates the night before, capping his recital with news he had just learnt himself – that the former peon Budhoo had been easily located, had put up a struggle when Dasher Dabholkar and his men made the arrest and had been found in possession of some of the Cabin Killer's earlier petty thefts.

'But Mr Rajinder,' Ghote concluded, 'I cannot conceal from you that all this leaves us in the matter of Mr Billy Patel's death exactly where we were starting.'

'Yes,' said Roger. 'Yes, I suppose it does. And it's no more use than it was before, I take it, me telling you that I simply did not do it.'

'No. No more use saying only.'

'So where were we, Inspector? Ah, yes. You were just trying to break me down by telling me that Tigga was accepting the attentions of our good friend Shantaram Das, and I—'

He broke off.

'Inspector,' he said, after he had gazed into thin air for perhaps six or seven seconds. 'Inspector, you dashed off to find Tigga before I had time to think about what you were saying.

And, Inspector, now that I've thought of it again, I've remembered. At last I've remembered.'

'What remembered?'

'What I did with that badge, Inspector. What I did with that badge.'

'Well, what were you doing with it? Speak up, man.'

'Inspector, it was after the presentation for Cocopuffs. I went to Shantaramji to tell him I had seen everything cleared up, and I remember putting my badge down on his desk. I even made some joke about not needing it any more now we were sure the client had accepted our idea about Shivaji's sword: *Cut through the cackle, get to the truth, Cocopuffs cannot be bettered.*'

'You put the badge on Mr Das's desk,' Ghote said impatiently. 'And what then?'

'Then – and this is why I forgot all about it – Tigga came into Shantaramji's cabin. He at once offered her a lift home in his car and she accepted even though she had earlier agreed to take a ride on the back of my scooter. Well, Inspector, I was so riled by this I burst out in anger, and we had a huge row I walked out. It all put the badge right out of my head. We only made up after the murder. It was when you yourself came into the office as a matter of fact. She called to me, and I asked if we were friends again.'

'Yes,' said Ghote eagerly. 'I remember that.'

He thought for a little.

'And you swear now,' he went on, 'that you left that badge with your name on it on Mr Shantaram Das's desk, and that you never saw it again?'

'Yes, Inspector,' Roger said. 'That's the absolute truth.'

Ghote stood up behind his desk. Decisively.

'I think I must talk once more with Mr Das.'

But he found at the Shalimar Associates offices that the plump and poetical new boss was not in his seat. Tigga was there however, and she told him that Shantaram Das – together with almost all the firm's staff – had gone over to Marine Drive where, for the start of the new Cocopuffs campaign, a huge hoarding was being erected with an immense Shivaji's sword cutting through the cackle in a swinging arc going right across the wide, traffic-whizzing road.

'It's going to be the biggest hoarding Bombay has ever seen,' she said, swept into momentary forgetfulness of the more serious things. 'It's terrific, really. Only someone like Billy Patel could ever have got all the permissions. The contacts he had were fantastic, just fantastic.'

'And Mr Das is there now, on Marine Drive?' Ghote asked sharply. 'With all the other senior executives?'

'Yes. Supervising the erection, and I imagine hopping about like a cat on hot bricks in case it doesn't work.'

Ghote turned to go.

'Listen,' Tigga said, 'I'll come with you. It can be quite a scene there, and I'll be able to get hold of Shantaramji for you. What's it all about anyway?'

'It is just something I want to ask him only,' Ghote said. 'A matter of not much importance, but something I need cleared up.'

Whatever he did, he was not going to give the girl any hope until he had something concrete to offer, even though he was ready now to consider Roger Rajinder no longer a suspect.

But his resolution lasted barely half the wriggling and weaving journey to the far end of Marine Drive where the Cocopuffs hoarding was going up. Tigga had sat beside him silent and looking so down in the mouth as, plainly, she thought of Roger still held for questioning, that at last he could bear it no longer.

'Miss Tigga, I should not be telling you this, but in utmost confidence let me give you one hint only. Tonight Mr Roger Rajinder could give somebody a ride home on his scooter.'

The smile that slowly spread over Tigga's pretty face, like the sun appearing after a day of monsoon downpour and warming the fresh earth, was reward enough.

Nothing more was said by either of them until the car drew up where, stretching at extraordinary length over the wide sweep of the road, a huge new wood-constructed bridge had appeared.

'Isn't it great?' Tigga burst out now more cheerful. 'Look, you can see the shape of Shivaji's sword even before all the panels are on at the front. It's going to be terrific, sweeping right across the road.'

'And it is for Cocopuff biscuits only?' Ghote asked.

'You bet. The greatest campaign Bombay has ever seen.'

Ghote sighed.

'Well, I suppose it is necessary,' he said.

He began looking for Shantaram Das. But among the groups of busy Sikh carpenters, the labourers from the country districts in their brightly coloured lungis, the crowds of idle onlookers and the many Shalimar Associates executives, even down to the dapper accountant, Tarlok Singh, he failed altogether to find him.

'But where please is Mr Das?' he asked Tigga sharply.

Tigga looked in her turn.

'Ah, there he is,' she said after a moment. 'Just behind the tower of the hoarding there.'

Ghote saw the plump poet then. He was in his element. Directing. Ordering. In his element as the new boss of Shalimar Associates. The position he had murdered to reach.

'Shantaramji, Shantaramji,' Tigga called out excitedly. 'Shantaramji, listen. Here's the Inspector again and good news. Good news. Roger's going to be freed. Freed. Yes, freed.'

Shantaram Das plainly heard her despite the noise of all the traffic streaming by at speed and the jabber of all the voices. He took a long look at the pair of them as they began to make their way towards him.

And then he put his head down and charged away in the direction of the traffic-swirling road.

'Shantaramji,' Tigga called, 'it's good—'

'He is absconding.'

Ghote ran forward, seething with fury at what he and the innocent, joyful Tigga had done to give the man warning.

There were people by the dozen between him and the heavy figure of the heir to Shalimar Associates. The gawping watchers that any activity in Bombay immediately attracts, the carpenters, their assistants carrying long lengths of rough timber, jeans-clad staff from the firm. Ghote ducked, weaved, shoved past them.

Shantaram Das had come to a halt at the edge of the road where the last of the great morning influx of traffic into the Fort business area was tearing at breakneck speed along the fine sweep of carriageway.

He would catch him yet.

Nimbly he jumped over an old beggarwoman in a greasy sari, brushed aside a boy in a pair of torn khaki shorts and plunged towards his quarry.

Then he saw the fat poet turn.

And despite his bulk, the man – swinging from the kerb in one lunging movement – darted back the way he had come and in an instant had reached the foot of the supporting tower of the hoarding and had heaved himself up into it.

Ghote swerved round towards him.

'Way! Way!' he yelled. 'Police! Police!'

He got little cooperation. But, he told himself, perhaps it did not matter. After all, Shantaram Das was trapped. He had got himself up on to all the criss-cross of bamboo and timber that formed one of the bases of the hoarding, but he would have to come down sooner or later. The later the better really. Given a little time, a whole circle of tough constables could be ringing the base of the scaffold.

Except – Ghote pushed and bullied his way nearer – except that the fat new Shalimar boss was steadily climbing still.

And then, looking up at the hoarding and assessing it properly for the first time, Ghote saw that it already formed a rough and dangerous sort of bridge right across the traffic-whizzing highway. Shantaram Das could perhaps, just perhaps, climb and clamber his way across it and escape before he himself could make his way through the eight lanes of daredevil traffic and get to the far side first.

There was only one thing to do.

Ghote put his head down, slid and weaved his way forward, reached the foot of the bamboo and timber tower and began in his turn to climb. The unfinished structure swayed beneath the force of his thrusting legs. But it held.

Already as he reached up each time for a new handhold he could feel the distant vibrations coming from where Shantaram Das, much heavier than himself, was climbing ahead of him.

Another heave or two, another hoist or two, and he had reached the tower's top. Ahead, appallingly frail, there stretched the narrow bridge itself, designed only to carry the huge shape of Shivaji's sword, much of it already in place in the form of great sheets of hardboard.

But Shantaram Das, he could see clearly now, was making his way quite rapidly forward along the slender swaying criss-crossed wooden tunnel, moving in a low crouch like a monkey, his white churidar-covered rear projecting behind him.

'Mr Das! Mr Das!' he called out. 'Stop now! Come back! It's not safe. You cannot escape!'

But if the fugitive heard him above the noise of the clacketing, racing traffic below, he showed no sign. Like a big active ape he clambered and crawled steadily onwards.

Ghote resumed his pursuit.

Beneath, as he too progressed in a monkey crouch, his hands splinter-jabbed from the rough wood he snatched at with every move, he saw the tops of hurrying cars and the yellow roofs of taxis zooming under him with dazzling speed. In his nostrils he caught the reek of petrol fumes, choking and sickening.

And ahead despite his bulk, Shantaram Das seemed to be progressing every bit as fast as he was himself.

At this rate the fellow would get to the ground on the far side sufficiently ahead to make good his escape.

Ghote lunged yet further forward for his next handhold, shut his mind to every risk, felt the frail structure sway ever more dangerously, plunged and plunged on.

The bobbing and thrusting white-clad rear in front of him grew bit by bit nearer.

Then, causing him to grip the rough wood in a freezing of fear, the whole slender bridge suddenly canted hard to the right.

We will go over.

The thought planted itself in his mind like a neon-pulsing slogan.

Death. The cars below. The crash on to a roof. The helpless sliding off. The wheels over his body.

And then, through sweat-blinded eyes, he saw just what he had forecast for himself. A heavy white shape tumbling rightwards. An arm flailing desperately. And then nothing. Nothing there at all.

But, below, the howls of a score of brakes jammed hard on. The booming noises as one car after another cannoned into whatever was in front.

Ghote raised his head and dared to look down.

He could see Shantaram Das's big sprawled white form on the black surface of the road just in front of a grey Ambassador.

He heard himself, still clutching hard on to the rough timber, give a little bark of an ironic laugh.

Live by the sword, die by the sword.

Well, Shantaram Das had hoped to live as well as Billy Patel by taking advantage of the sudden opportunity to get rid of him and have that convenient, newspaper built-up, ballooned-up figure of the Cabin Killer blamed. But instead he had died on Shivaji's sword when his hasty plan had proved not quite good enough, and his yet hastier attempt to involve Roger Rajinder – the badge which he must have put in his own pocket quietly slipped under Billy Patel's body with a sliding toe – had, too, come as unstuck.

Carefully, feeling decidedly sick, Ghote began making his way backwards along the narrow swaying tunnel behind Shivaji's sword. He reached the supporting tower and at last dropped down to the blessed safety of the firm ground.

Tigga was there at the foot of the tower waiting for him, her pretty face pale from shock.

'Hello, Miss Tigga,' he said. 'You know, it is very, very important to remember always "Murder Must Not At All Advertise".'

Then blackness rose up in his head like a swooshing fountain and he saw no more.

1984

9

The All-Bad Hat

Inspector Ghote of the Bombay CID was not a frequenter of record shops. But on this occasion he was on an important errand. It was soon to be his son Ved's birthday and Ghote's wife, Protima, had declared that the one thing the boy really wanted as a present was a record of the title song from the new hit movie *Sant aur Badmash*, the one in which two brothers are separated soon after their birth – one becomes a holy man, a saint, a sant, and the other becomes a deepest-dyed villain, a badmash. In the last reel they are reconciled.

But Ghote was not finding it easy to make his purchase. From loudspeakers in all four corners of the smart new shop – he had been told it was the best in Bombay – music was pounding out at maximum volume. His attempts to make anyone behind the counter hear had so far come to nothing.

At last he could stand the frustration no longer. He leant across the glossy counter, seized a young man behind it by the sides of his silk kurta and drew him close.

'Please to stop all this noise,' he demanded.

'Noise?' the young man said, or rather shouted. 'What noise is it?'

'That music. That damn music. Kindly get owner here to turn down volume.'

'I am owner,' the young man answered. 'Sole proprietor, Loafer's Delight Disc Mart.'

'Then you must turn down the volume,' Ghote shouted. 'Now.'

'Cool it, man,' the young proprieter shouted back. 'Be cooling it. That volume's good.'

'It is bad. Bad, I tell you. I am thinking it may be offence against the law.'

'The law? You are making me laugh, man.'

Ghote felt a jet of rage fountain up inside him.

123

'I am an Inspector of Police,' he shouted.

'That is swinging, man,' the proprietor riposted. 'And I am the son of the Minister for Home.'

'Please to behave,' Ghote answered sharply.

But whether the young man would have obeyed this injunction or not was never to be put to the test. Down near the entrance of the long, tunnel-like shop with its smart new racks of records and tapes and its dazzling posters decorating every wall, someone else was not behaving well.

In fact two tough-looking men, roughly dressed in contrast to the shop's smart clientele, were behaving extremely badly.

One of the record racks had already been deliberately knocked over. As the shop's young proprieter reduced the volume of his massive loudspeakers almost to nothing, more as a response to the trouble near the entrance than to Ghote's demand, Ghote was able to hear what one of the two newcomers was calling out to the other.

'Hey, Chandra bhai, these stands, see how easy they tip over.'

'Yes, yes,' the other man, a turbaned Sikh, called back. 'And these posters. So nice. But, look, already they are torn.'

They were not as he spoke. But two instants later they were torn indeed, ripped right off the walls by the man himself.

'Stop,' screamed the young proprietor. 'Stop. Those are imported. Two hundred rupees each.'

Rip. Rip. Rip. Another six hundred rupees went cascading to the floor.

'All right,' Ghote said.'I will deal with those two.'

He began making his way purposefully down the length of the narrow shop. But the place was too crowded for him to be able to get anywhere near the two trouble-makers before, with cheerful shouts of 'Sorry, Mr Loafer' and 'Goodbye, Mr Loafer Delight', they had reached the entrance and disappeared among the packed pavements of Mahatma Gandhi Road.

However, Ghote had had plenty of time to study the faces of the two goondas. Altogether forgetting Ved's birthday record, he had hurried back to CID Headquarters and there gone through the fat, tattered books of criminals in the Records section. It had not taken him long to find the two. The Sikh was one Iqbal Singh and the other was a certain Chandra Chagoo.

'I do not think I would have too much of difficulty to nab the pair of them, sir,' Ghote said to Assistant Commissioner Samant a quarter of an hour later.

'You are not even to try, Inspector.'

Ghote blinked.

'Not to try, ACP sahib? But already I am knowing the favoured haunts of those two. I can have them behind the bars in no time at all.'

'You are not to waste your time.'

Ghote stared at the ACP across his wide, semi-circular desk with its clutter of telephones, pen-sets and tea-cups. He really could not believe he had heard what he had.

'But, sir,' he pleaded, 'if you had seen those two goondas, the way they set about breaking up that place, sir. It was a matter of deliberate destruction at a Number One level.'

'No doubt, no doubt, Inspector. And you know why they were doing all that?'

'Protection racket, sir. The young fellow who owns the place was telling me afterwards. He had been asked to pay and said he would rely upon the police to protect him. It is a very black mark for us, sir.'

'And you know why a pair of goondas like that can get away with doing such things, Inspector?'

'No, sir.'

'It is because these two goondas that you were taking such trouble to impress on your memory, Inspector, are no more than the small fries only.'

'Small fries, sir?'

'Exactly, Inspector. You can nab them if you want, but when they come up before the Magistrate, what would we find?'

Ghote decided to leave the ACP to answer his own question.

'We would find that they are having alibis, Inspector. First-class alibis. Two, three, four seemingly respectable fellows willing to swear that at the time in question our two friends were not in Bombay even. And a damn fine advocate to back up the tale.'

'But— but, ACP sahib, alibis and advocates are costing very much of money. And those two did not look as if they are having more than two paisa to rub together.'

'Quite right, Inspector.'

'But then–'

'But the fellow they are working for has got all the paisa you could wish for.'

'And that is who, ACP?'

'Daddyji.'

'Daddyji, sir?'

'Yes, Inspector. Other names he has and has. But Daddyji he is known as always. If you had worked on protection racket cases before you would have known.'

'Yes, sir. He is running many, many such rackets then?'

'Not so many, Inspector.'

'But, sir, if he is not running many many, then how is he so wealthy that he can afford such alibis and advocates?'

'It is because of the kind of places he is specialising in protecting, Inspector. He likes only the best. Anything that is particularly fine. Best class places only.'

'I see, sir. Yes, that is bad.'

'He is bad, Inspector. Daddyji is bad. He is nothing less than an all-bad man.'

Until this moment Ghote had been following the ACP's explanations with all dutifulness. But these last words stuck in his craw. An all-bad man? All bad? He could not find it in himself to believe it.

And foolishly he ventured to express that doubt.

'But, sir, no man is altogether–'

'What is this, Inspector? You, a police officer. You have seen plenty of miscreants, I hope. Am I going to hear you tell me there is no such thing as an all-bad man?'

'But–'

Ghote thought better of it.

'I grant that most criminals are not all-bad. They are lacking in the guts to be. But that is not meaning that there are not all-bad men, and of them all, Inspector, the man by the name of Daddyji is the worst. The worst.'

'But, sir–'

'No. Let me tell a thing or two about Daddyji, Inspector. Have you got a father?'

'Sir, everybody is having a father. They may not still be–'

'Good. Well, now, perhaps you may not have had good relations with your father. But nevertheless you were treating him always with a certain respect, isn't it?'

'Yes, sir.'

'Daddyji has a father, Inspector. He used to run the gang that Daddyji now has. A pretty tough chap also. But then came the day when Daddyji thought it was time that he took over. Do you know where that father is now, Inspector?'

'No, sir.'

'Take a walk down to Flora Fountain, Inspector. There you would see a cripple man, propped up against the wall selling little clay figures that he is making.'

'Yes, sir. I am knowing him. Very very popular with tourists the figures he is making, most lively objects.'

'And damn close to falling under Indian Penal Code, Section 292.'

'Obscene books and objects, sir. Yes, sir, I think you are right. But – but what—'

'But it is not those that I am concerned with, Inspector. It is his legs.'

'His legs, sir?'

'I suppose you are too busy always looking at those figures. But that man's legs are smashed to pieces, Inspector. And it was his own son who was doing that.'

'I see, sir. He must be a very bad hat.'

'No, Inspector. An all-bad hat. An all-bad hat. And much too clever to be nabbed by one inspector only. So, leave him—'

He broke off as one of the phones on his wide desk shrilled out. He picked up the receiver.

'Samant. What is it? Oh. Oh, yes sir. Yes, Minister sahib. Yes? Yes, your son, Minister sahib. Yes, I see, sir. Yes, yes. Yes, at once. At once, Minister sahib.'

Slowly ACP Samant put down the receiver. He gave Ghote, standing neatly to attention on the far side of his desk, a slow, assessing look.

'So, Inspector, as I was telling, it is not going to be at all easy to pull in Daddyji. But we are going to do it. You are going to do it. He has a place down in Colaba. Go over there *ek dum* and get out of him something. Something to have him fairly and squarely on a first-class foolproof charge.'

And, before Ghote had time to reflect on the ACP's sudden about-turn, much less before he had managed to think how he was possibly going to get that evidence, he found himself outside the cabin perplexed.

127

Scarcely half an hour later Ghote was standing face to face with the man ACP Samant had pronounced to be all-bad.

Certainly, he thought, looking at the burly frame, the almost bald bullet head with the thick knife scar running above the left eyebrow and the expression of sullen coldness in the deep-set eyes, the fellow has all the appearance of somebody who is bad. Very bad even. But all-bad?

In spite of everything the ACP had said Ghote kept his reservations.

'Well,' he said, 'so you are the famous Daddyji I have heard and read a lot about. But you are not so big as I was expecting. You are not much taller than myself.'

'But twice as hard,' said Daddyji, his voice grinding out.

'Perhaps. But let me tell something. However hard or not hard I am, the CID itself is harder than you, Daddyji. Than you or anyone, than any man with a man's weaknesses.'

'Oh yes, Inspector? But I am here. And this is not Thana Gaol.'

'No, no, it is not. But the day for Thana Gaol is coming.'

'All kinds of days are coming. The day when elephants are flying, the day when the sea is drying up. But still I am able to do what I want.'

'Perhaps that time is going to end sooner than you think. I have a feeling that now you have gone too far.'

'I go where I like. Where do you think is too far, my little Inspector?'

'I think,' Ghote said slowly, 'the Loafer's Delight Disc Mart was too far. The owner is the son of the Minister for Home.'

But his threat, if threat it was, received only a roar of uninhibited laughter from the gang boss.

'Oh,' he said, wiping his eyes, 'that I was not knowing.'

'Not when you were ordering his shop to be pulled to pieces?' Ghote slipped in.

But his ruse was by no means clever enough.

'I order, Inspector?' Daddyji answered blandly. 'But why should you be thinking that?'

'Because that is your modus operandi,' Ghote replied. 'That is the pattern you are always working to, Daddyji. We know very much about you already.'

'You know nothing.'

'Oh, perhaps not enough to get a conviction today. But no

man is perfect, and one day you would make mistake.'

'Oh, yes, mistake and mistake I will make. But it will be no matter.'

'No matter?'

Daddyji shrugged.

'If I am making mistake,' he said, 'it would maybe cost me plenty plenty. But plenty plenty I have. So goodbye to catching Daddyji, Inspector.'

'Nevertheless,' Ghote said, 'I require you to answer certain questions.'

'Answers cost nothing.'

'If they are not true, they will cost you your freedom.'

But Daddyji only smiled.

'They will cost me only the price of making them true after, my little Inspector,' he said. 'And lies are cheap enough.'

'We shall see. Now, where were you at 3.15 pip-emma this afternoon?'

'That is easy. I was here. I am always careful to be with friends at such times, and I was talking with a police constable I am knowing.'

'At such times?' Ghote leapt in. 'Why were you saying "at such times"?'

Daddyji smiled again.

'At such times? At afternoon times only, Inspector. It is at such times that a man feels sad, and then it is good to talk. Especially with a police constable.'

'Very well. Then tell me, when did you last see two men by the names of Iqbal Singh and Chandra Chagoo?'

'Inspector, will you say those names again?'

'You are very well knowing them.'

'Inspector, I have never heard of any such persons. Who are they, please?'

'They are the men you instructed to break up the Loafer's Delight Disc Mart.'

Daddyji looked Ghote straight in the eye.

'And you would never be able to prove that, Inspector,' he said. 'You would never be able to prove that I have ever even met them.'

ACP Samant was not very pleased.

'And I suppose now,' he snapped, 'you are proposing to sit upon your bottom and say "no can do"?'

'No, sir,' Ghote answered firmly.

'No, sir. No, sir. Then what are you proposing to do, man?'

'Sir, from my examination of the material in Records I have come to the conclusion there is one good line still to take.'

'Records. Records. You are all alike. If it is hiding in Records with a good fan blowing down on you in the heat you are willing to work and to work. But if it is getting out into the hot streets you are thinking differently.'

'But, sir, I am about to go out into the hot— Into the streets, sir. To interview the owner of the only place so far to have defied Daddyji's goondas, sir. An establishment by the name of the Galerie Sodawaterwala.'

'Gallery? Gallery? What sort of place is that?'

'It is an art gallery, ACP sahib, and also a shop for the sale of curios and other objects.'

'Thank you for telling me, Inspector. And I suppose next you are going to inform that Sodawaterwala is an old Parsi name. Give me credit for knowing a little bit about some things, Inspector.'

'Yes, sir. No, sir. Sorry, sir.'

'Well, what for are you standing there, man? Get out there to this Sodawaterwala gallery and talk to the man.'

Mr Sodawaterwala seemed well named. He was a meek and mild looking individual, evidently with all the artistic leanings of the ancient Parsi community fully developed. But he had refused to pay Daddyji's men any protection money. Even after the police guard he had been given when he had reported the approach first had eventually been withdrawn.

'And nothing has happened since those men were withdrawn?' Ghote asked him, with surprise.

'Ah, no, Inspector. But you see I took certain steps.'

'Steps?'

Mr Sodawaterwala heaved a neat little sigh.

'Inspector,' he said, 'I must confess. I hired goondas of my own.'

'Criminal types? But, Mr Sodawaterwala . . .'

'Yes, yes. But what was I to do? The very day the police guard was withdrawn, I spotted on the far pavement there the very men who had earlier demanded money. But I am glad to

130

say, Inspector, that both the fellows I hired proved to be altogether charming chaps.'

'I am glad to hear.'

'Yes, yes. Goondas they may have been, but thoroughly willing and dependable fellows both.'

'They may have been, Mr Sodawaterwala? Are they then with you no more?'

'No, no. They are here always by day. But by night, I regret to say, I have been unable to find any others as dependable.'

'But have you left the premises unguarded at night?'

Mr Sodawaterwala suddenly smiled with tremendous impishness.

'No, indeed,' he said. 'Come this way, Inspector, and I will show you something.'

He lead Ghote to an upstairs office over the big gallery showroom, throwing open its door with a flourish.

And there, sitting on two stools, were what Ghote took to be at first sight a pair of the most villainous looking goondas he had ever met.

But then he stood peering in at the dimly lit room and looked again.

'They are not real?' he asked. 'They are dummies only?'

Mr Sodawaterwala giggled in glee.

'Exactly so, Inspector. Exactly so. A ruse I borrowed from my extensive reading of the crime stories of the West. The Saint, Sherlock Holmes and so forth. These are just such models as deceived the fierce Colonel Moran when Holmes returned from the dead.'

'You were making yourself?' Ghote asked, looking more closely at the extremely lifelike heads.

'No, no, my dear sir. I have no talent in that direction. Yet I am inclined to bet that you will never guess who did indeed make these altogether excellent figures.'

'One of the artists whose work you are selling?'

'No, no. Not at all, not at all.'

'Then I am unable to guess.'

'They were made, my dear sir, by none other than my sweeper boy.'

'A sweeper. But . . .'

'Yes, yes. But how could a sweeper, a boy of the lowest class, have such a talent? You are right to ask. But, Inspector, let it be a lesson to us. Never underestimate the abilities and complexity of any human being whatsoever.'

'He made them himself, without any assistance?' Ghote asked, looking again at the uncannily lifelike models, still only half able to believe that someone young and untutored could possess such ability.

'Something like a miracle, is it not?' the dapper little Parsi gallery owner said. 'And, more than this, the boy – he is about sixteen years of age only – came to me like a miracle.'

'Explain please, Mr Sodawaterwala.'

'Well, one morning a few weeks ago my old sweeper, who had been with me for years, announced suddenly that he was leaving. I offered him an increment. I even offered him a better place to sleep. He had the use of this cupboard here under the stair. Look.'

Mr Sodawaterwala led Ghote to a small door under the stairs and opened it with a flourish.

'You will meet my miracle –' he began.

Then his voice came to an abrupt halt.

'But . . . but this is extraordinary,' he said.

'What is it?' Ghote asked, alerted by the note of bewilderment in the Parsi's tone.

'The boy, Piloo. He has gone. Look, all his few possessions they are here no more. And his pictures. His pictures have gone.'

'What pictures are these?' Ghote asked.

'I was telling you, Inspector. Just the very day that my old sweeper left so unaccountably, Piloo came to me asking for a job. Quite soon I discovered that Piloo was a remarkable artist. He began to play with some scraps of modelling clay that were lying about and he made these really excellent small pictures. Scenes of everyday life, modelled in clay. I was going to get them on display even.'

'He knew this?'

'Yes, yes. Only three days ago I told him. And now he has gone. Vanished. And I really believe he would have become the Indian Hogarth.'

Ghote stood in silent tribute for a moment to this odd event in the gallery owner's life. But he could not waste more time. Pushing aside the boy's disappearance, he said, 'Mr Soda-waterwala, when I saw those dummies of your goonda guards an idea came into my head. Can I ask you tonight not to put them in their usual place?'

The gallery owner visibly paled.

'But, Inspector,' he said, 'in that case I very much fear I shall be visited by those fellows who threatened me. They will break up the gallery, perhaps even attack me myself.'

'That they should come into the gallery is exactly my object,' Ghote answered. 'But do not take away the dummies till a late hour. Say, after midnight. Before then I will come and conceal myself on the premises.'

'And catch the fellows red-handed?' Mr Sodawaterwala brightened.

'More than that I am hoping,' Ghote said. 'I hope to catch them and to get them to admit who sent them.'

'You think you can do that, Inspector?'

'I think I must do it, Mr Sodawaterwala.'

Ghote's mind was still filled with that determination as, just after eleven that night, he cautiously approached the darkened Galerie Sodawaterwala from the rear, the key to its back door which Mr Sodawaterwala had given him in his hand.

But he found the little door in the narrow dark lane unlocked. Worse, forced open.

With pounding heart he pushed into the echoing empty premises, flashing his pocket torch here and there. All seemed to be well. Nowhere was there any sign of the damage Daddyji's men were likely to have inflicted.

But then, from somewhere up above, he detected a sound. A muffled groan.

He swung the flashlight beam round, located the stairs, pounded up them. Pausing for a moment at the top he listened. And, yes, distinctly another groan.

He ran forward.

Mr Sodawaterwala was lying on the floor in the middle of his little upstairs office. His face was black and bloodied. One of his legs was twisted under him at an angle that it should never have been. Both his hands were a mess of open wounds.

Ghote knelt beside him.

'Mr Sodawaterwala,' he said, 'I am here. I will fetch help. Do not try to move. Where is your telephone?'

'In gallery,' the battered Parsi managed to say. 'Down . . .'

'Yes, yes. Downstairs. I am going. Lie back. Help will be here in a few minutes only.'

And indeed an ambulance arrived in answer to Ghote's urgent call in a commendably short time. But the interval had been long enough for Mr Sodawaterwalla to groan out to Ghote the details of what had happened.

'Daddyji' was the first word that he managed to mutter.

'Daddyji?' Ghote asked. 'Did he come himself? Was it him who did this to you?'

'He took pleasure . . . In telling . . . telling me.'

Ghote felt a renewed sense of angry determination.

'Then we shall get him,' he said. 'I am promising you that, Mr Sodawaterwala. But how was it that he knew this was a time to come? Were those dummies still in place?'

'Yes. Yes. Still there. As instructed. But Piloo–'

'Piloo? Your sweeper boy who disappeared this afternoon? What had he to do with this?'

'Brother.'

'Brother? I do not understand.'

'Piloo Daddyji's young brother. Daddyji told me. Told me made my old sweeper leave, put the boy in instead. Spy.'

Ghote, kneeling beside the broken body of the Parsi, thought for a little.

'But did you not tell it was some weeks since the boy came?' he asked at last. 'He had time to make the dummies, and for you to discover he was the Indian Garth-ho.'

'Ho-garth. Very famous British artist. Scenes of low life.'

'I am sorry. Hogarth. Yes, Hogarth. But why, if he was sent as a spy, did he not tell Daddyji long ago that you were not really guarded?'

'Because I had told him what a talent he had. He refused for a time to tell his brother.'

'Daddyji told you this?'

'Boasted. Said he was giving me extra because . . . Because of that.'

'Yes, that is very like the man,' Ghote said grimly. 'But now we would nab him, with your assistance we would do it.'

'No,' groaned the battered gallery owner.

'But – But – No, lie back, Mr Sodawaterwala.'

'Inspector, I will not give evidence against that man.'

'But, Mr Sodawaterwala, this is the one good chance we have. A man of your reputation, a stainless witness against that man.'

'Inspector. Not what I thought I was. Not a fighter for good through and through. Insp . . . He told me what he would do to me next time.'

It was with feelings of deep pessimism that Ghote reported next day to ACP Samant.

'Sir, Mr Sodawaterwala is recovering well in J. J. Hospital. But he is adamant, sir. He will not give evidence.'

The ACP grunted non-committally.

'And you say this boy, this Piloo, is Daddyji's younger brother?'

'Yes, sir. But if you are thinking that here is a way into that man's heart, I do not—'

'Heart? Heart? I tell you, Inspector, that sort of talk does not apply in the case of Daddyji. He is an all-bad hat. Understand that.'

'Yes, sir.'

'But the boy took away from the gallery these paintings or pictures or whatever?'

'Pictures in clay, sir. Mr Sodawaterwala believes they will make him the Indian Garth— The Indian Hogarth, sir.'

'I dare say. I dare say. But the point is that the clay was undoubtedly the property of Mr Sodawaterwala. So the boy stole it. And we are going to put him behind the bars for that.'

Ghote felt puzzled.

'But, sir, he was not anything to do with the raid on the Minister's son's record shop, sir.'

'But is the Minister to know that, Ghote? Is he? Is he? No, no, we tell Minister sahib that the boy was one of two brothers and that it has been convenient to bring a charge against one only, and we assure him that the culprit will catch a damn long term of Rigorous Imprisonment. That will get the Minister off our back, and that after all is the object of the exercise.'

'But, sir,' Ghote said, flooded with sudden dismay. 'Sir, the boy is the Indian Hogarth. If he is sent to prison, India will lose her Hogarth.'

ACP Samant brought his fist crashing down on to his desk

till every brass paperweight there jumped in the air.

'Inspector,' he stormed, 'unless you get down to Colaba and arrest that boy now India will lose her Inspector Ghote.'

So, in less than an hour Ghote was once again facing the formidable figure of Daddyji. A smiling, contemptuous Daddyji.

'I had a feeling that I would be seeing you soon, my little Inspector.'

'I expect so,' Ghote returned levelly. 'But I have not come to hear where you were at eleven pip-emma last night.'

That did surprise the boastful iron-tough crook.

'Not? Not? But you must want to know. I was far away. Out at Juhu Beach. With my friends Mahesh Khandwalla, Sudakar Dalvi, Mohamed Hai, Sudhir–'

'Stop. However much nonsense you are telling, however many names you are giving, I know better. You were at the Galerie Sodawaterwala then committing grievous bodily harm.'

Daddyji brightened at this. Here was a game where he knew the score.

'And you have witnesses?' he asked. 'As many as I have?'

'I have one witness. The best. I have the man you beat up.'

'And he will give evidence, is it?'

'Why would he not?'

Daddyji shrugged. Elaborately.

'How should I be knowing, my little Inspector, why this witness of yours will not tell the lies you are wanting? Perhaps it is that he is afraid.'

'Afraid of worse treatment from you,' Ghote stated blankly.

Daddyji looked back at him. He held out his wrists as if for handcuffs.

'You are going to arrest me for that then?' he asked.

'No,' Ghote said. 'Not you, Daddyji.'

Again he surprised the gang boss.

'Not me? Then who?'

'I have come to arrest your brother Piloo.'

'Piloo? But that's no good. Why, my witnesses will be speaking the truth for him.'

'Not when the charge is taking away feloniously from the Galerie Sodawaterwala a quantity of art material, viz six pictures in clay.'

Daddyji relaxed visibly. Plainly whatever he had been expecting Ghote to arrest Piloo for, it was not anything as trivial as this.

'Oh, but take, Inspector,' he said. 'Take the boy, take.'

'Take?'

'Yes. Take, take. For some pieces of mud clay he puts himself in danger. Why should I bother with him?'

'But he is your brother.'

'Brother, smother. What is brother? He is one of my men. Or until now he was.'

Ghote looked at the broad-shouldered crook.

'I should warn you, the boy is likely to get a long sentence. When someone as influential as the Minister has been insulted by him.'

'The Minister? What to do with Minister? Piloo can go to gaol for all his life. What am I caring?'

'But his pictures,' Ghote said.

'Those things. Pah!'

'But do you not know,' Ghote continued earnestly, 'that the boy has very, very great gifts. Mr Sodawaterwala says he will be the Indian Hogarth. Hogarth is a very, very famous English artist.'

'What is that to me? Here, you will be wanting your evidence, Inspector. Look under that charpoy there. That is where the boy put his bundle. You will find your pictures there.'

Ghote went and knelt beside the rope-slung bed, as much to hide his sense of disgust at Daddyji's behaviour – first his father, now his brother – as to get hold of the pictures. They were there, sure enough, and he dragged out the bundle and opened it up, thinking all the while, 'Yes, the ACP was right, Daddyji is an all-bad man. All-bad.'

'Hey!'

Daddyji's voice came loudly from over his shoulder.

'Hey, look at that. It is me. Just as I am. It is me playing cards with Iqbal Singh and that idiot Chandra Chagoo. See, he is losing as always. It is on his face. Wonderful, wonderful.'

Ghote looked more closely at the six hard-baked clay tablets. It was certainly true. Small though they were, it was clear beyond doubt that one of the card players was Daddyji and that on the miniature face of the man the gang boss had pointed out there was an expression of stupid chagrin, as if indeed he was losing at the game and could not understand why.

'Inspector?' Daddyji said, with a note of sudden calculation in his voice.

'What is it?' Ghote replied, prickling with suspicion.

'Inspector, I am going to ask you to do something for me.'

'For you? You dare to ask.'

Ghote thought with rising anger of how this man was truly all-bad.

'Inspector,' Daddyji was continuing, oblivious of Ghote's plain opposition. 'I am asking you to take these pictures now to Mr Sodawaterwala and to tell him that, of course, Piloo did not steal them. That he brought them here to show me only, to me, his brother who had raised him from a boy.'

'Take the pictures back? To Mr Sodawaterwala?'

Ghote felt deeply dismayed.

'Then there would be no charge against Piloo,' he said.

'That is right,' Daddyji answered cheerfully. 'And Piloo can go on and make more and more very good pictures like this. He can become the Indian Highlife.'

'Hogarth. But–'

And then an idea came to Ghote, an idea so good it was almost incredible.

'You are quite sure you are wanting me to take back these pictures?' he asked, trying to keep his voice neutral.

'But, yes, yes, yes. It is important for Piloo to have this chance. I may be a bad man, Inspector, but I am not all bad. I have some heart left for the boy.'

Quickly Ghote gathered up the little clay tablets, wrapped them and took them off.

He took them to Mr Sodawaterwala in his bed at the J. J. Hospital.

'And, if what Daddyji told me is true,' he said after he had handed them over, 'when you get back to your gallery you would find Piloo already back there, making more pictures like these.'

Mr Sodawaterwala smiled through his bruised and battered face. A smile of great gentleness.

'But that is wonderful, Inspector,' he said. 'Wonderful. And Daddyji himself insisted that you have the pictures? It is yet more wonderful. It restores my faith in humanity.'

'Yes,' Ghote said, 'it would seem that my own belief was all the time right. There is no such thing as the all-bad man. Even Daddyji has in him some spark of goodness. You know that his father, Piloo's father too, has a gift for modelling clay. He is making little, somewhat obscene figures to sell to tourists at Flora Fountain. So the strain of the artist comes to the surface if only in appreciation of what is good, even in a proud fellow like Daddyji.'

Mr Sodawaterwala smiled again.

'But in Piloo,' he said, 'that strain has gone to the heights. Do you know what I will do for him?'

'It would be something good I am sure.'

'I hope so. I am going to hold a first-class, Number One exhibition for him. And, just as soon as I can, I will go back and put these first six pictures of his in the window of the Galerie, as a foretaste.'

'Very good, Mr Sodawaterwala. Very good. And I will see that night and day there are four-five hefty constables guarding that window.'

'Guarding?' said Mr Sodawaterwala. 'But surely, Inspector, now that Daddyji has shown he is not all-bad there is no need for that.'

'But there is a need, very much of need,' Ghote replied. 'You see, one of those pictures is very important evidence.'

'Evidence? But there is no longer a question of Piloo having stolen any clay. That is ridiculous.'

'That is ridiculous, yes. But I will tell you what is not ridiculous: a charge of conspiring with two individuals, namely Iqbal Singh and Chandra Chagoo, to cause damage at the Loafer's Delight Disc Mart.'

Mr Sodawaterwala looked bewildered.

'But I do not understand,' he said. 'How can one of Piloo's pictures have anything to do with such a place as the Loafer's Delight Disc Mart?'

'Because that picture,' said Ghote triumphantly, 'shows Daddyji was a close acquaintance of those two men, something that up to now he was prepared to manufacture evidence to disprove. It shows the three of them playing cards together, clearly as clearly.'

'Then you are going to arrest Daddyji?' Mr Sodawaterwala asked. 'But you cannot do that now.'

Ghote looked down at him on the smooth white pillow of the hospital bed.

He sighed.

'Yes, Mr Sodawaterwala,' he said, 'I can arrest him and I will. Did you think I can let him go scot-free just because he gave Piloo his chance in life? Yes, even though it was in giving Piloo that chance he betrayed himself, I must arrest him nevertheless. All-bad or partly good, it is my duty to put him behind the bars and I will do it.'

1984

10

Hello, Hello, Inspector Ghote

– Hello, hello. Inspector Ghote?

  – Ghote speaking.

  – Oh, hello, Inspectorji.

  – Who is this? Who is there?

  – Oh, Inspectorji, it is I.

  – I? I? Who in all Bombay is I?

  – Inspectorji, it is Budhoo only.

  – Budhoo? Budhoo? Are you. . . ? Are you the Budhoo I am
sometimes meeting?

  – But, yes, Inspectorji, it is I, Budhoo.

  – Why are you using telephone? Such is not at all what we
were arranging, for when you were having something to tell.

  – No. No, Inspectorji, this is first time I have talked on
telephone ever at all. But, Inspectorji, I have watched and
watched Suleiman Dada when he was using, and now I have
seen how to do it.

  – But you are not telephoning from Suleiman Dada's posh
flat itself? Malabar Hill, Mount Pleasant Road?

  – Oh, Inspectorji, Suleiman Dada is shifting. Now he has flat
at Nepean Sea Road. But it is from there I am talking, I am not
at all knowing if other telephones are working just like
Suleiman Dada's.

  – But— But is the dada there? Are any of his goondas there
also? How dare you call me by name openly in front of such a
Number One anti-social?

  – Oh, Inspectorji, Inspectorji, I would not. Inspectorji, if I
was doing same Suleiman Dada would be slitting throat for me
ear to ear. That you must be knowing.

  – True enough, my friend. So why are you taking such a
damn bloody risk?

  – Oh, Inspectorji, Suleiman Sahib is out of station altogether. I am by myself here. That is what I am wanting to tell,

Inspector. Suleiman Dada has gone in great hurry-purry, and I am thinking that today is going to be Big Day . . .

– Speak up, man, speak up. I cannot hear. Shut off that damn radio.

– No radio, Inspector.

– Do not shout, man. Do not shout. Now, speak clearly. Did you say the Big Day?

– Yes, Inspector, Big Day.

– There has been a delivery?

– Oh, yes, Inspectorji, big-big delivery. To a godown at Indira Docks. Inspector, it is two thousand cartons of catfish itself. Frozen catfish.

– Catfish? But— Ah. No. It is that high-smelling stuff. So there are drugs placed inside for smuggling?

– Ji haan, Inspectorji. What else?

– And this is Big Day, you were saying? The Big Day I let you go free from that pocket-maar charge to learn all about?

– Ji, sahib. I am hearing Suleiman Dada say Number One Boss is wanting to check consignment himself. That fellow no one is at all knowing will be at the godown, Inspector.

– Yes, yes. But when, Budhoo? When? And just where in Indira Docks is this godown?

– Inspectorji, it is—

– Yes? Yes? Budhoo? Budhoo?

– Budhoo?

– Budhoo, you are there?

– Inspector, I think I am hearing someone . . . Inspector, it is—

Click

Tringg, tringg. Tringg, tringg

– Hello, hello. Is that V.P. Road Police Station? Inspector Ghote here.

– Police station? Are you saying police station?

– Yes, yes. That is V.P. Road Police Station?

– No, no. This is New Gentleman Restaurant only.

Click

Tringg, tringg. Tringg, tringg

– Hello. V.P. Road Police Station?

– V.P. Road Police Station.

– Is that V.P. Road PS? You are not at all sounding like a police station.

– I am hoping not. I am hoping not. This is the paan-shop on corner of Sukhlaji Street. Nice paans to munch, and nice-nice girls we are having all round. But policewallas, oh, no.

– Clear the line, clear the line. This is hundred per cent urgent.

Click

Tringg, tringg. Tringg, tringg. Tringg, tringg. Tringg, tringg . . .
 Click

Tringg, tringg. Tringg, tringg

– V.P. Road Police Station. Hello?

– Inspector Ghote, Headquarters CID here. Give me the Station House Officer, *ek dum, ek dum.*

– Yes, Inspector. Right away, Inspector.
Click, click, click

– Lock-up in-charge.

– Lock-up in-charge? What do you mean, lock-up in-charge?

– This is the lock-up. I am in-charge.

– But I am asking for Station House Officer. Get me put on to your SHO. Headquarters CID here. Jaldi, jaldi, jaldi.
Click, click, click

– Station House Officer, V.P. Road PS.

– Ah, thank God. Listen, this is Inspector Ghote, Headquarters CID. Now, I have a kabari in among Suleiman Dada's gang.

– Informer in there? First-class work, Inspector.

– Yes, yes. Never to mind that. Thing is, this fellow was telephoning me from Suleiman Dada's residence itself. Damn fool that he is. And in middle of call he told someone was coming and line was shut off. Now, I am thinking it was the dada himself coming and my fellow is in danger of his life only. So, can you get four-five men round there double-quick?

– Certainly, Inspector. It is a damn bad thing if it is getting known to one and all that a kabari has met a nasty fate. Where is it that he is?

– At Suleiman Dada's flat, Nepean Sea Road.

– And the flat is where, Inspector?

– You do not know yourself? You are having top-notch gang leader inside your area, and you are not knowing where he is residing?

– But, Inspector, I am thinking he must have just only come to Nepean Sea Road. I was hearing he was staying on Malabar Hill, no?

– He was, he was. But he has shifted.

– And now he is where? You are no more knowing?

– No. My fellow was saying Nepean Sea Road only.

– But, Inspector, there are twenty-thirty big flats-blocks there. How can we find just one flat only, when it is a matter of a damn hurry?

– Yes. Yes, it is hard I am— No. No. Wait. I have one clue. While I was talking with my kabari I was—

Click

– Switchboard? Switchboard? I have been cut off.

– You are calling, caller?

– Yes, yes. I have been cut off. Damn vital call. To V.P. Road PS.

– You were not cut off by me, caller. Kindly dial once more.

Tringg, tringg. Tringg, tringg

– Hello, hello, V.P. Road PS?

– V.P. Road PS here.

– Station House Officer. I was cut off. Urgent, urgent matter.

Click, click, click

– Hello. Lock-up in-charge speaking.

– No, no, no. Get me back to SHO. Hurry, hurry, hurry.

Click, click, click

– Station House Officer.

– Ah. It is Ghote again.

– Ah, yes, Inspector, we were cut off.

– I know, I know. Now, listen. While my kabari was talking I was having much difficulty to hear because of some damn music.

– A radio, Inspector?

– No, no. He was assuring there was no radio there. But I am thinking. Why would there be music at this time of day, very loud?

– Don't know, Inspector.

– A wedding, man. A wedding. Tell your men to go hell-for-leather only to Nepean Sea Road and to look out for a wedding party, those lamp-carrying fellows outside, anything. Then ask at the nearby block of flats for one Suleiman Sahib, or even for a newcomer only. Then they are to break in and be asking questions after. Okay?

– Tikh hai, Inspector. Tikh hai.

– Hello, hello, Inspector Ghote?

– Ghote speaking.

– Hello, Inspectorji. It is I, Budhoo. All is okay-okay, Inspector. Suleiman Dada was beating up, but your police-wallas came in nick of time. And they were arresting the bastard only.

– Arresting? Arresting? But how the hell is he going to go to his meeting with this Number One Boss nobody knows if he is behind the bars. How am I going to get my prize catch red-handed now? Budhoo, I am wishing one thing only.

– Yes, Inspectorji?

– That Suleiman Dada had taken the cord of that telephone and wrapped it round your damn neck.

Click.

1985

145

11

Nil By Mouth

Inspector Ghote ought, as he entered the guarded Cabin No 773 in the big noisy hospital, to have looked first of all at the criminal lying on the bed there, his kneecap shattered. But instead, his eye was caught for some reason by the boldly-printed card fastened to the top of his white tubular iron bed-head. 'Nil By Mouth' it said in thick black capitals in English, with below in devanagri script the same warning repeated in more immediately comprehensible terms: 'No food or drink allowed'.

He turned to the Sister, neat in her starched white head-dress and white overall with smart epaulettes, its cotton belt fastened with a wide metal buckle. 'Please,' he said, 'what for is it that he is not allowed food? Is it on police orders? We are wanting him to talk, you know.'

The Sister looked shocked.

'No, no,' she said. 'This man is a patient only here, whatever he may have done outside. Here it is Resident Medical Officer's orders that count only. Patient is in Nil by Mouth condition because operation is to take place at six pip-emma today.'

She turned away and stamped out, as if to re-emphasise that here within hospital walls it was the medical staff who gave orders not any policewalla.

Ghote looked at the man he had come to see, had come to interrogate. Ram Dharkar, small-time goonda. But a small-time muscleman who worked for a very, very big-time gang boss, the mystery man believed to be behind twenty-five well-organised bank dacoities in the past nine months. The man no one in Crime Branch had been able to get near.

But now, thanks to Ram Dharkar, they stood a chance. Because Dharkar had been found only five or six hours ago lying unconscious on a rubbish heap near the foul-smelling Chandanwadi Electric Crematorium, with his right knee smashed to pieces by a heavy lump of concrete left bloodily beside him. A clear case of a supposed informer having been punished and left as a lesson for any other gang member or hanger-on who might be thinking greedily of the large reward the banks of Bombay had, at last, collaborated to offer.

And the beauty of it was that Ram Dharkar had not been an informer at all. So, rightly aggrieved, he ought to be ready to talk and talk.

Ghote, who had been waiting for him to recover consciousness sitting for hours down in the crowded echoing entrance hall of the big hospital on a hard bench underneath a strident notice saying 'OPD Case Notes Will Be Issued From 7.30 am' – whatever that meant – had now at last been given the news by a white-capped ward-boy that Dharkar was in a condition to be interviewed.

He followed the boy then through long clackingly shrill corridors, up one wide-stone-stepped staircase and down another to a nursing station where he had been handed over to the starchy Sister who had taken him to Cabin No. 773 and Ram Dharkar, Ram Dharkar surely ready to talk, lying helpless on the bed within.

'Well, Ram,' Ghote said to him, 'you and I know each other of old, isn't it?'

The goonda on the bed made no reply, eyeing Ghote sullenly though wakefully.

'And how are you feeling?' Ghote asked, showing as much friendly concern as he could. 'The knee, it is giving pain, no?'

Again Ram Dharkar did not respond.

Ghote pulled up a sagging-seated grey canvas chair he had spotted in a corner by the little room's sole narrow window. He sat himself down and leant towards the injured man, who was, true enough, looking as if he was in not a little pain.

'Right then,' he said, 'let us be getting down to business. The Dada of your gang decided you were betraying one and all, isn't it? Well, we are damn well knowing such is not so. And the Dada, whoever he is, ought to be knowing as much also. Ram Dharkar was never a kabari.'

He looked for some sign of stirred pride in the goonda's lined face.

But there was nothing. Only that same sullen single expression.

He cleared his throat a little.

'No,' he said, feeling the falsity of the note of cheerfulness he was endeavouring to inject into his voice. 'No, that fellow should have known you better, Ram bhai. And look what he was doing to you instead. They tell me that however well is going the operation you are soon to have, you will find difficulty to walk for the rest of your life.'

No reaction.

Ghote sat and thought.

This he had not expected. The situation had seemed to him quite straightforward. The Dada behind the bank dacoities had made a mistake, his first and only mistake, but a big one. He had had Ram Dharkar cruelly punished for something he had not at all done. So, surely, Ram Dharkar would be avid for revenge. And revenge was there. He knew, he must know, who the Dada was and where he could be found. He had only to say and his chance to pay back the man who had had him crippled would be one hundred per cent secured.

But here the fellow was, obstinately silent. Saying nothing.

Ghote's glance fell again on the bed-head notice. 'Nil By Mouth.' Yes, that was what Ram Dharkar was so unexpectedly giving him himself, nil by mouth. Absolutely nil.

Why? Why?

And then he thought he had it.

'You are afraid?' he asked the goonda abruptly. 'Afraid, if you are talking, the Dada will finish off the job he was beginning?'

Ram Dharkar still did not reply, but his expression of stony nothingness changed. His eyes said, 'Yes'.

'But that is not so,' Ghote assured him eagerly. 'Think man, where you are. You are in one of the biggest hospitals in Bombay. You are in a cabin on your own. There is a constable on guard just outside that door. He has orders to let in just only two nurses and one doctor. You cannot be more safe.'

He thought then, from the faintly pensive expression on Ram Dharkar's face, that he had taken all this in and was at least considering it.

'Inspector, I do not dare.'

The words were croaked out. Yet Ghote took heart from them. At least the fellow was communicating. With patience and luck, he might be persuaded before long that it was safe to take the revenge that lay so easily in his power, as surely it was. The chances of any gang executioner sent by the Dada getting to his possible betrayer were one hundred-to-one against. More even.

And almost at once Ram Dharkar showed that he had committed himself to more than that one negative sentence.

'Inspectorji,' he said, his voice a little stronger. 'Get us a drink, no? I am thirsty-thirsty like hell.'

Ghote looked at the Nil by Mouth notice.

'Oh, I cannot do that, man,' he said. 'You are having operation soon and it is medical advice that you must take nothing before.'

'But a drink only. A little water. Inspectorji, it is damn hot in here. I am wanting just only one swallow of water. That cannot be doing any harm.'

Ghote wondered whether this in fact might not be true. Surely a single gulp of pure water would not make the operation due in five hours' time altogether dangerous?

He looked around the narrow cabin. But there was no jug of water or earthenware chatti to be seen. And, sure enough, the little room was appallingly hot.

'Well,' he said, glancing at the door, 'perhaps—'

But at that moment the door was pushed open and the two nurses presumably permitted to enter came in, wheeling a small trolley consisting of a padlocked metal chest on a stand.

'Dharkar, Ram,' said the more senior of the two. 'Medication has been ordered.'

She took a key from the bunch at her waist and solemnly unlocked the metal chest. Ghote saw that its interior was lined with pill bottles and jars by the dozen. The nurse consulted a sheet of paper and then selected one of the bottles.

'Excuse me,' Ghote said, prompted by a lingering resentment at the way the medical staff assumed that they and they only had a god-given right to do what they wanted when they wanted. 'Excuse me, but isn't it that this man is in Nil by Mouth condition?'

The nurse turned towards him, eyes sparking.

'Are you saying we do not know our duty?' she snapped. 'Tests have been carried out. Patient is not fit for immediate operation. The heart rate must be brought down.'

She turned to her colleague, showing her the label on the pill bottle.

'Digoxin 250 micrograms,' she said.

'Digoxin 250 micrograms,' the other nurse confirmed.

'One every four hours.'

'One every four hours.'

The senior nurse poured a little water from a vacuum flask in the medicine chest into a small plastic glass, handed Ram Dharkar a single white pill and the glass and watched him swallow the pill down.

When the pair of them had left Ghote turned to the injured goonda again.

'Well,' he said, 'you have had your taste of water after all.'

'And it is making it bloody worse,' Ram Dharkar responded. 'It is like giving a starving man one corner of a sweetmeat only.'

'Well,' Ghote answered, 'I suppose you must endure it. They did not take away that notice above your head.'

'But, Inspectorji, it is hot-hot. Feel only how hot I am.'

Ghote bent forward and took the goonda's calloused hand. It was thickly wet with sweat.

'Yes,' he said. 'Yes, you are hot. Even I am also.'

He glanced round the little room. Not even a fan to be seen.

'I tell you what,' he said. 'I would see if I can open that window.'

He got up and went across to the narrow opaque-glass affair. For a moment he wondered whether he had been sensible to make the offer. With the window open could Ram Dharkar, afraid for his life, make his escape through it should he himself have to leave the guarded cabin before he had finally got hold of that name? The fellow might think of it. He might. And then they would have lost their one golden opportunity.

But that was nonsense. Dharkar with his smashed kneecap would be totally incapable of getting through a window as narrow as this.

He thrust up its lower frame.

Nevertheless, having done so, he could not prevent himself putting his head out and making a careful survey of the escape possibilities.

No, he decided after a long look round, it really was safe enough. True, the window did overlook a lane inside the huge hospital compound. But, though technically at ground-floor level, it was in fact quite high up. A beggar, or some such, sitting crouched against the wall below, a piece of gunny laid out beside him to collect alms, looked from above quite small, his dirty-haired head like a dried coconut with the stump of one out-thrust leg – the fellow must be a leper, perhaps a patient from another department – looking like one of the flat bats dhobis used to beat washing clean. There was, certainly, a drainpipe running up the wall nearby, and an active man could probably scramble down that to the ground. But Ram Dharkar was the very opposite of an active man. No, it was safe enough.

Ghote turned from the window. Air less humidly hot than that in the room did seem to be drifting in.

'Better, heh?' he said to Ram Dharkar. 'Cooler, no?'

The goonda grunted unwilling assent.

'All the same,' he said, 'I am wanting-wanting something to drink.'

'Well, we would be seeing about that perhaps later.' Ghote answered with vague helpfulness. 'But now. Now let us talk about the man who had that done to your knee.'

'No.'

'But—'

'No, no, Inspectorji. I tell you he is not a person to be playing with, that one. If he had one idea only that I had given his name, or that I was thinking only – why, if he knew I was just only talking with you now – then it would be the finish of me straight away.'

'But think, man. How could he do that? When you are here, police guarded, in this hospital?'

'I am not knowing how. I am just knowing that he would do it.'

'But revenge. You could be taking revenge for what he has just done. Give us his name only, and where we could find, and in one hour, in one half-hour, he would be behind the bars and you would be here laughing.'

But Ram Dharkar merely turned his head away and lay silent.

Ghote sat on his uncomfortably sagging chair beside the bed and tried to think of some new line to take. But he felt that with every passing minute his chances of catching on to the injured goonda's desire for revenge – and, surely, surely he had that – were getting less.

At last the fellow stirred and gave a weary moan.

'So hot,' he said.

'Yes, it is hot. And if it had not been for your Dada you would not be here sweating it out, in pain, and on a crutch for the rest of your life also. So what is his name, man? What is his name?'

'A drink. I would give anything for one good, long, cool drink. Thandai, Inspector. You are knowing thandai?'

'Oh yes,' Ghote answered, trying for a new bond of sympathy. 'When I was a young man often I was taking thandai at that place at Kalba Devi where they are making specially. And very good it was, that milk, the ice crushed in and the mixed flavours, almond, pistachio, rose water, melon seeds.'

'And, Inspectorji, something else also?'

The injured goonda's voice had taken on a note of girlish coyness.

'Ah,' Ghote said, with a little laugh. 'The bhang that fellow is putting in sometimes, eh? The stuff that sends you into a nice, nice dream.'

'That is it, Inspector. That is it. Ah, what would I not give at just only this moment for a long, long drink of bhang thandai.'

And then an idea came into Inspector Ghote's head, an altogether wrong idea. But an idea of insidious appeal.

For a while he fought it down. He tackled Ram Dharkar once again, putting to him again all the arguments he had offered before. He could think of no others. But all his efforts seemed to be wasted. The goonda lay there on the bed, his face blankly inexpressive, occasionally letting out almost against his will a groan of pain and frustration. Then, right in the middle of one of Ghote's most complex, and most persuasive, sentences, the fellow brutally interrupted.

'Oh, shut up, shut up. What for are you going on and on? There is one thing only I am wanting, that bhang thandai. That only.'

And Ghote succumbed.

'Very well,' he said. 'If I am going out and smuggling in for you as big a drink of thandai as you have ever seen in your life, will you in exchange give me that name?'

The offer certainly got to the injured goonda. Ghote could positively see him swallowing down in anticipation that long, cool, refreshing and peace-bringing drink.

And, he thought, damn it all, that nurse said the operation had been delayed. So what real harm could there be in letting the fellow have something solid to drink? They must have left that Nil by Mouth card up there by mistake. He was not really endangering the man's life by letting him have his thandai.

And, when it came to it, he could always get the name out of him first and then throw the drink out of the window.

But would the fellow accept the offered bribe? Would he?

'Big-big? Double size?'

The bait had been taken. Right or wrong, it was to be done now.

And, perhaps, when he got back – getting the stuff was going to take him some little time – that notice would have been removed from the bedhead and Ram Dharkar would be able to have as much 'by mouth' as he liked. And if bhang would hardly be permitted by the hospital authorities, it would not do the fellow much harm. Might even do good, ease the pain.

'All right, my friend, I am off now. About half an hour, a little more perhaps. And you be thinking what you would be telling, no? Every detail you are able to remember. Then there will be no mistake in nabbing that Dada of yours.'

In fact, it took Ghote rather more than an hour to complete his errand. He realised first that he would need a good container to get the stuff into Ram Dharkar's cabin unobserved, something that would fit into his own briefcase. That took him some time to find amid the high-piled shops of Lohar Chawl with their heaps of crockery and glassware in orderly mounds, their bright plastic buckets piled in man-high towers, their steel or aluminium glasses in carefully constructed pyramids, their electric hot-plates and toasters tempting the middle classes and the pushing, gawping crowds buying and not buying, beating down prices and paying too much.

But at last he found a flat plastic flask with a screw top that looked as if it would hold a really sizeable amount of cooling thandai. Then he had to hurry down to Kalba Devi where the specialist in thandai had his stall. And there, since the day was scorchingly hot, he found a long, slow-moving line of customers waiting to be served, and had patiently to stand in it till he reached its head. He even had some trouble then persuading the thandaiwalla, cross-legged on a small bench beneath his cupboard-like, bright pink-painted stall, to pour the concoction into his plastic container, though one quick whispered word and the sight of a twenty-rupee note had sufficed to get him a mixture well laced with bhang.

Hurrying back to the hospital, Ghote began to worry that he might somehow be too late. Of course Ram Dharkar must still be there. That was one certain thing. The fellow could not move. But might he have somehow changed his mind? Might some thought of how the mysterious Dada could get at him despite all precautions have made him determined after all not to say one more single word?

Or could he, in the past hour, somehow have received a warning from the Dada? But how? No, it was impossible. A vision of a paper dart being flown in through that narrow open window momentarily crossed his mind. But that was ridiculous. Utter fantasy.

The constable on guard at the cabin's door being bribed to let someone in just long enough to deliver a threat? Well, it was possible. But he himself knew the fellow, a man near retirement, two yellow long-service stripes on his sleeve. As trustworthy as anybody in the force.

Nevertheless, entering the noisy, crowded entrance hall of the hospital – 'OPD Case Notes', the letters must stand for Out-Patients Department – he could not prevent himself from breaking into a walk not far short of a trot. Luckily he remembered how to get to Cabin No. 773, along one high, white-tiled corridor, his footsteps tapping out, up a wide set of stairs, along again, the white tiles here cracked and sometimes splashed with rust-red betel-juice stains, down another stair-case, past the nursing station, briefcase with its illegal guggling flask inside, a quick nod to the Sister on duty and there he was, outside the cabin, the grey-haired long-serving constable squatting beside its door scrambling up to salute him, alert as ever.

'No trouble, Constable?'

'No trouble, Inspector.'

And in. And there was Ram Dharkar lying on the bed, looking as if he had hardly moved in the past hour.

Looking, in fact, a good deal worse, Ghote thought, than when he had left him. But an hour more of pain, that would probably account for the clouded eyes, the yet greyer complexion. And the sight and smell of refreshing thandai – it ought still to be noticeably cool – should surely revive him.

'Well, man,' he said, infusing his voice with enthusiasm, 'thandai I have got. A big-big lot, more than you have ever had before I am betting.'

He unscrewed the top of the flask and held it just under Ram Dharkar's grey, unmoving face.

And got no response. No response at all.

He swirled the scented pink liquid in the flask and held it near the sick man again.

'Take, take,' he said. 'Take one good drink and then be telling me that name.' .

But Ram Dharkar lay unmoving.

Damn it, had the fellow gone right back to the beginning again? Had he, in that past hour, decided once more that he dared not speak? Not despite every precaution taken to guard him? Not despite his own promise to have the Dada nabbed within half an hour of learning his name and whereabouts? Not despite this offered illegal bribe?

Now suddenly, without warning, the goonda lying flat on the bed began to vomit.

Ghote was appalled. This was something he had not at all expected. And the fellow, he realised now, looked desperately ill. On the point of death even.

He tore across to the door of the little room, flung it open, saw with relief the Sister who had first shown him where the cabin was trotting down the corridor outside and shouted to her that Ram Dharkar was very, very ill.

In a moment she was beside the vomiting goonda's bed making a quick, professional analysis.

'Yes,' she said, 'he is serious. Very serious. Ring that bell, Inspector. We are going to need much more of help if he is not to expire.'

Ghote rang the bell, cursing himself for not having realised it was there before, and then retreated to the farthest corner of the narrow room while two other nurses and, soon, a doctor came on to the scene.

He watched, caught in horrified fascination, while they worked to save the dying man. And thoughts, grim thoughts, ran through his mind.

Ram Dharkar had been poisoned. He was sure of it if only from what he gathered from the terse questions and answers of the team round the bed. And if the fellow had been poisoned, then it was almost certain who was behind it. The Dada. The mysterious gang boss whose name he himself had counted on learning just a few minutes earlier. Somehow, he thought, word must have got back to this unknown master criminal that a Crime Branch Inspector had been closeted with the injured so-called informer for a considerable period. And the man had acted. Had acted with all the speed and decision with which the twenty-five bank dacoities he had planned had been carried out. He had, somehow, got poison into poor Ram Dharkar and, it looked, in time to shut his mouth for ever before he had spoken his name.

But how? How on earth had it been managed?

Then, suddenly, he thought he knew how it had been done. The nurses. The nurses with the wheeled medicines chest. They must have been bribed. Or substitutes must have replaced them and somehow, perhaps merely by the swiftness with which they had entered, they had tricked the old constable on guard at the door. And that single little white pill he himself had seen them administer, that must have been the poison. No wonder they had not taken away the Nil by Mouth notice. They had given the would-be betrayer all that was needed 'by mouth' to silence him for ever.

Abruptly then Ghote thrust away his suspicions. Through the leaning, busily working bodies of the nurses round the dying man he had caught a glimpse of Ram Dharkar's face. And his eyes, fixed magnetically on his own, seemed to be attempting to tell him something.

Regardless of the urgent medical work round the bed, he advanced towards it. And, yes, as he did so he was certain that Ram Dharkar was responding. If a look alone could do it, he was saying, 'Come, come, there is something I must tell.'

He got himself as close to the head of the bed as he could without actually impeding the nurse there. Ram Dharkar's eyes were, beyond doubt, begging him now to give him his utmost attention. Now, in all probability, knowing himself to be dying, knowing that he had been poisoned, he was at last determined to take revenge and name the Dada.

But the only sound that came from his vomit-flecked mouth was a feeble croak. Ghote turned his head and strove to catch every nuance. The dying man croaked out a noise again. But this was yet feebler than before.

156

Ghote felt a surge of pure anger. To have been defeated by his mysterious antagonist in this way. At the very last moment.

He leant yet nearer to the dying goonda, willing him and willing him into one last spurt of life, a moment of vigour just long enough to pronounce the name.

But not all his effort to hold Ram Dharkar in this world seemed to be helping. His eyes, clouded only until a few moments ago, now were plainly glazed over.

Ghote's mind raced. Perhaps after all he did not need to hear the name which, it was clear now, Ram Dharkar was never going to be able to speak. It was possible, surely, that the two false nurses, or the two bribed nurses, could be traced. Traced, arrested and interrogated. Interrogated, however toughly was necessary, until they squeaked. And if not able to name the mastermind Dada directly, be persuaded into giving enough information about who had given them their evil task, wittingly or unwittingly performed, for the trial to lead eventually to that mysterious lurking figure. It needed only one end of the thread to be in police hands and they could be sure, very nearly sure, of getting to the Dada.

He was so pleased by what he had worked out, contemplating even leaving the little room and the dying goonda at once to begin inquiries, that he almost failed to notice a change that had come about in the man on the bed.

But then he did notice.

Plainly Ram Dharkar's very last moments had come. A deep agitation was passing through him. But this final convulsion of energy was producing something that until now might have seemed altogether beyond him. He was jerking himself up into a sitting position. And, teetering precariously, he now flung out his right arm in a gesture of pointing. The forefinger was rigid as a rod of steel. And he was pointing, in a way that demanded compliance, at the narrow window of the little room, the window still open at the bottom from when Ghote himself had tried to bring in some cooler air.

Ghote looked at the window, looked back at Ram Dharkar. And saw in the hope in the man's now momentarily clearer eyes that he himself had begun to read correctly his last message.

There was more of it, too. With a supreme effort, keeping his gaze fixed on Ghote's face, the dying goonda made another gesture. He bunched the fingers on the hand that had pointed so dramatically at the window into a tight knot.

A knot that at once reminded Ghote of something. For a long moment his mind battered against the answer like a dull fly battering at a window-pane. And then he had it. A leper. Ram Dharkar's hand was unmistakably imitating the fingerless stump of a leper.

A leper. The leper. The leper he himself had seen, and had discounted, squatting beneath that very window. No, it was not those nurses, innocent and kind-hearted, who had brought that swift end of Ram Dharkar's life. It was this leper, or more likely imitation leper, who must have listened, keen-eared, to every word that had passed between Ram Dharkar and himself. The man who must have heard the promise of a drink of thandai and who, acting with speed and decision – why, yes, yes, he must be, he could only be the Dada himself in disguise – too had hurried off, obtained some cool drink that looked enough like proper thandai and had then swarmed up the drainpipe outside, in the way he himself had envisaged Ram Dharkar, if he had had full use of his legs, swarming down. Then, keeping his face averted, he had offered the drink to his half-conscious victim. The poisoned drink.

So, yes, at last from the dying man he had learnt all that he had wanted to know. He had learnt it nil by mouth.

Quietly Inspector Ghote withdrew from the poisoned goonda's deathbed. Quietly he made his way over to the still open window. Carefully he poked his head out just far enough to catch one glimpse of the dried-coconut disguised head of the supposed leper, crouching there waiting to know whether his daring plan had been successful.

The Dada himself. And not knowing one thing – that his disguise had been penetrated. That he was now dangerously exposed. That the arms of the law were on the point of being able to enfold him. The Dada. The mastermind.

Quietly as ever Ghote climbed up till his hands were grasping the top of the window and his feet were on its bottom ledge. The gap would be just wide enough, he saw with grim pleasure, to slide his body through.

He launched himself.

1987

12

A Present for Santa Sahib

Inspector Ghote put a hand to his hip pocket and made sure it was firmly buttoned up. Ahead of him, where he stood in the entrance doorway to one of Bombay's biggest department stores, the crowds were dense just two days before the festival of Christmas. It was not only the Christians who celebrated the day by buying presents and good things to eat in the huge cosmopolitan city. People of every religion were always happy to share in the high days and holidays in each other's calendars. When Hindus honoured Bombay's favourite god, elephant-headed Ganesh, by taking huge statues of him to be immersed in the sea, Moslems, Parsis and Christians delighted to join the enormous throngs watching them go by. Everyone had a day off too, and enjoyed it to the full for the Moslem Idd holiday.

But the crowds that gathered in the days before any such celebration brought always trouble as well as joy, Ghote thought to himself with a sigh. When people came in their thousands to buy sweets and fireworks for Diwali or to acquire stocks of coloured powders to throw and squirt in the springtime excitement of Holi, they made a very nice golden opportunity for the pickpockets.

He had, in fact, caught a glimpse just as he had entered the shop of a certain Ram Prasad, a well-known jackal stalking easy prey if ever there was. It equally had been the sight of the fellow, spotting him himself and turning rapidly back, that had made him check that his wallet was secure. It would look altogether bad if an Inspector of Crime Branch had to go back minus one wallet and empty-handed to the wife who had as usual commissioned him to buy a present for her Christian friend, Mrs D'Cruz, in return for the one they had received at Diwali.

And he had another little obligation, too, on this trip to the store. Not only was there a gift to get for Mrs D'Cruz but there was a visit to pay to Santa Claus as he sat – voluminously wrapped in shiny red coat, a silky red cap trimmed in fluffy white on his head, puffy cottonwool beard descending from his chin, sack of presents tucked away beside him – in his special place in the store.

Ghote was not actually going to line up with the children waiting to be given, in exchange for a rupee surreptitiously handed over by a hovering mother, a bar of chocolate or a packet of sweets from the big sack. Santa was an old friend who merited a word or two of greeting. Or, if not exactly a friend, he was at least someone known for a good long time.

In fact Santa – his actual name was Moti Popatkar – was a small-fry con-man. There was no getting past that. For all save the ten days each year leading up to Christmas, he made a dubious living from a variety of minor anti-social activities. There was the fine story he had for any British holidaymaker he happened upon – his English was unusually good, fruit of a mission school education long ago – about how he had been batman to an Army officer still living in retirement in India and how he needed just the rail fare to go back and look after Colonel Sahib again. Or he would offer himself as a guide to any lone European tourist he could spot, and sooner or later cajole them into buying him potent country liquor at some illicit drinking den.

It was at one such that Ghote had first met him. A visiting German businessman had complained to the police that, on top of being persuaded into handing over to his guide a much bigger tip than he had meant to give, he had also been induced to fork out some fifty rupees for drinks at a place tucked away inside a rabbit-warren building in Nagandas Master Road called the Beauty Bar.

There was not much that could be done about the complaint, but since the businessman had had a letter of introduction to a junior Minister in the State Government, Ghote had been detailed to investigate. He had dutifully gone along to the Beauty Bar, which proved to be very much as he had expected, a single room which a shabby counter in one corner, its walls painted blue and peeling, half a dozen plastic-topped tables set about. Where sat a handful of men, white-capped office messengers, a khaki-uniformed postman delaying on his round, a red-turbaned ear-cleaner with his little aluminium case beside him, an itinerant coldwaterman who had left his barrel pushcart outside. All hunched over smeary glasses of clear fluid.

But one of the drinkers seemed to answer to the description the German businessman had given of his guide. And, at the first sharp question, the fellow had cheerfully admitted that he was Moti Popatkar and that, yes, he had brought a German visitor to the place the day before.

'Exciting for him, no?' he had said. 'Seeing one damn fine Indian den of vice?'

Ghote had looked at the peeling walls, at a boy lackadaisically swiping at one of the table tops with a sodden heap of darkly grey cloth, at the two pictures hanging askew opposite him, one of an English maiden from some time in the past showing most of her breasts, the other of the late Mrs Gandhi looking severe.

'Well, do not let me be catching you bringing any visitor from foreign to such a fourth class place again,' he said.

'Oh, Inspectorji, I would not. In nine-ten days only I would be Santa Claus.'

So then it had come out what job Moti Popatkar had every year in the run-up to Christmas.

'And I am keeping same,' he had ended up. 'When I was first beginning, too many years past, the son of Owner, who is himself Ownerji now, was very much liking me when his mother was bringing him to tell his wishings to old Santa. So now Manager Sahib cannot be giving me one boot, however much he is wanting.'

There had been then something in Moti Popatkar's cheerful disregard of the proper respect due to a police inspector, even of the cringing most of his like would have adopted before any policewalla, that had appealed to a side of Ghote which he generally felt he ought to keep well hidden. He felt a trickle of liking for this fellow, however much he knew he should disapprove of anyone who led visitors to India into such disgraceful places, and however wrong it seemed that such a good-for-nothing should wear the robe, even for a short period, of a figure who was after all a Christian saint, to be revered equally with Hindu holy man or Muslim *pir*.

So, visiting Santa's store a few days later to get Mrs D'Cruz her present, he had gone out of his way to have a look at Moti Popatkar, happy-go-lucky specimen of Bombay's riff-raffs, impersonating Santa Claus, Christian holy man of bygone days.

There had been a lull in the stream of children coming to collect chocolate bars and breathily whisper wishes into Santa's spreading cottonwool beard at the time, so he had stayed to chat with the red-robed fellow for a few minutes. And every successive year since he had found himself doing the same thing, for all that he still felt he ought to disapprove of the man behind the soft white whiskers. The truth was he somehow liked his irresponsible impudent approach to life and to his present task in particular.

Only last year Father Christmas had had a particularly comical tale to tell.

'Oh, Inspectorji, you have nearly seen me in much, much trouble.'

'How is that, you Number One scallywag?'

Moti Popatkar grinned through his big white beard, already looking slightly grimy.

'Well, you know, Inspector, I am half the time making the *baba log* believe they will be getting what for they are wishing, and half the time also I am taking one damn fine good look at the mothers, if they are being in any way pretty. Well, just only ten minutes past, a real beauty was coming, Anglo-Indian, short skirt an' all. Jolly spicy. And – oh, forgive, forgive God above – I was so much distracted I was giving her little girl not just only one bar of chocolate but a half-kilo cake of same. And then – then who should come jumping out from behind but Manager Sahib himself? What for are you giving away so much of Store property, he is demanding and denouncing. Then – oh, Inspector, I am a wicked, wicked fellow. You know what I am saying?'

'No?'

'I am saying, quick only as one flash of lightning, "But, Manager sahib, that little girl has come with her governess. She is grand-daughter of multi-millionaire Tata, you are knowing." '

Ghote had laughed aloud. He could not help himself. Besides, the Manager, whom he had once had dealings with, was a very self-satisfied individual.

'But then, Inspectorji, what is Manager sahib saying to me?'

'Well, tell.'

'He is saying, "Damn fool, you should have given whole kilo cake".'

And Ghote had felt then his Christmas was all the merrier. Mrs D'Cruz had got a better present than usual, too.

So now he decided to pay his visit to Santa Claus before he went present-buying. But when he came to the raised platform on which Father Christmas was installed, his fat sack of little gifts on the floor beside him, he found the scene was by no means one of goodwill to all men.

Moti Popatkar was sitting in state as usual on his throne-like chair, his bright red shiny robe as ever gathered round him, his floppy red hat with the white trimming on his head. But he was not bending forward to catch the spit-laden whisperings of the children. Nor was he rocking back and issuing some Ho, ho, hos. Instead he was looking decidedly shifty under his cottonwool beard, and in front of him there was standing the Store Manager, both enraged and triumphant.

A lady dressed in a silk sari that must have cost several thousand rupees was standing just behind the Manager holding the hand of a little girl, evidently her daughter, plainly bewildered and on the verge of tears.

'You are hearing what this lady is stating,' the Manager was shouting as Ghote came up. 'When she was bringing this sweet little girl to visit Santa Claus there was in her handbag one note-case containing many, many hundred-rupee notes. But, just after leaving you, she was noticing the handbag itself was wide open and she was shutting same – click – and then when she was wanting to pay for purchase made at Knick-knacks and Assorted counter, what was she finding? That note-case had gone.'

Instinctively, Ghote felt at his hip again. But *thik hai*, no *pocket-maar* had been light-fingered with his wallet.

'But, no, Manager sahib. No, no. I was not taking any note-case. Honest to God, no.'

Yet Moti Popatkar's protestations had about them – there could be no doubting it – a ring of desperation.

'I am going to search you, here and now only,' the Manager stormed.

'No!'

'Yes, I am saying.'

And the Manager darted a hand into each of the big, sagging

pockets of the shiny red robe one after the other. Only to withdraw from the second holding nothing more incriminating than a fluff-covered *paan* which Santa Claus had had no opportunity to pop into his mouth and chew.

'Open up robe,' the Manager demanded.

Ghote stood watching, a feeling of grey sadness creeping over him, as Moti Popatkar, now dulled into apathy, allowed Santa's robe to be tugged open and eager fingers to dip into shirt pocket and trouser pockets beneath.

But they found nothing more in the way of evidence than the fluff-fuzzed *paan* already brought to light.

The Manager, furiously baffled, took a step back. Moti Popatkar behind his spreading white beard – distinctly pulled apart during the search – had still not regained anything of his customary good spirits.

The Manager turned to offer explanations to the complaining customer.

Ghote gave a deep sigh.

'Look into Santa's sack, Manager sahib,' he said.

'Ah! Yes. Yes, yes.'

The big sack was jerked wide. The Manager plunged to his knees.

'Wait,' Ghote shouted suddenly.

The Manager turned and looked up.

'You should let a police officer handle this,' Ghote said.

He stepped up on to the platform and knelt in his turn beside the gaping sack. Then, very carefully, he felt about inside it, easing his fingers past bars of chocolate, little bags of sweets.

At last he rose to his feet.

Between the tip of the forefinger of his right hand and its thumb he was holding a crocodile-skin note-case frothed at the rim with big blue one-hundred rupee notes.

'Mine,' exclaimed the watching lady customer.

Beside her, her daughter burst into tears.

'Inspector,' the Manager said, 'kindly charge-sheet this fellow.'

'Well, Manager sahib,' Ghote replied, 'I am thinking I should not do that until I have evidences. Fingerprint evidences.'

'But . . . but we have caught him red-handed only.'

'Are you sure, Manager sahib? Were you actually observing

this Santa placing the note-case inside his sack? And, more, did you not observe his manner when you were accusing? He was not at all his usual chirpy self. Now, if he was thinking that by hiding himself this note-case in his sack he would altogether trick you because you would not look there, I am believing he would have found something cheeky to be saying. It was because he was not that I was suddenly realising what must have happened.'

'And what was that, Inspector?' the rich customer demanded.

'Oh, madam, you could not be knowing, but just only as I was entering this store I was catching sight of one Ram Prasad, notorious pickpocket. And he also was catching sight of myself, and *ek dum* he was turning round and making his way more into the store. It was soon after, I am thinking, that he was dropping the note-case he had already lifted from your open handbag into this sack. This Santa must have spotted him doing that, but been unable to prevent and Ram Prasad will have had the intention of removing his loot when he had seen that I myself had left the store. I do not have much of doubt that it will be his fingerprints, which we have had ten-twelve years upon the file, that will be found on his very nice shiny crocodile-skin surface.'

And it was then that, behind the bedraggled cottonwool of his beard, Santa sahib gave a wide, wide smile.

'Ho, ho, ho,' he chuckled.

1988

165

13

The Purloined Parvati and Other Artefacts

The Assistant Commissioner was angry. Inspector Ghote could be in no doubt of it. That voice, he thought, so loud it must be heard through entire Bombay.

The ACP had thumped the glass-topped surface of his desk, too.

'It is not good enough. Not good enough by one damn long chalk.'

'No, sir. No, ACP sahib.'

'The clear-up rate for Crime Branch has fallen almost to zero.'

Ghote thought of stating the exact figure which, if it was somewhat down on the year before, was still well above that zero. But he realised that putting it forward would hardly calm the ACP's wrath. In fact, it might have the very opposite effect.

'Yes, sir,' he said.

'And you, Ghote, are as much responsible as any. More even. More.'

Again Ghote was aware of a lack of precise factuality in the ACP's charge. But this time he did not even produce a word in acknowledgement.

'Look at the business of the Gudalpore Temple theft,' the ACP stormed on, as unappeased by silence as he had been by sycophantic agreement. 'How long is it since we were receiving the tip-off that the loot was held in Bombay for inspection by some damn unscrupulous foreign buyers? Two months? Three months? Four?'

Once more Ghote decided that silence was best. It was not.

'How long? I am asking you, Inspector. How long? Three months, four?'

'It is seven weeks, three days, ACP sahib.'

'Exactly. Seven weeks, eight, and what results have you succeeded to get?'

'Sir, it is not at all easy. We have had no more than that one tip-off itself. No hint even of where the loot may be hidden. No reports of any suspicious foreigners coming to camp in Bombay.'

'No this, no that. What good are your noes and woes to me, Inspector? It is results I am wanting. A most valuable statue of Goddess Parvati was stolen in broad daylight and numerous artefacts also.'

'Artefacts, sir?' Ghote blurted the question out before he had had time to see it would be a mistake to display ignorance of what exactly the English word meant.

'Yes, man, artefacts. Artefacts. Whatsoever they are.'

The ACP snatched the metal paperweight inscribed with his initials off one of the formidable piles of documents on his desk and began a scrabbling hunt through it. At last he produced a long list badly reproduced on mauvish paper, and slammed the paperweight back before the breeze from the big fan behind him could play havoc with the pile.

He began reading aloud.

'One Goddess Parvati, tenth-twelfth century, sandstone, height 147 centimetres, seated upon a representation of a *tipai* in the semi-lotus position with the left arm resting upon the knee and the right in an attitude of blessing. Plus four God Ganeshas, terracotta, height 22 centimetres, 23 centimetres, 25 centimetres and 28 centimetres respectively. Plus one Goddess Sarasvati, bronze, 12 centimetres, tail of peacock partly missing. Plus two Krishnas, fluting, no heights stated. Plus eighteen other artefacts, various.'

He looked up.

'Eighteen artefacts, Ghote, and you have not been able to locate even one.'

'No, sir.'

'Well, it is not good—'

The ACP's observations were interrupted by the shrilling of one of the three telephones on his wide-spreading desk. He picked it up.

'*Haan?*'

An urgent voice squeaked out.

'No,' the ACP barked back. 'No, I am not able to see. Every

damn foreigner coming here has some letter of introduction from a Minister and thinks they can bother me with their every least wish. I have appointment. Lions Club luncheon. One hundred per cent important.'

He slammed the phone down.

'Ghote,' he said, his voice much less furious than it had been a minute earlier, 'there is some Professor Something-or-other wanting to make some complaint or protest or demand. Deal with it, yes?'

'Yes, sir. Yes, ACP sahib. Right away, sir.'

Ghote clicked heels smartly and left, buoyed up with relief at the unforeseen rescue.

Fate, it soon began to seem, was to be yet kinder to him. The foreign professor turned out to his surprise to be not the venerable man he had envisaged but an English lady, stout of person, red of face, bristly of eyebrow and clad in skirt and jacket of some tough pale brown material resembling the sail of a Harbour dhow. She had no sooner announced herself as 'Professor Prunella Partington, good day to you' than she stated in a ringingly British voice that she had just seen in Bombay 'a Parvati statue that ought quite certainly to be in its proper place in the temple of Gudalpore'.

Ghote could hardly believe his ears. Was this – this lady actually speaking about the very statue of Goddess Parvati, 147 centimetres in height, stolen from the Gudalpore Temple and hidden ever since somewhere in Bombay awaiting a foreign buyer? The very idol, together with other artefacts, that he had just been rebuked by the ACP for not having located?

'Madam,' he said, his heart thumping in confusion, 'what, please, is the height of said statue?'

'Height? Height? How the devil should I know?'

'But you have stated that you have just only seen same, madam.'

'Course I have. Wouldn't come round to Police Head-quarters fast as I could, would I, unless I had?'

'But, then, the height of same?'

'Oh, I suppose about five feet. Far as I remember when I examined it at Gudalpore ten years ago. Statue of Parvati, seated on a stool in the semi-lotus position. Sandstone.'

'Madam, this is sounding altogether like one idol stolen from that same temple seven-eight weeks back, together with other art— art— other objects, madam.'

'Well, obviously it's been stolen from Gudalpore, and someone had better come along pronto and arrest the fellow who stole it.'

'You are knowing who it is? Please, kindly state where he is to be found.'

'In that appalling sham museum of his, of course. Where else?'

'But, madam, you are altogether failing to name that appalling sham museum.'

'Nonsense, my good chap. Course I named it. Look, here's the place's piffling brochure.'

From her large leather handbag, stoutly clasped, the professor – was she Professor Mrs or Professor Miss Prunella, Ghote wondered – produced a slim pamphlet printed in a shade of deep pink.

Ghote read.

Hrishikesh Agnihotri Museum of Indology. This Museum is serving the nation for the past two and a half decades playing an important role by displaying classical, traditional and also folk arts to fulfil aesthetic, scientific and practical aims. It is containing different specimens in various fields, viz. Physics, Chemistry, Botany, Chiromancy, Phonology, Anthropology, and Archaeology. The Museum may also organize from time to time seminars, lecture series, conferences and meetings for research and study on Mythology, Tantra, Yantra, Mantra, Astro-Geomancy, Physiognomy, Palaeontology, Gemology, Alchemy and several other arts and sciences originating in India in ancient and medieval times. Founded by Shri Hrishikesh Agnihotri. Chairman of the Board of Trustees: Shri Hrishikesh Agnihotri.

He looked up at the burly form of the British professor.

'But this is sounding cent per cent *pukka*,' he said, much impressed by all the -ologies and -ancies. 'It is seeming not at all of sham.'

'Poppycock, my good man. Poppycock. A hodge-podge like that? Fellow must be an utter charlatan. You'll think so pretty quick when you see him. Come on.'

'But madam,' Ghote said, still reserving judgement, 'in any

169

case it is not possible at once to come on. If your detailed description of the idol of Parvati is correct, I am admitting there is a prima facie case against one Mr Hrishikesh Agnihotri. But if I am to nab the gentleman certain procedures must be followed.'

'And in the meantime the fellow will take to his heels, accompanied by that dreadful dumb brute he keeps about the place.'

'There is another miscreant also?'

'I should jolly well say there is. Just as I'd spotted the Gudalpore Parvati this hulking creature came out of a little door just behind it. Well, I'd seen quite enough anyhow, so I came straight round here. I've got a letter from your Minister of Health, Family Planning, Gaols and the Arts, you know.'

'Yes, yes, madam. And I am promising fullest cooperation itself. But, kindly understand, under Criminal Procedure Code it is necessary to have any arrest witnessed by two *panches*, as we are calling them.'

'Independent evidence? Well, wouldn't I be that?'

'No, madam. Very regret. You would be witness for prosecution only.'

The professor drew her bristly eyebrows together in thought for a moment. Then she brightened.

'Got just the chap for you,' she said. 'You could call him an expert on Indian art even. Staying at my hotel, as it happens. Name of Edgar Poe.'

Ghote felt a faint stirring at the back of his mind.

'Edgar Poe?' he asked. 'It is the gentleman who is writing the famous story of "The Pit and the Pendulum"?'

'Good God, no, man. Edgar *Allan* Poe must have been dead over a hundred years. This chap's another kettle of fish. Dealer in antiques. As a matter of fact, it was because of him that I went to that appalling museum at all. Heard him talking to an Indian friend over breakfast this morning. Sitting at the next table. Mentioned the place, and I thought it might be worth a quick look-see. Suppose it was, in a way, since I spotted the Gudalpore Parvati. But Mr Poe and his friend would make first-class – what-d'you-call-'ems – pinches.'

'Madam, it is *panch. Panch.*'

'Never mind all that. Thing is, we could be round there in

ten minutes if you get a move on, pick them up and get over to that place.'

'No, madam, no. I am thinking that it is not altogether a fine idea. Your Mr Poe would be kept here in India perhaps many, many months waiting to give evidence. No, I would instead obtain some very, very suitable persons.'

The professor shrugged her burly shoulders.

'As you like, Inspector, as you like. But do hurry up or our birds will have flown the coop.'

Resenting obscurely being put under this pressure, Ghote picked up his phone, got through to the nearby Tilak Marg Police Station – whose good offices he relied on in situations like this – and requested that an officer should come round as quickly as possible with two of their regular *panches*.

'And, listen,' he added, 'do not send the sort of fellows you are using when it is just only a question of pulling in some chain-snatcher. This is a Number One important business. So find some *panches* claiming full respect, yes? This is a fifty-sixty lakh theft case. More.'

He got quick and complete agreement. Fifty-sixty lakhs was big money.

But when the two witnesses and a sub-inspector met them outside the little Press Room hut near the entrance to the Headquarters compound, Ghote saw at once that they were by no means the respectable citizens he had so carefully specified. One was a very old man with a mouth that hung slackly open to reveal a single long yellow tooth, probably a retired office peon to judge by the raggedy khaki jacket that covered his bare chest. The other, though much younger, was scarcely more presentable, a *pinjari*, one of the itinerant fluffers-up of cotton mattresses who go about Bombay advertising their services by loudly twanging the single taut wire of the harp-like instrument they use in their work. An object he was possessively clutching.

Nor was Sub-Inspector Jadhav more likely to impress the British professor, Ghote thought. He was a stocky, cocky fellow who at once attempted to take charge of the whole operation.

'I am bringing four-five constables, Inspector,' he said. 'You were not requisitioning, but for a job like this you would be needing some fellows who know how to get a suspect ready to talk.'

171

'No, I was not requisitioning,' Ghote snapped out. 'And let me remind you, I am in charge of this operation, SI.'

He turned to the little group of tough-looking uniformed men at the sub-inspector's heels.

'Report back to your station *ek dum*,' he barked. 'At the double, at the double.'

Turning, he bundled the two *panches* and the sub-inspector into the back of the jeep he had waiting, opened its front door for the British professor, scrambled in himself and told the driver to go as fast as he could under the professor's directions to the Hrishikesh Agnihotri Museum.

The place proved to be a large dilapidated-looking house, heavy with ornate wooden carving in the style of Gujarati mansions of some hundred years earlier. They mounted the impressive steps and Ghote knocked thunderously on the solid wide door.

No answer came.

'What did I tell you, Inspector?' the professor snorted. 'Flown the coop, both of them.'

Ghote, fighting off a sinking feeling that the culprits had indeed made off, hammered on the door once more.

'Better I should go round the back, Inspector,' SI Jadhav said. 'You often catch fellows who are absconding that way. Pity we were not bringing some more men.'

Keeping half an eye on Jadhav to make sure he did not start to act on his own initiative, Ghote raised his hand to knock yet again. But as he did so, he heard beyond the thick door the slap-slap-slap of someone approaching with feet in loose-fitting *chappals*.

A moment later the door was opened a cautious inch or two.

The man who peered out at them was plainly the Museum's Founder and Chairman of Trustees. Learning and respectability were written on him from head to toe, from his wizened agedness, from the gold-rimmed spectacles half-way along his thin and inquisitive nose, right down to his mis-matched *chappals*, one pale brown leather, the other black.

'Public admitted at a fee of rupees three per person,' he said, apparently altogether failing to recognise the British professor he had seen little more than an hour earlier.

'I am not at all public,' Ghote returned sharply. 'It is police. I am wishing to examine your premises for the purpose of

172

ascertaining whether there is to be found upon same one idol of Goddess Parvati, together with various other— er— artefacts.'

Whether it was the production of this last impressive word or the explicit mention of a statue of Parvati, Ghote's statement appeared to stun the museum's Founder and Chairman. His mouth opened. And shut. He fell back a pace.

Swiftly Ghote pushed the heavy front door wide and stepped into a narrow entrance hall lined with a series of tall glass-fronted cupboards. He turned to Professor Prunella, close at his heels.

'Kindly lead at once to wheresoever the idol of Parvati is to be found,' he said.

Unhesitatingly the professor marched off. Following, Ghote took in that the tall cupboards to either side were crammed and jammed with an extraordinary variety of objects. One contained vases, of all shapes and sizes, china, brass, enamelled. Another was a jumble of clocks, elegant old European ones, cranky alarms, even a plastic kitchen-timer. A third was apparently filled with measuring devices, ancient sticks marked with notches, lengths of cord regularly knotted, rulers in bundles, even some round metal spring-loaded tapes.

On they went through an archway and into a series of tiny, floor-to-ceiling-filled rooms, each devoted, it seemed, to one or other of the many -ologies and -ancies the museum served the nation by preserving. The Founder and Chairman came clacking after them on his mis-matched *chappals*, uttering from time to time little squeaks of protest or dismay.

SI Jadhav, swaggering along with his two disreputable *panches*, showed – whenever Ghote chanced to look back for a moment – a hair-raising tendency to swipe at any object that looked as if it might be easy to topple, a display of china European Farm animals, a pile of inkwells of all sorts heaped one on the other, even a chair made entirely out of glass in a room devoted wholly to such furniture. The aged first *panch* broke out into a wild cackle of laughter every now and again and his younger companion, the *pinjari*, apparently felt that the higgledy-piggledy dignity of his surroundings obliged him to pause at the entrance to each successive little room and emit from his fluffing instrument one loud resounding twang.

Ghote thanked his stars that the British professor was too

173

intent on her onwards rush to the possibly stolen Parvati to pay attention to the rest of his party.

At last they came to a narrow downwards-leading flight of stairs, each step used to display some other object from the museum's collection, four or five different hookahs, a framed picture of an English cottage, turned sideways, a small board hung with various patterns of padlock.

At the stairs' foot they plunged once more into another series of little rooms. Professor Mrs or Miss Prunella seemed to know her way, unerring as a bloodhound on the scent.

In the gloom here the Founder and Chairman stopped his squeaks, regained his voice and began to shoot out vague explanations of the riches under his control. 'Opal water,' he said, gesturing abruptly to a tall glass jar half full of some cloudy liquid. 'Where there is poison there is also nectar, that is a mathematical truth.' Then in the next little chamber, 'Alchemy Department. We are doing many experiments to turn copper into gold. Gold into copper also.' And in a room containing coins and banknotes of every conceivable kind – Ghote had to stop and prevent the *pinjari* secreting a heap of little silver pieces – 'Kindly notice the Arab currency notes, all misprinted, very, very rare.' And in yet another room, its walls lined with narrow shelves on which rested, dustily, stones of every colour and shape, 'One thousand different, full of scientific importance, magical point-of-view, astrological point-of-view.'

This last utterance was finally too much even for relentlessly forward-marching Professor Prunella. She turned briefly and barked out over her shoulder, 'Charlatan. Poppycock.'

Ghote, alternating during the whole of their clattering progress between being impressed by the sheer quantity of learned objects and feeling darts of doubt over the Founder's claims about them, felt grateful that the professor made no further assertions of her uncompromising beliefs until they came, at last, to a faded loop of red rope barring their way.

Professor Prunella unhesitatingly thrust it aside, as doubtless she had done on her earlier visit. Striding forward a pace or two into the denser gloom of an ill-lit short corridor, she reached up and clicked on a light switch.

'There,' she said.

Behind, the *pinjari* gave not one but a whole succession of reverberant twangs on his instrument.

Screwing up his face in an effort to blot out all awareness of the sound, Ghote could not but recognise that, a yard or two further down the corridor, there stood an idol of Parvati, the 'princess of the fish-shaped eyes' herself. Seated on the representation of a stool. With one leg tucked under, half way towards the lotus position.

'It is from the Gudalpore Temple?' he asked Professor Prunella.

'Stake my life on it. It's my subject, you know. This is going to make one hell of a paper for *Indian Sculpture Studies*.'

Ghote turned, with curious reluctance, to the Founder and Chairman.

'Sir,' he said, 'are you able to account for the presence here of one object that appears to have been removed from the Temple of Gudalpore without due and proper authorisation?'

The aged amasser of all the varied objects they had seen licked at his thin lips. He cast a peering long, searching look over the rounded limbs and tall-crowned head of the stone goddess.

'The making of this museum,' he muttered, 'has been my life-long work.'

'That is not an answer,' Ghote replied, forcing himself to unrelenting severity despite a prickle of doubt somehow running through him like an underground tremor, unaccountable but not to be ignored.

He waited for the old man to speak again. But he seemed to find it difficult to produce any further words.

'Come, Inspector,' Professor Prunella said with a snort of indignation, 'you have my word for it. This is the Parvati from Gudalpore and nowhere else.'

And as if to emphasise her certainty she gave the rounded form of the goddess a resounding slap across her shoulder.

Ghote winced.

'Good, good,' exclaimed the *pinjari* suddenly in broad Marathi. 'I would give a beauty like that more slaps than one.'

Ghote hoped profoundly that the professor's Indian studies had not given her an acquaintance with local vulgarities.

Apparently they had not, because she simply contented

herself with keeping the slapping hand on the goddess's shoulder in a distinctly proprietorial manner.

Ghote turned again to the Founder.

'Sir,' he said, 'you have not yet given proper answer to my request concerning this idol.'

'No,' the old man shot out, as if the single word of denial had been a hard bubble deep within him whose passage at last could not be resisted. 'No, no, no. Who can say where such a fine object can have come from? This Parvati may have been in my store-room many, many years.'

Ghote found himself in a dilemma. The Founder and Chairman's response had clearly not been wholly satisfactory, yet clearly, it was nevertheless a denial that this idol of Parvati, one after all among many thousands that must exist all over India, was the very selfsame object that had once been in the Gudalpore Temple. Equally, on the other hand, the British lady professor had declared uncompromisingly that it was the Parvati from Gudalpore. She herself had seen it there. Yet might she be mistaken? That had been ten years ago, after all. And then one had a duty as an Indian not to accept each and every statement a Westerner cared to make as a holy truth. A patriotic duty even, though difficult.

'Inspector,' Professor Prunella snapped out now, 'arrest this man.'

It almost decided Ghote. He was damned if he was going to carry out an arrest on the order of a Westerner, an *angrezi* even, relic of the British Raj and, worse, a woman. But on the other hand . . .

Then he heard cocky sub-inspector Jadhav come clicking to attention as if to acknowledge orders from a senior officer he was showing the utmost willingness to comply with.

No, if the Founder and Chairman was to be arrested on a charge of concealing property knowing it to have been stolen, then that task was not going to fall to a little jumped-up fellow from Tilak Marg Police Station. It was—

But suddenly from immediately behind the tall statue of the fish-eyed princess there came the rending squeal of heavy wood on stone and a small door there was abruptly thrust open. In the narrow doorway there stood a bare-chested man of huge proportions, bullet-headed, heavy-jowled, arms loose-hanging.

176

Instinctively Ghote stiffened, expecting instant attack.

'Ah, Manik, there you are,' the Founder and Chairman said with sudden cheerfulness. 'Just when I am wanting you.'

The hulk in the doorway answered only with a grunt, though he seemed to have understood.

'Manik, have you moved this Parvati idol?' the Founder and Chairman asked. 'Where was it kept before?'

He turned to Ghote.

'You will hardly believe it,' he said urgently, 'but the Museum has accumulated so many important objects in so many fields of Indology that at times even I begin to forget where and when they were acquired.'

The declaration had the effect, for no conceivable reason, of causing the old, slack-mouthed ex-peon *panch* to break out into another of his long cackling laughs. Was it – could it be? – Ghote thought, somehow a mocking comment on what the old museum owner had said?

And should he act on it?

He was saved, however, from feeling he had been swayed by any such ridiculous motive by the explosive shrilling of a large bell clamped to the wall nearby connected to a telephone elsewhere in the old building.

'Some person offering some new object for the Collection,' the Founder immediately claimed. 'Or perhaps they are wanting to arrange some seminar.'

He made as if to go and answer.

Ghote quickly stepped across and laid a detaining hand on his arm. He was not going to risk a possible malefactor making off.

'Go and answer it,' the old man said to Manik. 'I really must give this gentleman and lady my fullest attention.'

The silent hulk shuffled off in the direction of the stairs.

'SI, go with him,' Ghote snapped. 'See he makes no attempt to leave.'

Turning from making sure the sub-inspector had obeyed, Ghote saw that the Founder and Chairman had slipped though the little narrow doorway behind the Parvati statue.

Brushing past the substantial form of the British professor, still laying claim to the goddess, Ghote dived through the doorway in pursuit.

But he found that the old man was not making for any tiny

back entrance, as he had feared. Instead, he was moving from one object to another in the dimly-lighted store-room, peering at representations of gods and goddesses, some so thickly covered in dust as to be almost unrecognisable, others clearly to be seen as elephant-trunked or many-armed or many-headed, playing flutes, astride peacocks, chipped here, broken almost in half there, complete to the last detail elsewhere.

'Sir,' he said, firmly as he could, 'what are you doing? I am not at all satisfied by your answers till date. Kindly accompany me back to the idol in question and give detailed assurances.'

For a moment it looked as if the old man was going to ignore him. But he straightened up at last and without explaining breathed a heavy sigh and made his way out to stand on the other side of the disputed Parvati from the stout competing form of Professor Prunella, still with her hand on the goddess's shoulder.

Ghote felt that the pair of them were somehow presenting to him his dilemma as a living picture. Which of the two had the real right to possess Parvati? Was it the imperious lady professor, bringing to her claim all the overwhelming confidence of the West? Or was it this old man, steeped in the philosophies of the East, seeing this Parvati as one among the many, many accumulations of a lifetime of gathering objects to illustrate and enhance the concept of Indology?

And yet, had there not been something distinctly doubtful about the way he had advanced his claim to possession of the fish-eyed princess? But, there again, the British professor had surely been more aggressive in her demands than was altogether right. She had spoken of a contribution to – what was it? – the *Indian Sculpture Studies* as if that meant more to her than anything else.

So could she have . . .? But, then, could he not . . .?

He was unable, in his dilemma, to prevent himself looking with fervent prayerfulness to the goddess herself as if from her stone lips the answer might somehow come.

And it did.

Because suddenly he realised there was a way of making sure this Parvati was the Gudalpore Parvati. An almost certain way.

Sub-inspector Jadhav had just returned, sullen now, shepherding in front of himself the huge silent bulk of the man Manik.

'SI,' Ghote said to him, 'keep sharp watch on each and every person here. I would not be one moment.'

And without waiting for any acknowledgement of the order, he set off at a run through all the little crammed and crowded rooms of the basement area, past the thousand different dusty stones, past the misprinted Arab currency, past the alchemic apparatus, past the tall jar of opal water. He took the stairs two at a time, ignoring padlocks, hookahs, everything. On he went, still hurrying as fast as he dared, past glass chairs and bedsteads, past china farm animals – how did they reflect Indology? No matter – past the heaped pile of different inkwells.

Till at last he came to the entrance hall. And to the glass-fronted cupboard that contained measuring instruments from the most distant past to the present day. Without hesitation, he wrenched open its door, reached up and took from its place one of the neat modern measuring tapes he had seen almost without seeing it as Professor Prunella had hurried them towards her quarry, and to the tape he added, as a last-second afterthought, one of the straight notched sticks from the most distant past.

Then, in even less time than it had taken him to get to the cupboard, he ran back to where the disputed Parvati stood. The Founder and Chairman had not budged from his place at one side of the stone goddess, nor had the British professor moved from her position on the other side. Each silently asserted possession firmly as before.

'Excuse, please,' Ghote said.

And he brushed the two claimants aside, took the notched stick he had seized and laid one end on the topmost stone jewel of the princess's crown. Then he swivelled the stick's other end till it touched the nearest point on the wall behind and made there a tiny scratch on the plaster.

Next, swiftly kneeling, he took the spring-loaded tape, zipped it open and measured the exact distance between his scratched mark and the floor beneath.

The tape, he found with sudden relief, was marked in centimetres, rather than inches. And in a moment he was able to look up and proclaim triumphantly, 'One hundred and forty-seven.'

'One hundred and forty what, for heaven's sake?' Professor Prunella boomed. 'Have you gone dotty, Inspector?'

'Madam,' Ghote replied, still kneeling on the floor. 'Not one hundred and forty, but one hundred and forty-seven. One hundred and forty-seven centimetres, the exact height of the idol of Parvati stolen from the Gudalpore Temple and reported on first-class authority to be kept hidden in Bombay for inspection by foreign buyer or buyers, unknown. That statue is undoubtedly here.'

'You're telling me nothing I haven't been saying all along,' Professor Prunella answered, puffing her chest out to wonderfully new dimensions. 'Arrest this man. Haven't I told you it's your duty half a dozen times already?'

Ghote rose to his feet, taking a deep breath. As he had knelt checking the exact figure on his measuring tape, a number of things he had observed in his brief time in the Hrishikesh Agnihotri Museum had formed into a pattern in his head. A satisfying coherent pattern.

'Madam, Sir' he said looking from the majestic form of the British professor to the bewildered Founder and Chairman. 'There is not only the question of one Parvati idol itself, there is the question of other artefacts also.'

'What—'

'Madam, from the Gudalpore Temple there were also stolen four terracotta representations of God Ganesha, that is with the elephant head as you must very well be knowing, plus also one Goddess Sarasvati riding as per custom upon a peacock, in this case with tail partly missing, plus again two God Krishnas playing upon flutes together with eighteen other artefacts, various. Madam, in this store-room just only behind where I am standing I have observed, as also has Mr Agnihotri, each and every one of these items, notably free from dust. So, madam, what is to be learnt from this?'

'Why, damn it, that this fellow has stolen the whole lot from Gudalpore.'

'Not so, madam. I have told. Mr Agnihotri was just only examining these items. He was not attempting further to conceal same. No doubt he was wishing that, like this Parvati idol, there were objects he had at some faraway time acquired, but he found in the core of his heart that they were not. No, madam, he was not responsible for having these things stolen.'

'Then who the deuce? No, wait. I know. My Mr Poe's Indian guest at breakfast this morning.'

'No, madam, no. The person who hid all these loots here is the man strong enough to move from place to place one Goddess Parvati in sandstone, 147 centremetres in height. The same person who also, though he is appearing dumb, can very well answer telephones and could also communicate with accomplices suggesting to them to hide Parvati among so many other gods and goddesses. It was a most clever device used, I am thinking, by Mr Edgar Allan Poe in the story by the name of "The Purloined Letter".'

He shot out an order to Sub-Inspector Jadhav.

'Take him to your station and charge-sheet him, in my name, with concealing twenty-six various artefacts knowing them to have been stolen.'

'Artefacts, Inspector?' the SI inquired, a frown on his face even as he grabbed the hefty and bewildered Manik.

'Yes, man, artefacts. Artefacts. Are you not knowing what are artefacts?'

1988

14

Light Coming

All the anger of youth blazed in young Ved's eyes.

'Oh, Dada,' he shouted, neck stringy with rage, 'did you never do any wrong? Were you always and always one good-good police inspector?'

'Ved,' his mother exclaimed, bristling with shock. 'How dare you? When you know you are in the wrong also. Taking that sweetmeat I was keeping and keeping for your father. He ought to beat you.'

'Well,' Inspector Ghote said, offering Protima a placatory smile, 'let me perhaps instead tell a story.'

And despite the sharp look he got back, tell his story he did.

It happened, Ghote said, when he was a boy himself, a little younger than Ved was now, in the days when his father had been the schoolmaster in a remote village. A village so remote that, when he himself had been born, it had not even had electricity.

'Up to the age of ten only I had not seen any light that did not come from a flame. Still now when I am thinking of my boyhood I see men moving through the night with burning flares, just only dispelling the darkness. Then you were feeling that this was what light was doing, sending back the dark. Now it is something you are feeling you have some definite right to have.'

'Yes,' Ved said, yet at the edge of sulkiness, 'but what is the story?'

'Ah, it is what happened when at last electricity was coming. One day there arrived into the village a jeep with on it the words *Ele Dept* and inside a burra sahib with one sola topee on his head. Of course, we boys were not then knowing what all this was. But we soon learnt. The sahib was there to take measurements for digging the ditch for the cable that was to bring us this marvel electricity.'

The excitement had kept the village buzzing for weeks. Debate had raged. Some had prophesied dire effects from breathing air mixed with mysterious electricity. Others had seen a glorious new world when everything at night would be seen as plainly as in the full sun. Fears and jokes. The great sport of the evening at the chaikhana was telling the proprietor he would no longer be able in the all-revealing light to make his tea with too little milk. And Ghote's father had given his pupils special lessons on electricity, the new wonder.

'But I am afraid the utmost result of those was that we boys thereafter went round the village the whole time shouting two English words, "Light coming, light coming".'

'So,' said Ved, 'when it was coming what was happening?'

'Oh, but you cannot imagine what the coming itself was meaning to us. It gave us entertainment all the day, from when we were let out of school till when we were driven by the darkness to go to bed.'

'Yes, yes,' Protima put in. 'In those days no boys were allowed to stay up till late-late listening to radio and watching television.'

'No. But nevertheless we had plenty to amuse us,' Ghote said.

There had been the arrival of the truck bearing a huge drum of silvery cable, 'and we boys went rushing to see it, like one flock of sparrows only, elbowing and pushing to get a better view, though there was nothing to stop us seeing all we wanted by standing still only. And then there was the Engineer sahib, taking pleasure to push us back. And we boys – I was one of the most daring even – taking pleasure also to get as near to the truck as we could. And the orders shouted as the big-big drum was rolled to the ground, and the opposing orders, shouted more loudly. Oh, it was one hundred per cent tremendous.'

Then there had been the weeks of the digging of the ditch and opportunities for jumping down into it. And there had been following round the Engineer sahib as he superintended the work, treading almost on his heels and imitating his stomach-outthrust walk. And there was the raising of the poles on which the new lamps were to be placed, with even the women enrolled to help heave on the ropes that hoisted them. And there had been more hours of keen-eyed, mystified watching while the wiringwalla connected up the big main fuse-box placed in the safety of the chavadi where the village headman had his one-room office. And finally there had come the ceremonious departure of the three unneeded old iron lamp-posts which each evening the village lamplighter had climbed up to with his ladder and his guarded flame. They had been carried away 'with much of singing, like a funeral procession only'.

'Yes, but—'

'No, no. I am coming presently to what I was wanting to tell.'

Eventually all the work had been completed. In the schoolmaster's house and others of the better-off light fittings had been installed, switches placed with care, bulbs fitted. 'Then it was my delight to stand and switch. On, off. On, off. On, off. It must have been altogether very, very annoying to each and every person in the house. So in the end I was forbidden absolutely to touch any switch whatsoever. When it was the time in the evening for light it was to be my father only who would click the switch.'

'I know, you did it once, Dada? You were beaten also?'

'Oh, that would not be too much of a story, if it was just only that.'

No, the excitement of 'Light coming' had not ended with the coming of the light itself. Something as important in the history of the village could not go by without proper and due recognition. 'Our MLA was to come to perform opening ceremony.'

'Ved, you are knowing what is MLA?' Protima asked.

'Oh, everybody is knowing that. Member, Legislative Assembly. Member, Legislative Assembly.'

So at last the great day had come. Or rather the great evening because, although the village had had and used the electric light for five or six weeks, it could not truly be there without being switched on officially. And this, of couse, could be done only when there was darkness to be, at the throw of a switch, triumphantly banished. 'May this light, symbol of progress, progress for the village, and progress also for our free and independent India. . .' the great man had intoned, standing garlanded in front of the whole assembled village.

'Or, if I am to be altogether accurate, the whole assembled village with one only exception. Myself. I do not know to this day what it was that had come over me. But I was not sitting

184

cross-legged on the ground with the other children at the front of the rows of attentive listeners to the great sahib. Where I was? I was inside the chavadi, near that big fuse-box. And no sooner had MLA sahib thrown the switch that, officially, was bringing light to our benighted village than I myself and no other pulled out the fuse, as I had seen the wiringwalla do when he was testing.'

'And after, Dadaji?' Ved finally asked, awe in his voice, almost shock.

It was a reaction echoed in Protima's expression, if not aloud.

'After? After there was very much of confusion. More even than I had in my most wild dream expected.'

'And after that? You were beaten-beaten?'

Ghote smiled.

'No, my son. I was not. For the one and simple reason that from that day to this no one has ever known who played that abominable prank.'

It was then that he saw in his son's eyes, as he had hoped to see, light coming.

1988